LEGACY FROM A LOST RACE

The Tar-Aiym had been dead for perhaps a million years. Once they had fought against and then ruled the galaxy. But now they had vanished, leaving only the legend of their final artifact—the lost Krang.

Nobody knew what the Krang might be, but everyone wanted it. Until it was found . . .

Then it turned out that the Krang had a purpose, and that the Krang had power and a will of its own . . .

Also by Alan Dean Foster
available now from Ballantine Books:

The
TAR-AIYM
KRANG

Alan Dean Foster

A Del Rey Book

BALLANTINE BOOKS • NEW YORK

To
Larry Thor
and
John W. Campbell, Jr.
Mentors

A Del Rey Book
Published by Ballantine Books

ISBN 0-345-28165-9

Manufactured in the United States of America

First Edition: March 1972
Fourth Printing: June 1979

First Canadian Printing: March 1975

Cover art by Darrell Sweet

Chapter One

The Flinx was an ethical thief in that he stole only from the crooked. And at that, only when it was absolutely necessary. Well, perhaps not absolutely. But he tried to. Due to his environment his morals were of necessity of a highly adaptable nature. And when one is living alone and has not yet reached one's seventeenth summer, certain allowances in such matters must be made.

It could be argued, if the Flinx were willing to listen (a most unlikely happenstance), that the ultimate decision as to who qualified as crooked and who did not was an awfully totalitarian one to have to make. A philosopher would nod knowingly in agreement. Flinx could not afford that luxury. His ethics were dictated by survival and not abstracts. It was to his great credit that he had managed to remian on the accepted side of current temporal morality as much as he had so far. Then again, chance was also due a fair share of the credit.

As a rule, though, he came by his modest income mostly honestly. This was made necessary as much by reason of common sense as by choice. A too-successful thief always attracts unwanted attention. Eventually, a criminal "law of diminishing returns" takes over.

And anyway, the jails of Drallar were notoriously inhospitable.

1

Good*Alan Dean Foster*

Good locations in the city for traveling jongleurs, minstrels, and such to display their talents were limited. Some were far better than others. That he at his comparatively slight age had managed to secure one of the best was a tribute to luck and the tenacity of old Mother Mastiff. From his infancy she had reserved the small raised platform next to her shop for him, driving off other entrepreneurs with shout or shot, as the occasion and vehemence of the interloper required. Mother Mastiff was not her real name, of course, but that was what everyone called her. Flinx included. Real names were of little use in Drallar's marketplaces. They served poorly for identification and too well for the tax-gatherers. So more appropriate ones were rapidly bestowed upon each new inhabitant. Mother Mastiff, for example, bore a striking resemblance to the Terran canine of the same name. It was given in humor and accepted with poor grace, but accepted, nevertheless. Her caustic personality only tended to compliment the physical similarity.

The man-child had been an orphan. Probably involuntary, as most of his ilk were. Still, who could tell? Had she not been passing the slave coops at that time and glanced casually in a certain direction, she would never have noticed it. For reasons she had never fully understood she had bought it, raised it, and set it to learning a trade as soon as it was old enough. Fortunately his theatrical proclivities had manifested themselves at quite an early stage, along with his peculiar talents. So the problem of choosing a trade solved itself. He proved to be a keen if somewhat solemn observer, and so his own best apprentice. Fine and well, because the older performers always became more nervous in his presence than they cared to

2

admit. Rather than admit it, they pronounced him unteachable, and left him to his own devices.

She had also taught him as early as was practical that in Drallar independence was ever so much more than an intangible thought. It was a possession, even if it would not fit into one's pocket or pouch, and to be valued as such. Still, when he had taken to her word and moved out to live on his own, the sadness lingered with her as a new coat of paint. But she never revealed it to him for fear of communicating weakness. Not in her words nor in her face. Urged on affectionately but firmly he was, much as the young birds of the Poles. Also she knew that for her the Moment might come at any time, and she wanted it to brush *his* life as lightly as possible.

Flinx felt the cottony pain of a sugar-coated probe again in his mind; the knowledge that Mother Mastiff was his mother by dint of sympathy and not birth. Coincidence was his father and luck his inheritance. Of his true parents he knew nothing, nor had the auctioneer. His card had been even more than usually blank, carrying not even the most elementary pedigree. A mongrel. It showed in his long orange-red hair and olive complexion. The reason for his orphanhood would remain forever as obscure as their faces. He let the life flood of the city enter his mind and submerge the unpleasant thoughts.

A tourist with more insight than most had once remarked that strolling through the great central marketplace of Drallar was like standing in a low surf and letting the geometrically patient waves lap unceasingly against one. Flinx had never seen the sea, so the reference remained obscure. There were few seas on Moth anyway, and no oceans. Only the uncounted, innumerable lakes of The-Blue-That-Blinded and shamed azure as a pale intonation.

The planet had moved with unusual rapidity out of its last ice age. The fast-dwindling ice sheets had left its surface pockmarked with a glittering lapis-lazuli embroidery of lakes, tarns, and great ponds. An almost daily rainfall maintained the water levels initially set by the retreating glaciers. Drallar happened to be situated in an exceptionally dry valley, good drainage and the lack of rainfall (more specifically, of mud) being one of the principal reasons for the city's growth. Here merchants could come to trade their goods and craftsmen to set up shop without fear of being washed out every third-month.

The evaporation-precipitation water cycle on Moth also differed from that of many otherwise similar humanx-type planets. Deserts were precluded by the lack of any real mountain ranges to block off moisture-laden air. The corresponding lack of oceanic basins and the general unevenness of the terrain never gave a major drainage system a chance to get started. The rivers of Moth were as uncountable as the lakes, but for the most part small in both length and volume. So the water of the planet was distributed fairly evenly over its surface, with the exception of the two great ice caps at the poles and the hemispheric remnants of the great glacial systems. Moth was the Terran Great Plains with conifers instead of corn.

The polyrhythmic chanting of barkers hawking the goods of a thousand worlds formed a nervous and jarring counterpoint to the comparatively even susurrations and murmurings of the crowd. Flinx passed a haberdashery he knew and in passing exchanged a brief, secret smile with its owner. That worthy, a husky blond middle-aged human, had just finished selling a pair of *durfarq*-skin coats to two outlandishly clad outworlders ... for three times what they were worth. Another saying trickled lazily through his mind.

"Those who come unprepared to Drallar to buy skin, inevitably get."

It did not offend Flinx's well-considered set of ethics. This was not stealing. *Caveat emptor.* Fur and fibers, wood and water, *were* Moth. Can one steal seeds from a tomato? The seller was happy with his sale, the purchasers were pleased with their purchase, and the difference would go to support the city in the form of welfares and grafts anyway. Besides, any outworlder who could afford to come to Moth could damn well afford to pay its prices. The merchants of Drallar were not to any extent rapacious. Only devious.

It was a fairly open planet, mostwise. The government was a monarchy, a throwback to the planet's earlier days. Historians found it quaint and studied it, tourists found it picturesque and frozepixed it, and it was only nominally terrifying to its citizens. Moth had been yanked abruptly and unprepared into the vortex of interstellar life and had taken the difficult transition rather well. As would-be planetbaggers rapidly found out. But on a planet where the bulk of the native population was composed of nomadic tribes following equally nomadic fur-bearing animals who exhibited unwonted bellicosity toward the losing of said furs, a representative government would have proved awkward in the extreme. And naturally the Church would not interfere. The Counselors did not even think of themselves as constituting a government, therefore they could not think of imposing one on others. Democracy on Moth would have to wait until the nomads would let themselves be counted, indexed, labeled, and cross-filed, and that seemed a long, long way off. It was well known that the Bureau of the King's Census annually published figures more complementary than accurate.

Wood products, furs, and tourism were the planet's principal industries. Those and trade. Fur-bearing creatures of every conceivable type (and a few inconceivable ones) abounded in the planet's endless forests. Even the insects wore fur, to shed the omnipresent water. Most known varieties of hard and soft woods thrived in the Barklands, including a number of unique and unclassifiable types, such as a certain deciduous fungus. When one refered to "grain" on Moth, it had nothing to do with flour. The giant lakes harbored fish that had to be caught from modified barges equipped with cyborg-backed fishing lines. It was widely quoted that of all the planets in the galaxy, only on Moth did an honest-to-goodness *pisces* have an even chance of going home with the fisherman, instead of vice-versa. And hunters were only beginning to tap *that* aspect of the planet's potentialities . . . mostly because those who went into the great forests unprepared kept an unquieting silence.

Drallar was its capital and largest city. Thanks to fortuitous galactic coordinates and the enlightened tax policies of a succession of kings it was now also an interstellar clearing-house for trade goods and commercial transactions. All of the great financial houses had at least branch headquarters here, reserving their showier offices for the more "civilized" planets. The monarch and his civil service were no more than nominally corrupt, and the king saw to it that the people were not swamped by repressive rules and regulations. Not that this was done out of love for the common man. It was simply good business. And if there were no business, there would be no taxes. No taxes would mean no government. And no government would mean no king, a state of affairs which the current monarch, his Driest Majesty King Dewe Nog Na XXIV, was at constant pains to avoid.

Then too, Drallar could be smelled.

In addition to the indigenous humans, the business of Drallar was conducted by half a hundred intelligent races. To keep this conglomeration of commerce pulsing smoothly, a fantastic diversity of organic fuels was demanded. So the central market place itself was encircled by a seemingly infinite series of serving stands, auto-chefs, and restaurants that formed in actuality one great, uninterrupted kitchen. The resulting combination of aromas generated by these establishments mingled to form an atmosphere unduplicated anywhere else in the known galaxy. On more refined trade stops such exotic miasmas were kept decently locked away. In Drallar there was no ozone to contaminate. One man's bread was another man's narcotic. And one man's narcotic could conceivably make another being nauseous.

But by some chance of chemistry, or chemistry of chance, the fumes blended so well in the naturally moist air that any potentially harmful effects were canceled out. Left only was an ever-swirling thick perfume that tickled one's throat and left unexpecting mouths in a state of perpetual salivation. One could get a deceptively full and satisfying meal simply by sitting down in the center of the markets and inhaling for an hour. Few other places in the Arm had acquired what might best be described as an olfactory reputation. It was a truth that gourmets came from as far away as Terra and Proycon merely to sit on the outskirts of the marketplace and hold long and spirited competitions in which the participants would attempt to identify only the wisps of flavor that were wafted outward on the damp breeze.

The reason for the circular arrangement was simple. A businessman could fortify himself on the outskirts and then plunge into the whirl of commerce without having to worry about being cut down in the midst of an important transaction by a sudden gust of, say, pungent *prego*-smoke from the bahnwood fires. Most of the day the vast circle served admirably well, but during the prime meal hours it made the marketplace resemble more than ever that perspicacious tourist's analogy of the ebb and flow of a sea.

Flinx paused at the stand of old Kiki, a vendor of sweets, and bought a small *thisk*-cake. This was a concoction made from a base of a tough local hybrid wheat. Inside, it was filled with fruit-pieces and berries and small, meaty *parma*-nuts, recently ripened. The finished product was then dipped in a vat of warmish honey-gold and allowed to harden. It was rough on the teeth, but, oh, what it did for the palate! It had one drawback: consistency. Biting into *thisk* was like chewing old spacesuit insulation. But it had a high energy content, the *parma*-nuts were mildly narcotic, and Flinx felt the need of some sort of mild stimulant before performing.

Above the voices and the smells, above all, Drallar could be viewed.

The edifices of the marketplace were fairly low, but outside the food crescents one could see ancient walls, remnants of Old City. Scattered behind and among were the buildings where the more important commerce took place. The lifeblood of Moth was here, not in the spectacular stalls below. Every day the economies of a dozen worlds were traded away in the dingy back rooms and offices of those old-new structures. There the gourmet restaurants catered to the rich sportsmen returning from the lakes, and turned up their noses and shut their windows against the plebian effluvia assailing them from the food stalls below. There the taxidermists plied their noisome arts, stuffing downy Yax'm pelts and mounting the ebony nightmare heads of the horned Demmichin Devilope.

Beyond rose the apartment houses where the middle and lower classes lived, those of the poorer characterized by few windows and cracking plaster, and those of the better-off by the wonderful multistoried murals painted by the gypsy artists, and by the brilliant azurine tiles which kept the houses warm in winter and cool in summer. Still farther off rose the isolated tower groupings of the rich inurbs, with their hanging gardens and reinforced crystal terraces. These soared loftily above the noise and clamor of the commonplace, sparkling as jeweled giraffes amid each morning fog.

Rising from the center of the city to dominate all was the great palace of the rulers of Drallar. Generations of kings had added to it, each stamping a section here, a wing there, with his own personality. Therein dwelt King Dewe Nog Na and his court. Sometimes he would take a lift to the topmost minaret, and there, seated comfortably on its slowly revolving platform, leisurely survey the impossible anthill that constituted his domain.

But the most beautiful thing about Moth was not Drallar, with its jeweled towers and chromatic citizenry, nor the innumerable lakes and forests, nor the splendid and variegated things that dwelt therein. It was the planet itself. It was that which had given to it a name and made it unique in the Arm. That which had first attracted men to the system. Ringed planets were rare enough.

Moth was a winged planet.

The "wings" of Moth doubtless at one time had been a perfect broad ring of the Saturn type. But at some time in the far past it had been broken in two places—possibly the result of a gravitational stress, or a change in the magnetic poles. No one could be certain. The result was an incomplete ring consisting of two great crescents of pulverized stone and gas which encircled the planet with two great gaps separating them. The crescents were narrower near the planet, but out in space they spread out to a natural fan shape due to the decreasing gravity, thus forming the famed "wing" effect. They were also a good deal thicker than the ancient Saturnian rings, and contained a higher proportion of fluorescent gases. The result was two gigantic triangular shapes of a lambent butter-yellow springing out from either side of the planet.

Inevitably, perhaps, the single moon of Moth was designated Flame. Some thought it a trite appelation, but none could deny its aptness. It was about a third again smaller than Terra's Luna, and nearly twice as far away. It had one peculiar characteristic. It didn't "burn" as the name would seem to suggest, although it was bright enough. In fact, some felt the label "moon" to be altogether inappropriate, as Flame didn't revolve around its parent planet at all, but instead preceded it around the sun in approximately the same orbit. So the two names stuck. The carrot leading a bejeweled ass, with eternity forever preventing satisfaction to the latter. Fortunately the system's discoverers had resisted the impulse to name the two spheres after the latter saying. As were so many of nature's freaks, the two were too uncommonly gorgeous to be so ridiculed.

The wing on Drallar's side was visible to Flinx only as a thin, glowing line, but he had seen pictures of it taken from space. He had never been in space himself, at least, only vicariously, but had visited many of the ships that landed at the Port. There at the feet of the older crewmen he listened intently while they spun tales of the great KK ships that plied the dark and empty places of the firmament. Since those monster interstellar craft never touched soil, of course, he had never seen one in person. Such a landing would never be made except in a dire emergency, and then never on an inhabited planet. A Doublekay carried the gravity well of a small sun on its nose, like a bee carrying pollen. Even shrunk to the tiny size necessary to make a simple landing, that field would protect the great bulk of the ship. It would also gouge out a considerable chunk of the planetary crust and set off all sorts of undesirable natural phenomena, like tsunamis and hurricanes and such. So the smaller shuttle ships darted yoyolike between traveler and ground, carrying down people and their goods, while the giant transports themselves remained in Polyphemian exile in the vastnesses of black and cold.

He had wanted to space, but had not yet found a valid reason to, and could not leave Mother Mastiff without anyone. Despite unceasing bellows asserting to her good health she *was* a hundred and something. To leave her alone simply for a pleasure trip was not a thought that appealed to him.

He tugged his cloak tighter around his shoulders,

half-burying Pip in the folds of thick fur. As human-
inhabited worlds go, Moth was not an exceptionally
cold planet, but it was far from tropical. He could not
remember the time when he had not been greeted
upon awakening by a wet and clammy fog. It was a
dependable but dampish companion. Here furs were
used more to shed water than to protect from bitter
chill. It was cold, yes, but not freezing. At least, it
snowed only in winter.

Pip hissed softly and Flinx absently began feeding
him the raisins he'd plucked from the *thisk*-cake. The
reptile gulped them down whole, eagerly. It would
have smacked its lips, if it'd had any. As it was, the
long tongue shot out and caressed Flinx's cheek with
the delicate touch of a diamond cutter. The minidrag's iridescent scales seemed to shine even brighter
than usual. For some reason it was especially fond of
raisins. Maybe it relished their iron content.

He glanced down at the plus window of his personal cardmeter. They weren't broke, but neither were
they swimming in luxury. Oh, yes, it was definitely
time to go to work!

From a counter of her variegated display booth,
Mother Mastiff was pleading amiably with a pair of
small, jeweled thranx *touristas*. Her technique was
admirable and competent. It ought to be, he reflected. She'd had plenty of time in which to perfect it. He
was only mildly surprised at the insectoid's presence.
*Where humans go, thranx also, and vicey-versy, don't
you know?* So went the children's rhyme. But they
did look a bit uncomfortable. Thranx loved the rain
and the damp, and in this respect Moth was perfect,
but they also prefered a good deal less cold and more
humidity. Paradoxically, the air could be wet and to
them still too dry. Every time a new hothouse planet

12

turned up they got ecstatic, despite the fact that such places invariably possessed the most objectionable and bellicose environments. Like any human youngster, he'd seen countless pictures of thranx planets: Hivehom, their counterpart of Terra, and also the famous thranx colonies in the Amazon and Congo basins on Terra itself. Why should humans wear themselves-out in an unfriendly climate when the thranx could thrive there? They had put those inhospitable regions to far better use than man ever could or would have—as had humans the Mediterranean Plateau on Hivehom.

Indeed, the Amalgamation had worked out very well all around.

From the cut of their necklaces these two were probably from Evoria. Anyhow the female's tiara and ovipositor glaze were dead giveaways. Probably a hunting couple, here for some excitement. There wasn't much to attract thranx to Moth, other than recreation, politics, and the light metals trade. Moth was rich in light metals, but deficient in many of the heavier ones. Little gold, lead, uranium, and the like. But silver and magnesium and copper in abundance. According to rumor, the giant thranx Elecseed complex had plans to turn Moth into a leading producer of electrical and thinkmachine components, much as they had Amropolous. But so far it had remained only rumor. Anyway, inducing skilled thranx workers to migrate to Moth would necessitate the company's best psychopublicists working day and night, plus megacredits in hardship pay. Even off-world human workers would find the living conditions unpalatable at best. He didn't think it likely. And without native atomics there'd be a big power problem. Hydroelectricity was a limited servant due to the lack of white

water. It formed an intriguing problem. How to generate enough electricity to run the plant to produce
electrical products?

All this musing put not credit in one's account nor
bread in one's mouth.

"Sir and madame, what think ye on my wares? No
better of the type to be found this side of Shorttree,
and damn little there." She fumbled, seemingly aim-
less, about her samples. "Now here's an item that
might appeal to ye. What of these matched copper
drink-jugs, eh? One for he and one for she." She held
up two tall, thin, burnished copper thranx drinking
implements. Their sides were elaborately engraved
and their spouts worked into intricate spirals.

"Notice the execution, the fine scroll work, sir," she
urged, tracing the delicate patterns with a wrinkled
forefinger. "I defy ye to find better, yea, anywheres!"

The male turned to his mate. "What do you say, my
dear?" They spoke symbospeech, that peculiar mixture of Terran basic and thranx click-hiss which had
become the dominant language of commerce throughout the Humanx Commonwealth and much of the rest
of the civilized galaxy besides.

The female extended a handfoot and grasped the
utensil firmly by one of its double handles. Her small,
valentine-shaped head inclined slightly at an angle in
an oddly human gesture of appraisal as she ran both
truehands over the deeply etched surface. She said
nothing, but instead looked directly into her mate's
eyes.

Flinx remained where he was and nodded knowingly at the innocent smile on Mother Mastiff's face.
He'd seen that predatory grin before. The taste of her
mind furnished him with further information as to
what would inevitably follow. Despite a century of

intimate familiarity and association with the thranx there still remained some humans who were unable to interpret even the commoner nuances of thranx gesture and gaze. Mother Mastiff was an expert and knew them all. Her eyes were bright enough to read the capital letters flashing there: SALE.

The husband commenced negotiations in an admirably offhand manner. "Well . . . perhaps something might be engendered . . . we already have a number of such baubles . . . exorbitant prices . . . a reasonable level. . . ."

"Level! You speak of *levels?*" Mother Mastiff's gasp of outrage was sufficiently violent to carry the odor of garlic all the way to where Flinx stood. The thranx, remarkably, ignored it. "Good sir, I survive at but a subsistence level now! The government takes all my money, and I have left but a pittance, a pittance, sir, for my three sons and two daughters!"

Flinx shook his head in admiration of Mother Mastiff's unmatched style. Thranx offspring always came in multiples of two, an inbred survival trait. With most things terrene and human there had been little or no conflict, but due to a quirk of psychology the thranx could not help but regard human odd-numbered births as both pathetic and not a little obscene.

"Thirty credits," she finally sighed.

"Blasphemous!" the husband cried, his antennae quivering violently. "They are worth perhaps ten, and at that I flatter the craftsman unmercifully."

"Ten!" moaned Mother Mastiff, feigning a swoon. "Ten, the creature says, and boasts of it! Surely . . . surely, sir, you do not expect me to consider such an offer *seriously!* 'Tis not even successful as a jest."

"Fifteen, then, and I should report you to the local

magistrate. Even common thieves have the decency to work incognito."

"Twenty-five. Sir, you, a cultured and wealthy being, surely you can do better than taunt and make sport of an old female. One who has doubtless fertilized as many eggs as you . . ." The female had the grace to lower her head and blush. The thranx were quite open about sex . . . theirs or anyone else's . . . but still, Flinx thought, there *were* lines over which it was improper to step.

Good manners it might not have been, but in this case at least it appeared to be good business. The male harrumphed awkwardly, a deep, vibrant hum. "Twenty, then."

"Twenty-three five, and a tenth credit less I will not say!" intoned Mother Mastiff. She folded her arms in a recognizable gesture of finality.

"Twenty-one," countered the male.

Mother Mastiff shook her head obstinately, immovable as a Treewall. She looked ready to wait out entropy.

"Twenty-three five, not a tenth credit less. My last and final offer, good sir. This pair will find its own market. I must survive, and I fear I may have allowed you to sway me too far already."

The male would have argued further, on principle if for nothing else, but at that point the female put a truehand on his b-thorax, just below the ear, and stroked lightly. That ending the bargaining.

"Ahhh, Dark Centers! Twenty-five . . . no, twenty-three five, then! Thief! Assaulter of reason! It is well known that a human would cheat its own female-parent to make a half-credit!"

"And it is well known also," replied Mother Mastiff smoothly as she processed the sale, "that the thranx

16

are the most astute bargainers in the galaxy. You have gotten yourself a steal, sir, and so 'tis you and not I the thief!"

As soon as the exchange of credit had been finalized, Flinx left his resting place by the old wall and strolled over to the combination booth and home. The thranx had departed happily, antennae entwined. On their mating flight? The male, at least, had seemed too old for that. His chiton had been shading ever so slightly into deep blue, despite the obvious use of cosmetics, while the female had been a much younger aquamarine. The thranx too took mistresses. In the moist air, their delicate perfume lingered.

"Well, mother," he began. He was not indicating parentage—she had insisted on that years ago—but using the title bestowed on her by the folk of the markets. Everyone called her mother. "Business seems good."

She apparently had not noticed his approach and was momentarily flustered. "What? What? Oh, 'tis you, cub! Pah!" She gestured in the direction taken by the departed thranx. "Thieves the bugs are, to steal fom me so! But have I a choice?" She did not wait for an answer. "I am an old woman and must sell occasionally to support myself, even at such prices, for who in this city would feed me?"

"More likely, mother, it would be you who would feed the city. I saw you purchase those same mug-spirals from Olin the Coppersmith not six days ago ... for eleven credits."

"Ay? Harrumph," she coughed. "You must be mistaken, boy. Even you can make a mistake now and then, you know. Um, have you eaten yet today?"

"A *thisk*-cake only."

"Is that the way I raised ye, to live on sweets?" In

her gratefulness for a change of subject she feigned anger. "And I'll wager ye gave half of it to that damned snake of yours, anyway!"

Pip raised his dozing head at that and let out a mild hiss. Mother Mastiff did not like the minidrag and never had. Few people did. Some might profess friendship, and after coaxing a few could even be persuaded to pet it. But none could forget that its kind's poison could lay a man dead in sixty seconds, and the antidote was rare. Flinx was never cheated in business or pleasure when the snake lay curled about his shoulder.

"Gentle, mother. He understands what you say, you know. Not so much what as why, really."

"Oh surely, surely! Now claim intelligence for the monster! Bewitched it is, perhaps. I believe it that latter, at least, for I can't deny I've seen the thing react oddly, yes. But it does no work, sleeps constantly, and eats prodigiously. You'd be far better off without it, lad."

He scratched the minidrag absently behind the flat, scaly head. "Your suggestion is not humorful, mother. Besides, it *does* work in the act. . . ."

"Gimmick," she snorted, but not loudly.

"And as to its sleeping and eating habits, it is an alien thing and has metabolic requirements we cannot question. Most importantly, I like it and . . . and it likes me."

Mother Mastiff would have argued further except that they had gone through uncounted variations of this very argument over the years. No doubt a dog or one of the local domesticated running-birds would have made a more efficacious pet for a small boy, but when she'd taken in the maltreated youngster Mother Mastiff'd had no credits for dogs or birds. Flinx had stumbled on the minidrag himself in the alley behind their first shack, rooting in a garbage heap for meats and sugars. Being ignorant of its identity, he'd approached it openly and unfearing. She'd found the two huddled together in the boy's bed the following morning. She had hefted a broom and tried to shoo it off, but instead of being frightened the thing had opened its mouth and hissed threateningly at her. That initial attempt constituted her first and last physical effort at separating the two.

The relationship was an unusual one and much commented upon, the more so since Alaspin was many parsecs away and none could recall having heard of a minidrag living unconfined off its native world before. It was widely surmised that it had been the pet of some space trader and had gotten loose at the shuttleport and escaped. Since the importation of poisonous animals was a felony on most planets, Moth included, few were surprised that the original owner had not made noisy efforts to reclaim his property. In any case it had harmed no one (Flinx knew otherwise, and better than to boast the fact) and so none in the marketplace protested its presence to the authorities, although all wished with a passion it would go elsewhere.

He moved to change the subject.

"How are you equipped for credit, mother?"

"Fah! Poorly, as always. But," and this with a sly, small grin, "I should be able to manage for a while off that last transaction."

"I'd wager," he chuckled. He turned to survey the chromatically colored crowd which flowed unceasingly around and in front of the little shop, trying to gauge the proportion of wealthy tourists among the

19

everyday populace. The effort, as usual, made his head ache.

"A normal day's passings or not, mother?"

"Oh, there's money out there now, all right! I can smell it. But it declines to come into my shop. Better luck to you, perhaps, lad."

"Perhaps." He walked out from under the awning and mounted the raised dais to the left of the shop. Carefully he set about rearranging the larger pots and pans which formed the bulk of Mother Mastiff's cheaper inventory to give himself sufficient room to work.

His method of enticing an audience was simple and timeworn. He took four small *brana* balls from a pocket and began to juggle them. These were formed from the sap of a tree that grew only in Moth's equatorial belt. Under the sun's diffused UV they pulsed with a faint yellow light. They were perfect for his needs, being solid and of a uniform consistency. A small crowd began to gather. He added a fifth ball now, and began to vary the routine by tossing them behind his back without breaking rhythm. The word was passed outward like invisible tentacles, occasionally snatching another person here, another there, from the fringes of the shuffling mob. Soon he had acquired his own substantial little island of watchful beings. He whispered softly to the minidrag, almost buried in the soft fur.

"Up, boy."

Pip uncurled himself from Flinx's shoulder, unfurling his leathery wings to their fullest extent. In spite of its rarity the crowd recognized the lethal shape and drew back. The snake soared into the air and performed a delicate, spiraling descent, to settle like a crown around the boy's head. It then proceeded to catch each ball and toss it high into the air, changing the shape but not the rhythm of the act. The unbroken fluorescent trail took on a more intricate weave. A mild pattering of applause greeted this innovation. Jugglers were more than common in Drallar, but a young one who worked so deftly with a poisonous reptile was not. A few coins landed on the platform, occasionally bouncing metallically off the big pans. More applause and more coins when the snake flipped all five balls, one after another, into a small basket at the rear of the dais.

"Thank you, thank you, gentlebeings!" said Flinx, bowing theatrically, thinking, now for the real part of the act. "And now, for your information, mystification, and elucidation . . . and a small fee" (mild laughter), "I will endeavor to answer any question, *any* question, that anyone in the audience, regardless of his race or planet of origin, would care to tempt me with."

There was the usual skeptical murmuring from the assembly, and not a few sighs of boredom.

"All the change in my pocket," blurted a merchant in the first row," if you can tell me how much there is!" He grinned amid some nervous giggling from within the crowd.

Flinx ignored the sarcasm in the man's voice and stood quietly, eyes tightly shut. Not that they had to be. He could "work" equally as well with them wide open. It was a piece of pure showmanship which the crowds always seemed to expect. Why they expected him to look inward when he had to look outward remained ever-puzzling to him. He had no real idea how his answers came to him. One minute his mind was empty, fuzzy, and the next . . . sometimes . . . an answer would appear. Although "appear" wasn't quite

21

right either. Many times he didn't even understand the questions, especially in the case of alien questioners. Or the answers. Fortunately that made no difference to the audience. He could not have promised interpretations. There!

"Good sir, you have in your pocket four tenth pieces, two hundredth pieces ... and a key admitting you to a certain club that. . . ."

"Stop, stop!" The man was waving his gnarled hands frantically and glancing awkwardly at those in the crowd nearest him. "That will do! I am convinced." He dug into his pocket, came out with a handful of change, thrust the troublesome key back out of sight of the curious who leaned close for a look. He started to hand over the coins, then paused almost absently, a look of perplexity on his face. It changed slowly to one of surprise.

"By Pali's tide-bore, the whelp is right! Forty-two hundredths. He's right!" He handed over the coins and left, mumbling to himself.

Flying coins punctuated the crowd's somewhat nervous applause. Flinx judged their mood expertly. Belief had about pulled even with derision. There were naturally those who suspected the merchant of being a plant. They granted he was a very convincing one.

"Come, come, gentlebeings! What we have here is larvae play. Surely there are those among you with questions worth tempting my simple skill?"

A being at the back of the crowd, a Quillp in full post-mating plumage, craned its thin ostrichlike neck forward and asked in a high, squeaky voice, "In what summer-month my hatchlings come about will?"

"I am truly sorry, sir, but that is a question that involves the future, and I am not a clairvoyant." The creature sighed unhappily and prepared to leave the gathering. At this sign of mortality on Flinx's part a number of others seemed inclined to go with the tall Ornithorpe. Flinx said hurriedly, "But I hope fervent all *five* of your hatchlings successful are!"

The Quillp whirled in surprise and turned goggling eyes on the small stage. "How did you know that number my circle had?" In its excitement it spoke in its native tongue and had to be reminded by a neighbor to shift to symbospeech.

"I make it a policy not to reveal professional secrets." Flinx yawned with calculated elaboration. "Come, a real question, gentlebeings. I bore quickly. Miracles I cannot produce, though, and they usually bore anyway."

Two humans, big, muscular fellows, were pushing their way ungently to the stage. The one on Flinx's left wore glasses—not for their antique therapeutic value, but because in some current fashion circles it was considered something of a fad. He extended a credcard.

"Can you accept this, boy?"

Flinx bridled at the "boy," but extracted his cardmeter. "Indeed I can, sir. Ask your question."

The man opened his mouth, paused. "How do I know what to pay you?"

"I can't set value on my answers, only on your question. Whatever you deem it worth, sir. If I give no answer I will refund your credits." He gestured to where the minidrag rested alertly on his shoulder. "My pet here seems to have a feel for the emotional states of others which is quite sensitive. Even more so than myself. A swindler, for example, exudes something that he is especially sensitive to. I am rarely swindled."

The man smiled without mirth. "I wonder why?"

He dialed a setting on the card, extended it again. "Will a hundred credits do?"

Flinx was quick to stifle his reaction. A hundred credits! That was more than he sometimes made in a month! For a moment he was tempted to lower the figure, mindful of the laugh Mother Mastiff might have if she found out. Especially after his comments on *her* pricings this morning. Then he reminded himself that, after all, the man had set the price and surely would not cheat himself. He tried but could detect no trace of humor about the man. Nor his companion. Quite the contrary. And he hadn't heard the question yet. What if he couldn't answer it?

"A . . . a hundred credits would be most satisfactory, sir."

The man nodded and stuck his card in the little black meter. The compact machine hummed softly and the amount, one-oh-oh-zero-zero, clicked into place on its tiny dial. There was a brief pause and then it buzzed once, the red light on its top glowing brightly. It noted that the amount of so-and-so, card number such-and-such, was good for the amount dialed, and that credits numbering one hundred (100) had been transferred to the account of one Philip Lynx (his given name in the city records) in the Royal Depository of the sovereign Republic of Moth. Flinx returned the box to its place in his pouch and looked back to the two expectant men.

"Ask your question, sirs."

"My companion and I are searching for a man . . . a friend . . . whom we know to be somewhere in this part of the city, but whom we have been unable as yet to contact."

"What is there distinctive about him?" Flinx asked from under closed eyes.

The other man spoke for the first time. His voice revealed an impatience that his mind confirmed. It was brusque and low-pitched. "He is not tall . . . thin, has red hair like yourself, only darker and tightly curled. Also his skin is not so dark as yours. It is mottled, and he has wet eyes."

That helped. Redheads were not plentiful in Drallar, and the reference to "wet eyes" indicated a man with a high sexual potential. The combination ought to be easy to locate. Flinx began to feel more confident. Still, Drallar was large. And there was the shuttleport to consider, too.

"Not enough. What else?"

The two looked at each other. Then the bigger one spoke again. "This man is dressed in navigator's clothes. He has with him . . . probably on his person . . . a small map. A star map. It is hand-drawn and very unprofessional looking. He usually keeps it in his blouse, which bulges slightly in consequence."

Flinx concentrated harder. So, a shift in the internal abstract, an angle resolved. . . . He opened his eyes, looked up in surprise. His gaze roved over the rear of the silent crowd and came to rest on an individual at the back. A redheaded man, not tall, with mottled skin, wet eyes, and a slight bulge over his heart. Not surprisingly, Flinx sensed paper therein. As soon as their eyes met the man's went wide. He broke and plunged into the market mob. At the ensuing commotion the big man turned his head and strained to see through the mass. He clasped a hand on his companion's shoulder and pointed urgently. They started off in the direction of the disturbance, forcing the other members of the assembly out of their way with far more strength than tact.

Flinx almost called to them, but the action turned

to a shrug instead. If this form of an answer satisfied the two, he certainly wasn't going to argue the matter. A hundred credits! Without even committing himself. And the loose coin on the dais for Mother Mastiff. He waved an impulsive hand at the crowd.

"Thank you ever so for your attention, gentlebeings. For today, at least, the show is over."

The assemblage began to melt back into the flow of traffic, accompanied by not a few groans of disappointment from would-be questioners. With the unexpected dramatic build-up he had been given by the two strangers he probably could have milked the remainder for a pile, but his gift was capricious and possessed of a tendency to tire him quickly. Best to halt with an unchallanged success. This windfall entitled him to a serious celebration, and he was already impatient to get on with it.

"Pip, if we could take in what we took today on a regular basis, the king would make me royal treasurer and you his official guardian." The snake hissed noncommitally, the jet-black eyes staring up at him. Ink boiled in those tiny poolings. Apparently government work didn't have much appeal.

"And you are no doubt hungry again." This produced a more positive hiss, and Flinx chuckled, scratching the minidrag under its leather-soft snout. "That's what I thought. However, I feel that something of a more liquid nature is in order for myself. So we will make our way over to Small Symm's, and I will guzzle spiced beer, and you may have all the pretzels your venomous little carcass will hold!" The snake wagged its tail at this, which involved its quivering all over, since it was mostly tail in the first place.

As they made their way over the cobblestone back

26

street he began mentally to reproach himself for not playing the crowd longer. He still felt that to overuse his talent would be to burn it out. But there were times when one had to be businesslike as well as cautious, a point Mother Mastiff had made to him many times. Still, he had slept late today and gotten started later than was usual. It would probably have proved difficult to hold the crowd much longer anyway. In Drallar darkness had a tendency to disperse people rapidly, and it was even now quite black out. Besides, he had a hundred credits in his pocket! Effectively, not actually, since it was in his account at the depository. So why worry? Did the sun fight to gather new hydrogen?

He had almost reached the dimly lit bar when he tasted the sounds. They came filtering out of the alleyway to his left, a hole dark as the gullet of a giant pseudo-sturgeon from one of the Great Northern Lakes. It sounded very much like a fight. A questing probe brought back overtones of fear/anger/terror/greed/bloodlust. Fighting in fun was accompanied by much cursing and shouting. None were uttered in a battle to the death since the participants were too busy and too intent of purpose to waste the breath. Only humans fought quite that silently, so he knew they were not a part of the city's alien populace. There was that peculiar muteness of thought . . .

Flinx did not mix in such conflicts. In a city like Drallar where fat bellies and empty purses coexisted in abundance, one's own business remained healthy so long as one minded it. He had taken one step toward the peace of the bar when Pip uncoiled himself from his shoulder and streaked into the alley.

Even at his comparatively young age, Flinx could curse fluently in fourteen languages. He had time for only five before he was hurtling into the blackness after his pet. It was only in precaution that he drew the thin stiletto from its boot sheath without breaking stride.

Now he could perceive three forms in the dim light from the cloud-masked stars and the city-glow. Two were large and stood upright. The other was slight of build and lay with a recognizable stillness on the ground. One of the others bent over the prostrate body. Before it could carry out its unknown purpose, it jerked and roared loudly in the quiet.

"GODDAMN!"

The man began flailing wildly at a thin, leathery shape which dived and swooped at his head. The other pulled the wicked shape of a neuronic pistol from a shoulder cup and tried to sight on the rapidly moving object. Flinx had no time to think. With vague thoughts of forcing the man to the ground and knocking him out, he leaped onto the man's back. The thick ropes of broad muscle he felt beneath the man's blouse rapidly squelched that idea. The man lurched. In another second he'd be smashed against the wall of the nearest building. The thin blade plunged once, instinctively. The big man buckled horribly and crashed to the ground like a great tree. Flinx had already left the dead hulk before it reached the pavement.

The other whirled to meet this new menace as his companion pitched forward onto his face. Cursing, he fired in Flinx's direction. Rolling like mad, the youth had made the cover of a broken metal crate. Fortunately the man's night vision didn't seem as good as his own. Even so, the near miss sent a painful tingle up his leg. An almost-hit with the ugly weapon would cause a man literally to shake himself to death in a series of uncontrollable muscular spasms. A direct hit to the heart or brain would kill instantly. Supposedly such weapons were outlawed on Moth. Obviously the law could be circumvented. The man rayed the area to his left. It was a mistake. Unhampered, Pip had the time he needed. The minidrag spat once.

It was not a gesture of defiance, but of death. The flying snakes or "miniature dragons" of Alaspin are akin to a few other carnivorous creatures. Among these is the *Hemachacus*, or spitting cobra, of Terra. The latter has forward-facing fangs, and instead of injecting its venom via a bite, can spit it to a surprising distance with remarkable accuracy. The Alaspinian minidrags, however, have no fangs. Only small cutting teeth for biting. Little work has actually been done on them on their seldom visited planet, but they apparently, eject their poison through a narrowing tube of cartilaginous material running along the roof of the mouth. Muscles running the length of the jaw and along the neck force the venom even farther than the Terran types, and with greater accuracy. Fortunately the minidrag has a relatively mild disposition and attacks only when threatened. Pip's actions were therefore unusual but not incomprehensible.

The man gave vent to a shockingly shrill, soul-tearing scream and sank to his knees, clawing at his eyes. The venom was corrosive as well as killing. It was not fatal unless it got into the bloodstream, and so by rubbing at his eyes the man effectively killed himself. In thirty seconds he had become incapable of even that.

In another thirty he was incapable of doing anything at all.

Pip returned to his familiar resting place. As he settled his coils around Flinx's shoulder, the boy could feel the unnatural tension in the reptile's muscles. There was a brief urge to bawl the minidrag out good and proper, but his narrow escape and the fact that the snake had once again saved his life put it off. Time pressed. Still shaking slightly from muscular reaction of his own, he crept from his hiding place to the results of an undesired action.

The only sounds in the alley were the ruffling whispers made by the always moist air flowing over the silk-cool stones and the steady plop, plop, plop of blood flowing from the wound in the back of the man the stiletto had finished. There remained the third body. In spite of everything, he had been too late to help the small man. His neck had been broken cleanly. Unmoving, the sightless eyes reflected the silent stars.

There was just sufficient light for him to make out the man's brilliant red hair.

A crumpled piece of plastic lay clutched in a spasmodically frozen hand. Flinx pried it from his grasp, bending open the lifeless but still stubborn fingers. Above him lights began to come on as the cautious inhabitants of the alleyway decided it was safe to trust their precious selves to the quiet uncertainty of the night. Prudence had been served and now curiosity had taken over. It was time for him to leave. Now that the locals had bestirred themselves and the action had been resolved the local constabulary would be arriving. Although they would take their time, they would get here nonetheless. It would not do to be found standing over three lifeless bodies, all of them blatantly outworld. Especially when one of them had registered a hundred credits to his account only this afternoon.

He didn't like stealing from the dead, but anything

that small that could cause the death of three men in one night was too important to leave to the discretion of the police. Without more than a casual glance at it, he shoved the rumpled sheet into his pouch.

The police arrived shortly after he had exited the mouth of the alley. A sudden increase in the babble of thoughts and voices told him that the bodies had been discovered. For locals action was time-defined and pedantic. When the police discovered that the three corpses were outworlders, a search pattern would be put into effect with small delay. Murder was not conducive to increased tourism. He hurried a mite faster toward the bar.

Small Symm's establishment was notable not so much for its food and drink, but rather for the reputation it enjoyed as being one of the few places in Drallar where a being could go at night, get comfortably drunk, and still be assured of retaining the same amount of body fluid that he had commenced the evening with. Small Symm himself was well aware of the business this favorable standing attracted to his place and so labored mightily to maintain it. He did not know it, but if his business had been a country on Terra several odd centuries ago, it would have been called Switzerland.

As Small Symm stood well over two meters tall and weighed in the neighborhood of a hundred and fifty kilos, few felt inclined to dispute his neutrality. Those who had yearnings to contented themselves with imbibing elsewhere and commenting on the inordinate size of the barkeep's ears.

There were no drinking laws on Moth. Only sober ones, as the saying went. As far as the judges were concerned one could proceed directly from the mother's breast to a bottle of Old Yeast-Bubble's best mash

31

brew liquor. The end result of this oft-commented upon degenerate policy was a thriving local industry and a surprisingly small number of alcoholics.

However, there had been a few who had commented at times on Flinx's comparative youth and thereby questioned his right to imbibe fermented spirits. One particular person, a traveling sinspinner from Puritan, had been especially obnoxious in this respect. Small Symm had lumbered over and politely advised the fellow to mind his own business. Holding fast to the tenets of his faith (and being a bit tipsy himself), the man had told Symm in no uncertain terms what he could do with his suggestions. The next thing he knew, his right arm had been neatly broken in two places. As gently as possible. The outworlder had gone straight to the police and the police had objected . . . after all, an outworlder, respected . . . but not too vigorously. Especially after Symm had picked up their paddycraft and jammed it immovably into a sewer opening. After that Flinx and Symm both found themselves little troubled by minions of either God or Cop.

The giant was pleased to see him. Not the least of the things they had in common was the fact that both were technically orphans.

"A dry hearth, young master! And how does the world find you tonight?"

Flinx took the seat at the end of the bar. "It finds me well enough, enormous one. Well enough so that I will have a bottle of your very finest Burrberry beer, and a cauldron of pretzels for my friend."

He rubbed the snake under the jaw and Pip's eyes slitted in appreciation. There were times when he would swear he could hear the thing purr. But since no one else could, he never made it a point of discussion.

Symm's eyebrows went up slightly. Burrberry was expensive, and potent. He was far more concerned about the youth's ability to handle the former, however. The red ale was imported all the way from Crnkk, a thranx planet, and packed quite a kick for even a full-grown human. But he fetched it, and the pretzels for the minidrag.

When he returned, the snake did not wait for an invitation, but dived immediately into the bowl and began wallowing around in the salty twists, its tongue darting and flicking with machinelike rapidity at the big halite crystals. Like many things in Drallar, even the pretzels disdained subtlety. Flinx reflected again that for an undeniably carnivorous animal, his pet was notoriously fond of grain products. The minidrag's culinary adaptability had been one reason why it had been able to thrive so well in the city. There had been times when meat had been scarce, and vermin as well, and he and Mother Mastiff had watched in wonderment as the reptile happily downed large portions of salted bread or *pime,* the cheap cornlike growths that infested many of Moth's softwoods.

Flinx hefted the delicately formed bottle and poured the cherry-red brew, watching it foam pinkly over the lip of the mug. Brewing was one of the thranx's most polished abilities. It was too late for the few perpetual drunkards and too early for most night crawlers. Small Symm satisfied himself that his other customers were taken care of and hunkered himself over the bar, leaning on crossed arms like hirsute trees. He watched silently as the boy downed a long draught of the effervescent liquid, then began

33

on the remainder with short, caressing sips. Now and
then a satisfied hiss would come from the region to
their right, among the pretzels.

The barkeep's eyebrows jumped again when Flinx
elected to pay for the nourishments in coin. "Business
has been so good, then?"

"It has, it has. Believe it or not, old friend, I made a
hundred credits today. Honestly, too!" The recent
memory of three bodies in an alley came back to him.
"Although now I am not so glad I did, maybe."

"That is a strange thing to say." The giant poured
himself a tiny yttrium cognac. "I am happy for you,
but somewhat disappointed also, for it will mean that
you will not need the job I've lined up for you."

"Oh? Don't be in such a hurry, massive one. And
don't try to psych me, either. I am solvent at the
moment, true, but money has a tendency to slip un-
noticed from my fingers. I give too much away, also.
And I have the old woman to think of, although by
now she might own the city fountains, despite her
protestations of poverty."

"Ah. Mother Mastiff, of course. Well, possibly you
would be interested, then. I can at least promise you
some intriguing company." He gestured behind Flinx.
"The third booth. Two most extraordinary person-
ages."

Flinx turned to look at the small, cloth-covered
booths which lined the back of the establishment.
Business and pleasure, sometimes mixed, were often
conducted in those shrouded enclaves. He peered
harder in the fuzzy light. Most people could not have
discerned anything at even that short distance, but
Flinx did not look with his eyes alone. Yes, there were
indeed two figures in the indicated booth. And yes,

from what he could see of them they did form an odd pair.

One was a very tall human. His face was not sallow, but composed mostly of acute angles, like knife blades protruding out from under the skin. His hair seemed to be graying at the temples and back, a natural turning of color, and one streak of pure white ran all the way from front to back. The eyes were sharply slanted, almost mongoloid, and as black as most of his hair. They were made to appear mildly incongruous by the bushy eyebrows which met over the bridge of the nose. The mouth was small and thin-lipped, and the body, while not skinny, had the slenderness of careful diet more than vigorous exercise. He was heavily tanned on the visible portions of his body, the tan that Flinx had come to recognize as belonging to men who had been long in space and exposed to greater amounts of naked ultraviolet than most.

If the man was unusual, his companion was twice so. Although Flinx had not seen so very many thranx, for they did not congregate in Drallar, he had seen enough to know that the one lounging across from the man was by far the oldest he'd ever come across. Its chiton had faded from a normal healthy pale blue to a deep purple that was almost black. The antennae drooped to the sides and were scaly at the base. Even at this distance he could perceive how the shell below the wing cases (both sets were present: unmated, then) was exfoliating. Only the glowing, jewellike compound eyes glittered with a gold that signified youth and vigor. A pity that he could not perceive even deeper.

The cloth effectively cut off their conversation at this distance, but now and then the insect would make a gesture with a truehand and the human would nod solemnly in response. Flinx found the liquor hampering him. Almost angrily, he turned back to his friend.

"You were right, Symm. An odd coupling to find here."

"They've been in every night for four nights running now, and they drink steadily, although it seems to have about as much effect on them as water. But to the point. As is plain to a *Mottl*-bird, they are strangers here. Yesterday they first began inquiring after a guide, saying that they wish to see more of the city. I was at a loss to help them until I thought of you. But now, since you are grown as rich as the king. . . ."

"No, no. Wait." Flinx was feeling expansive. Perhaps it was the beer. "They should be good for a few stories, if nothing else. Yes, I'll assume the conveyance."

Symm grinned and ruffled the boy's hair roughly. "Good! I thought a glimpse of them might persuade you, as your interest in things off-world is notorious. Why it should be, though, the Tree knows! Wait here, I'll go tell them."

He went out from behind the bar and over to the booth. Through the faintly puce haze induced by the beer he could see the giant part the curtain and murmur to the two beings within.

"Well," he muttered to himself. "One thing's helping, anyways. At least they're not common tourists. Perhaps I'll be spared the agony of watching them chortle over buying shiploads of junk at three times the honest price." He made a sound that was a long hiss ending in a popped bubble. A scaly, smug head popped up from the bowl of demolished pretzels, which had shrunken considerably in volume. The minidrag slid out onto the table and up the proffered arm, curling into its familiar position on Flinx's shoulder. It burped once, sheepishly.

Symm returned with the two off-worlders in tow. "This youth is called Flinx, sirs, and offers to be your guide. A finer or more knowledgeable one cannot be found in the city. Do not be misled by his comparative youth, for he has already acquired more information than is good for him."

Here at close range Flinx was able to study his two charges better. He did so, intently. The tall human was a fair sixth meter shorter than the huge Symm, but the thranx was truly a giant of its kind. With its upper body raised as it was now, its eyes were almost on a level with Flinx's own. The entire insect was a full 2 meters long. One and a half was normal for a male of the species. That their eyes were busy in their own scrutiny of him he did not mind. As a performer he was more than used to that. But he found himself looking away from those great golden orbs. Meeting them was too much like staring into an ocean of shattered prisms. He wondered what it was like to view life that way, through a thousand tiny eyes instead of merely two large ones.

When the man spoke, it was with a surprisingly melodious voice. "How do you do, youngster. Our good dispenser of spirits here informs us that you are practically indispensable to one who wishes to see something of your city."

He extended a hand and Flinx shook it, surprised at the calluses there. As the effects of the mildly hallucinogenic brew wore off, he became increasingly aware of the uniqueness of the two beings he was going to be associating with. Each exuded an aura of something he'd not encountered before, even in his wanderings among the denizens of the shuttleport.

"My name is Tse-Mallory ... Bran. And this, my companion, is the Eint Truzenzuzex."

The insect bowed from the "waist" at the introduction, a swooping, flowing motion not unlike that of a lake-skimmer diving for a surface swimming fish. Another surprise: it spoke Terranglo, instead of symbospeech. Here was a learned and very polite bug indeed! Few thranx had the ability to master more than a few elementary phrases of Terranglo. Its inherent logical inconsistencies tended to give them headaches. The insect's pronunciation, however, was as good as his own. The rasping quality of it was made unavoidable by the different arrangement of vocal cords.

"High metamorphosis to you, youth. We've been in need of a guide to this confusing city of yours for several days, actually. We're very glad you've agreed to help us out of our difficulty."

"I'll do what I can, gentlesirs." This flattery was embarrassing.

"We would prefer to start at dawn tomorrow," said Tse-Mallory. "We're here on business, you see, and a more intimate acquaintance with the city is a prerequisite which we have put off too long already. We were expecting a guide to meet us, actually, but since he has apparently changed his mind, you will have the commission."

"We are staying at a small inn a short distance down this same street," added Truzenzuzex. "Its sign is three fishes and ..."

"... a starship. I know the place, sir. I'll meet you at first-fog—seven hours—tomorrow, in the lobby."

The two shook hands with him once again and

made as if to take their leave. Flinx coughed delicately but insistently. "Uh, a small detail, sirs."

Tse-Mallory paused. "Yes?"

"There is the matter of payment."

The thranx made the series of rapid clicking sounds with its mandibles which passed for laughter among its kind. The insects had a highly developed, sometimes mischievous sense of humor.

"So! Our guide is a plutocrat as well! No doubt as a larvae you were a hopeless sugar-hoarder. How about this, then? At the conclusion of our tour tomorrow—I daresay one day will be sufficient for our purposes—we will treat you to a meal at the finest comestabulary in the food crescent."

Well! Let's see now, twelve courses at Portio's would come to . . . well! His mouth was watering already.

"That'll be great . . . sufficient, I mean, sirs." Indeed, it would!

Chapter Two

Flinx was of course not a guide by profession, but he knew ten times as much about the real Drallar as the bored government hirelings who conducted the official tours of the city's high spots for bemused off-worlders. He'd performed this function for other guests of Small Symm more than once in the past.

These, however, had proved themselves rather outré *touristas*. He showed them the great central marketplace, where goods from halfway across the Arm could be found. They did not buy. He took them to the great gate of Old Drallar, a monumental arch carved from water-pure silicon dioxide by native craftsmen, and so old it was not recorded in the palace chronicles. They did not comment. He took them also to the red towers where the fantastic flora of Moth grew lush in greenhouses under the tender ministrations of dedicated royal botanists. Then to the tiny, out-of-the-way places, where could be bought the unusual, the rare, and the outlawed. Jeweled dishware, artwork, weaponry, utensils, gems, rare earths and rare clothings, tickets to anywhere. Scientific instruments, scientists, females or other sexes of any species. Drugs: medicinal, hallucinogenic, deadly, preservative. Thoughts and palm-readings. Only rarely did either of them say this or that small thing

40

about their surroundings. One might almost have thought them bored.

Once it was at an antique cartographer's, and then in a language incomprehensible to the multilinguistic Flinx.

Yes, for two who had seemed so needful of a guide, they had thus far shown remarkably little interest in their surroundings. They seemed far more interested in Flinx and Pip than in the city he was showing them. As late afternoon rolled around he was startled to realize how much they had learned about him through the most innocent and indirect questioning. Once, when Truzenzuzex had leaned forward to observe the minidrag more closely, it had drawn back warily and curled its head out of sight behind Flinx's neck. That itself was an oddity. The snake's normal reaction was usually either passivity or belligerence. This was the first time Flinx could recall it's displaying uncertainty. Apparently Truzenzuzex made little of the incident, but he never tried to approach the reptile closely again.

"You are an outstanding guide and a cheerful companion," the thranx said, "and I for one count myself fortunate to have you with us." They had moved along until they were now quite a distance from the city's center. Truzenzuzex gestured ahead to where the tower homes of the very wealthy stretched away in landscaped splendor. "Now we would wish to see the manicured grounds and hanging gardens of Drallar's inurbs, of which we have both heard so much."

"I'm afraid I cannot manage that, sir. The grounds of Braav inurb are closed to such as I, and there are groundkeepers—with guns—who are posted by the walls to keep the common folk from infesting the greens."

41

"But you *do* know the ways within?" prodded Tse-Mallory.

"Well," Flinx began hesitantly. After all, what did he really know of these two? "At night I have sometimes found it necessary to . . . but it is not night now, and we would surely be seen going over the walls."

"Then we shall go through the gate. Take us," he said firmly, shutting off Flinx's incipient protests, "and we will worry about getting past the guards."

Flinx shrugged, irritated by the man's stubbornness. Let them learn their own way, then. But he mentally added an expensive dessert to the evening's meal. He led them to the first gateway and stood in the background while the large, overbearing man who lounged in the little building there came over toward them, grumbling noticeably.

It was now that the most extraordinary event of the day took place. Before the obviously antagonistic fellow could so much as utter a word, Truzenzuzex put a truehand into a pouch and thrust under the man's eyes a card taken from somewhere inside. The man's eyes widened and he all but saluted, the belligerence melting from his attitude like wax. Flinx had never, never seen an inurb guard, a man widely noted for his cultivated rudeness and suspicious mannerisms, react so helplessly to anyone, not even the residents of the inurbs themselves. He grew even more curious as to the nature of his friends. But they remained basically unreadable. *Damn* that beer! It seemed to him that he had heard the name Tse-Mallory somewhere before, but he couldn't be certain. And he would have given much for a glimpse of the card Truzenzuzex had so negligently flashed before the guard.

The way was now quite unopposed. He would at

least have the opportunity of seeing some familiar things for the first time in the light of day. At leisure, too, without having to glance continually over his shoulder.

They strolled silently amid the emerald parklike grounds and tinkling waterfalls, occasionally passing some richly dressed inhabitant or sweating underling, sometimes startling a deer or phylope among the bushes.

"I understand," said Tse-Mallory, breaking the silence, "that each tower belongs to one family, and is named thusly."

"That's true enough," replied Flinx.

"And are you familiar with them?"

"Most, not all. Since you are curious, I'll name the ones I do know as we pass them."

"Do that."

It seemed silly, but they were paying, so who was he to argue the practicality? A fine wine joined the dinner menu. . . .

". . . and this," he said as they drew abreast of a tall black-glazed tower, "is the House of Malaika. A misnomer, sir. As I understand, it means 'angel' in a dead Terran language."

"No Terran language is 'dead,' " said Tse-Mallory cryptically. Then, "He who is named Maxim?"

"Why, yes. I know because I've performed here for parties, several times past. This next, the yellow. . . ."

But they weren't listening, he saw. Both had halted by the black tower and were staring upward to where the rose-tinted crystal proto-porches encircled the upper stories and overhung the lush greenery of the hanging vines and air-shrubs.

"It is fortuitous," he heard Truzenzuzex remark, "that you know each other. It might or might not

43

facilitate certain matters. Come, we shall pay a call on your Mister Malaika."

Flinx was completely taken aback. Was this why they had hired him in the first place? To come this far to an impossibility? Next to the king and his ministers, the trader families of Drallar, nomads who had taken their talents off-planet, were the wealthiest and most powerful individuals on the planet. And some might possibly be wealthier, for the extent of the great fortunes was not a subject into which even the monarch could inquire with impunity.

"It is a slight acquaintance only, sirs! What makes you believe he will do anything but kick us out? What makes you believe he'll even see us?"

"What makes you think we can enter an oh-so-restricted inurb?" replied Truzenzuzex confidently. "He will see us."

The two began to head up the paved walkway toward the great arch of the tower entrance and Flinx, exasperated and puzzled, had little choice but to follow.

The double doorway of simple carved crystal led to a domed hallway that was lined with statuary and paintings and mindgrams which even Flinx's untrained eye could recognize as being of great value. There, at the far end, was a single elevator.

They halted before the platinum-inlaid wood. A woman's voice greeted them mechanically from a grid set off to one side.

"Good afternoon, gentlebeings, and welcome to the House of Malaika. Please to state your business."

Now they would finish this foolishness! The message was all very nicely put, the surroundings pleasant. Out of the corner of an eye he could see a screen, delicately painted, ruffling in the slight breeze

of the chamber's ventilators. Beyond which no doubt
the muzzle of a laser-cannon or other inhospitable
device was already trained on them. It was comfortably cool in the hall, but he felt himself nonetheless beginning to sweat.

"Ex-chancellor second sociologist Bran Tse-Mallory
and first philosoph the Eint Truzenzuzex present
their compliments to Maxim of the House of Malaika
and would have converse with him if he is at home
and so disposed."

Flinx's mind parted abruptly from thoughts of
making a run for the entrance. No wonder they'd
gotten past the gate guard so easily! A churchman
and a pure scientist. High-ranked at that, although
Tse-Mallory had said "ex". Chancellor second—that
was planetary level, at least. He was less sure of
Truzenzuzex's importance, but he knew that the
thranx held their philosophs, or theoreticians, in an
esteem matched only by that of the honorary Hive-
Mothers and the Chancellor Firsts of the Church
themselves. His mind was deluged with questions, all
tinged by uncertainty as much as curiosity. What
were two such eminences doing slumming in a place
like Small Symm's? Why had they picked him for a
guide—a youth, a nothing—when they could have had
a royal escort by a king's minister? That answer he
could read clearly. Incognito; the one word said much
and implied more. At the moment, what dealings did
two such sophisticated minds have with a solid, earthy
merchant like Maxim Malaika?

While he had been dazedly forming questions without answer, a mind somewhere had been coming to a
decision. The grid spoke again.

"Maxim of the House of Malaika extends greetings,
albeit astonished, and will have converse immediately

with the two honorsirs. He wishes the both of you
. . ." there was a pause while a hidden eye somewhere scanned, ". . . the three of you to come up. He
is now in the southwest porchroom and would greet
you there soonest."

The grid voice clicked off and immediately the
rich-grained doors slid back. Man and thranx stepped
unbidden into the dark-pile interior. Flinx debated a
second whether to follow them or run like hell, but
Tse-Mallory decided for him.

"Don't stand there gawking, youth. Didn't you hear
it say he wished to see the *three* of us?"

Flinx could nowhere detect malignance. He stepped
in. The elevator held them all more than comfortably.
He'd been in this house before, but if there was one
thing he was certain of it was that he was not now
being summoned to provide entertainment. And this
was not the servants' entrance he'd used before. The
soft *fsssh* of air as the doors closed sounded explosive-
ly loud in his ears.

They were met at the end of their ride by a tall
skeleton of a man dressed in the black and crimson of
the Malaika family colors. He said nothing as he conducted them to a room Flinx had not seen before.

The far end of the room looked open to the sky.
Actually it was one of the great crystal proto-porches
which made this section of Drallar resemble so well a
bejeweled forest. He quivered momentarily as he
stepped out onto what appeared to be slick nothingness. The two scientists seemed unaffected. He had
been on one of these before, when performing, but it
had been opaque. This one was perfectly transparent,
with just a hint of rose coloring, all the way to the
ground. He looked up and the vertigo passed.

The furnishings were all in red and black, with

here and there an occasional bright color in some imported article or work of art. Incense hung cloyingly in the air. In the distance the sun of Moth had begun to set, diffused by the perpetual thin fog. It got dark early on Moth.

On one of the numerous big fluffy couches sat two figures. One he immediately recognized: Malaika. The other was smaller, blond, and quite differently formed. The majority of her covering was formed by her waist-length hair.

The voice that rumbled out of the thick-muscled neck was like a dormant volcano stirring to life. "*Je?* Our visitors are here. You run along, Sissiph, dear, and make yourself more pretty, *ndiyo?*"

He gave her a crushing peck on the cheek and sent her from the room with a resounding swat on the most prominent portion of her anatomy. He's got a new one, thought Flinx. This one was blonde and a bit more ripely curved than the last. Apparently the trader's tastes were expanding along with his belly. In truth, though, it showed only slightly as yet.

"Well! Well," boomed Malaika. His teeth flashed whitely in the ebony face, sparkling amidst wisps of curly beard. He was up to them and shaking hands in two steps. "Bran Tse-Mallory and the Eint Truzenzuzex. *Usitawi. The* Truzenzuzex?"

The insect performed another of its slow, graceful bows. "I plead guilty of necessity to the accusation." Flinx took the time to admire the insect's abilities. Due to the nature of their physiology the thranx were usually extremely stiff in their movements. To see one bow as did Truzenzuzex was exceptional.

When the Humanx Commonwealth was in the process of being formed, humans had marveled at the scintillating blue and blue-green iridescence of the

47

thranx body coloring and swooned at the natural perfume they exuded. They had wondered miserably what the thranx would see in their own dun-colored, stinky soft selves. What the thranx had seen was a flexibility coupled with firmness which no thranx could ever hope to match. Soon traveling dance companies from humanoid planets had become among the most popular forms of live entertainment on the thranx colonies and homeworlds.

But from the thorax up, at least, Truzenzuzex gave the impression of being made of rubber.

Malaika finished shaking hands with both and then gave Flinx another little surprise. The merchant extended his head and touched nose to antenna with the insect. It was the nearest a human could come to the traditional thranx greeting of intertwining antennae. But then, he reminded himself, a man who did business with as many races as had Malaika would know every gesture as a matter of course . . . and commerce.

"Sit down, sit down!" he roared in what he undoubtedly thought to be a gentle tone of voice. "What do you think of my little *mwenzangu* there, eh? Companion," he added, seeing the puzzlement on their faces. He jerked his head in the direction taken by the departed girl.

Tse-Mallory said nothing, the twinkle in his eyes being sufficient. Truzenzuzex went further. "If I read current human values aright, I should venture to say that such a proportion of marmoreal flesh to the width of the pelvic region would be viewed as more than usually aesthetic."

Malaika roared. "Stars, you *are* a scientist, sir! Powers of observation, indeed! What can I give you both to drink?"

"Ginger ale for me, if you have a good year."

"Fagh! I do, but 'pon my word, sir, you've mellowed if you're the same Tse-Mallory I've heard tell of. And you, sir?"

"Would you by any chance have some apricot brandy?"

"Oh ho! A gourmet, as well as a man of science! I believe we can accommodate you, good philosoph. But it will necessitate a trip to the cellars. I don't often receive such a discerning guest." The shadow which had conducted them from the elevator still stood wraithlike at the back of the room. Malaika waved to it. "See to it, Wolf." The sentinel bowed imperceptibly and shuffled from the room, taking something in the atmosphere with him. More sensitive to it than the others, Flinx was relieved when the man's presence had gone.

Now, for the first time, that hearty voice lost some of its bantering tone. "*Je?* What brings you two here, to Drallar? And so very quietly, too." He glanced keenly from one imperturbable face to the other, stroking that rich Assyrian beard slowly. "Much as my ego would be flattered, I cannot believe that such a stealthy entrance to our fair city has been effected purely for the pleasure of making my company." He leaned forward expectantly in a manner that suggested he could smell money at least as well as Mother Mastiff.

Malaika was not as tall as Tse-Mallory, but he was at least twice as broad and had the build of an over-age wrestler. Shockingly white teeth gleamed in the dusky face which bore the stamp of the kings of ancient Monomotapa and Zimbabwe. Massive, hairy arms protruded from the sleeves of the one-piece semisilk dressing gown he wore casually belted at the

49

waist. Legs to match, as solid looking as a Mothian ironwood tree, thrust out from the pleated folds at the knees. The short, knobby toes on the splayed feet bore a close resemblance to the woody parasites that often infested such growths. At least, they did on one foot. The other, Flinx knew, ended at the knee. Fueled by credits, the prosthetic surgeons had labored their best to make the left match its natural counterpart on the right. The match was not quite perfect.

The real one, Flinx had learned from a talkative young woman at one of Malaika's parties, had been lost in the man's youth. He had been on a fur-gathering expedition to the planet of a minor sun in Draco when his party had been attacked by an ice-lizard. Being rather stupidly caught away from their weapons, they had watched helplessly as the car-nivore instinctively sought out the weakest member of their party, the youthful female accountant. Malaika alone had intervened. Lacking a suitable weapon, he had choked the beast to death by the simple expedient of jamming his left leg down its throat. It was the sort of extreme stunt that one wouldn't expect of the pragmatic merchant. Unfortunately, by the time they could get him to sufficient hospital facilities the limb had been torn and frozen beyond repair.

"We neither intended nor expected to deceive you, friend Malaika. We happen in fact to be on the trail of something we have good reason to think you would find of value, yes. To us, however, it means much more than a paltry few hundred million credits."

Flinx swallowed.

"But," Tse-Mallory continued, "our personal re-sources are limited, and so we are forced, however reluctantly, to seek an outside source of aid. One with an open credit slip and a closed mouth."

"And so you've wound your way to me. Well, well, well! It seems I'm to be flattered after all. I wouldn't be truthful if I said I were not. Nonetheless, you must of course prove that what you wish me to provide credit for is going to be profitable to me ... in hard credit, not philosophical intangibles ... your pardon, friends. Tell me more about this thing which is worth much more than a mere few millions of credit."

"We assumed that would be your reaction. Any other, to tell the truth, would have made us suspicious. It is one of the reasons why we feel we can deal openly with your type of person."

"How comforting to know that you regard me as so obviously predictable," Malaika said drily. "Do go on."

"We could have gone to a government organization. The best are all too often corrupt, despite Church pronouncements. We could have gone to a large philanthropic organization. They are too prone to shock. In the end we decided it would be best to go where the promise of much credit would insure the exclusivity of our enterprise."

"And supposing that I do agree to put up the *fedha* for this venture, what guarantee have you that I will not kill you outright if it proves successful and return with the object of search and two cancelled checks?"

"Very simple. First, odd as it may sound, we know you to be both reliable and reasonably honest in your business dealings. This has proved among the best of your wares in the past and should again, despite the bloodthirsty image your publicists enjoy presenting to the gullible public. Second, we don't know what we're looking for, but we will know it when we find it. And there is an excellent possibility that we will find nothing at all. Or worse, something will be found

51

which will still remain worthless to us because of its incomprehensibility."

"Good! Any other thoughts and *I* would have become suspicious! I become more and more curious. Elucidate for the benefit of my poor, ignorant trader's mind. Why me, *por favor?*"

Truzenzuzex ignored the pun and made the thranx equivalent of a shrug. "Someone was necessary. As already mentioned, your reputation in a business noted for its back-stabbing made my ship-brother select you." Another revelation, thought Flinx. "And Moth itself is close to our objective ... in a relative sense only, so it would do you little good and much expense to try to find it on your own. Also, another vessel departing Moth would mean nothing, with its constant flux of star travel. Our course would not be suspect from here, whereas elsewhere it might engender unwanted cogitation. Traders, however, often fly peculiar tangents to throw off competitors."

At this point the drinks arrived. Conversation was suspended by mutual consent as the debaters sipped at their refreshments. Flinx sampled Tse-Mallory's mug of ginger ale and found it delicious, if mild. Malaika drained at least half the contents of a huge tankard in one gulp. He rubbed his foamy lips with the sleeve of an immaculate gown, staining it irreparably. Knowing the fabric's worth in the marketplace, Flinx couldn't help but wince.

"I again apologize for my denseness, sirs, but I would have whatever it is the competition is to be thrown off of spelled out to me." He turned to face Tse-Mallory directly. "And although you are apparently no longer associated with the Church in an official capacity, sociologist, I confess I am curious to know why you did not approach them seeking aid."

"My dealings with the United Church, Malaika, have not been overclose for a number of years now. My parting was amicable enough, but there was a certain amount of unavoidable bitterness in certain quarters over my leaving that . . . matters would be complicated, shall we say, should I reveal our knowledge to them at this time. Such would be necessary to secure their aid."

"Um. Well, that's blunt enough. I won't prod a sore. Maybe we should get on to. . . ." He paused and looked to his right. Tse-Mallory and Truzenzuzex followed his gaze with their own.

Flinx shifted his position on the floor uncomfortably. He had managed to hear as much as he had by remaining utterly inconspicuous while in plain sight, an art he had learned from a certain patient and very sneaky old man. Aided by his own odd abilities, it had served him importantly more than once. These three, however, were far more observant than the folk one encountered in the marketplace. He could see clearly that he would have to leave. Why not voluntarily?

"Uh, sirs, I could do with some . . . if you, honored host, would point me in the direction of a pantry, I will endeavor to make myself instantly and painlessly nonpresent."

Malaika chuckled deafeningly. "Astuteness is laudable, youth. So instead of sending you home . . . I could wonder where *that* might be . . . you go back to the hall, to your right, second door. You should find in there enough nourishment to keep even you busy for a few minutes!"

Flinx uncurled from his lotus position on the floor and departed in the indicated direction. He felt their eyes and minds on him until he was out of view, at

which point the pressure relaxed. Malaika's convivial-
ity did not fool him. He might already have heard
more than would prove healthy. He was intensely
interested in the answers to a good many questions
that Malaika was now undoubtedly putting to his
guests, and entertained thoughts of locating a good
listening place at a thin section of wall. However, the
death's head had reappeared and stationed himself
by the entrance to the porch-room. The blue eyes had
passed over him once, as though he were not worthy
of a second glance. Flinx bridled, then sighed. He
would have to make do with what he could pick up
without visual contact. Might as well enjoy the other
opportunity while he had it. He walked on.

The pantry was all of fantastic. He almost forgot the
unusual progression of incidents that had brought him
here while he gorged himself and the minidrag on the
store of luxuries. He had gotten as far as debating
between Terran champagne and pine mint from Bar-
rabas when a short series of extremely odd thoughts
drifted across his open mind. He turned and noticed
that the door to the room on his right was slightly
open. The teasing sub-vocalizations came from beyond there. He did not for a moment doubt that that
door should be securely locked. Cautiously, with a
quick glance at the kitchen entrance, he made his
way over to the door and slid it back another inch.

The room next to the kitchen was narrow but long.
It probably ran the whole length of this radius of the
tower. Its function, at least, was unmistakable. It
was a bar. With an eye towards locating an even
more palatable drink and his curiosity piqued he
prepared to enter, only to catch himself quickly.

The room was already occupied.

A figure was hunched over by the opposite wall, its

head pressed tightly against it. He could make out the outlines of a ventilating grid or something similar on the other side of the head. The face was turned away from him and so hidden. The metal and wood he could see there was thin and light. The voices from the next room sounded clearly to him even from where he stood in the kitchen.

He eased the door back as slowly and easily as possible. Apparently totally engrossed in the conversation taking place on the other side of the wall, the figure did not notice his quiet approach. The grid itself could now be seen to be much larger than would be required for ventilating purposes. It looked loose and was probably hinged. Garbage could be passed through it from the other room, and thence shifted to nearby disposal units. He had a hunk of spiced Bice cheese in one hand and a pheasant leg between his teeth. His free hand started down for the stiletto hidden in his boot, then paused. The thoughts of the figure did not have the coldness nor the death-clear logic of the professional spy or assassin. Quite the contrary. Deaf killers were also rare, and this one had *still* refused cognizance of his presence.

He made a rapid decision and brought back a foot, delivering a solid blow to the upthrust portion of the unbalanced figure below. It uttered a single screech and shot through the grill into the room beyond. In a split second he had regretfully discarded both pheasant and cheese and rolled through after it, coming up on his feet on the other side. The startled faces of Malaika, Tse-Mallory, and Truzenzuzex were already gazing in astonishment at the scene. The figure stood opposite him, rubbing the injured portion. It cursed him steadily and fluently. He noticed absently as he dodged the fingers which drove for his larynx that the figure was very much that of a woman. It matched the thoughts he had picked up. Reluctantly he assumed a defensive pose, legs apart, knees slightly bent, arms out and forward. Pip fluttered nervously on his shoulder, the pleated wings unfurling preparatory to the minidrag's taking flight.

The woman made another motion as if to attack again, but was frozen by the bellow which came from Malaika's direction.

"ATHA!" She turned to face him.

The big merchant strode over to stand between them. His eyes went from one to the other, finally settling hard on Flinx.

"Well, *kijana?* I suggest something profound, and quickly!"

Flinx tried to keep his voice as even as possible, despite the adrenalin pumping through his system.

"I was in the pantry and happened to notice the door to the room next to it was open" (never mind why he had noticed it). "Looking in, I saw a figure . . . that figure . . . hunched over next to a grill. The room most certainly ought to have been locked. I assumed that this was not part of your normal method of conducting private business talks and so I decided to force the issue—and the person—into the open, where the air is clearer. I'm sorry if I've broken a fetish or taboo of yours."

"What!" Then he caught the humor of it and grinned. "Think I'm a weirdie, eh, *kijana?*"

"It was a thought, sir."

"*Adabu*! No, you did right, Flinx." He turned a furious gaze on the girl. She shrank back slightly under that withering visage but the obstinate glare never left her face. Somehow she found the where-withal to look righteous.

"Goddamn you, girl, double-damn and collapsed drives, I've told you about this, before!" He shook his head in exasperation. "Again, *kwa ajili ya adabu*, for the sake of manners, I forgive it. Get out to the port and check out the shuttle."

"It was checked again only last week and nothing was wrong with. . . ."

"Agggh!" He raised a hand the size of a ham. "I . . . strongly . . . suggest . . . that you . . .!" She skittered by the descending hand and sped for the exit. The look she sent Flinx on the way out was brief, but hot enough to melt duralloy. Malaika caught his breath and seemed to calm himself somewhat.

"How much of what she heard did you hear?"

Flinx lied. In the situation he considered it more than ethical. "Enough."

"So, so!" The merchant considered. "Well, perhaps it will work out for the better. You'll probably turn out to be the sharpest one aboard, lad, but I'd stay clear of Atha for awhile. I'm afraid your method of making first greetings will never replace shaking hands!" He shook with laughter at his own witticism. He put out an arm as if to embrace Flinx's shoulders, drew it back hastily at a warning gesture from Pip.

"She works for you?" It was a rhetorical question. But Flinx was curious to know what position the girl held that could inspire such trust on Malaika's part that he could treat her as he had without fear of reprisal.

"Atha? Oh yes." He looked in the direction taken by the girl. "You wouldn't think a *mwanamke* that ferocious would have the patience to make starship copilot at her age, would you? She's been with me in that capacity for six years now."

Flinx resumed his former position on the floor. In

reply to Tse-Mallory's inquiring gaze, Malaika said, "I've decided that our young friend will accompany us on the journey. I know what I'm doing, gentlesirs. If the trip is long and tedious he will provide relief for us, and he's sharp as a whip besides. He also has some peculiar abilities which might prove useful to us, despite their capriciousness. It is a subject to which I have meant to give more attention in the past, but have never found the time." Flinx glanced up interestedly, but could detect nothing beyond the merchant's veneer of surface geniality. "In any case, he is too poor and not rich enough to pose a threat to us. And I believe him to be disgustingly honest. Although he has had ample opportunity to steal from my house he has never done so . . . as far as I know."

"His honesty was never in question," said Truzenzuzex. "I've no objection to the lad's presence."

"Nor I," added Tse-Mallory.

"Then, sociologist, if you would continue with your narrative?"

"Actually, there is not much that is new to tell. Would that there were. As you might know my companion and I gave up our respective careers and regular pursuits some twelve odd years ago to research jointly the history and civilization of the Tar-Aiym."

"Some talk of your work has filtered down to my level, yes. Do continue. Naturally I am interested in anything that has to do with the Tar-Aiym . . . or their works."

"So much we—naturally—supposed."

"Pardon, sir," interrupted Flinx. "I know of the Tar-Aiym, of course, but only by rumor and book. Could you maybe tell me more, please?" He looked properly apologetic.

Since Malaika offered no objection, perhaps himself

not considering such information redundant, Tse-Mallory agreed.

"All right then, lad." He took another long swig of his drink. "As near as we have been able to determine, some 500,000 Terran-standard years ago this area of the galaxy was, as it is now, occupied by a large number of diverse and highly intelligent races. The Tar-Aiym were by far the strongest of these. Most of their time and effort was apparently absorbed in warring with their less powerful neighbors, as much for the pleasure of it, it seems, as for the wealth it brought them. At one time the Tar-Aiym empire covered this section of space to a depth of four quadrants and a width of at least two. Maybe more.

"Any reason we could put forth to explain the total disappearance of the Tar-Aiym and most of their subject races would be mostly conjecture. But working painstakingly with bits and pieces of myth and rumor, and a very few solidly documented facts, researchers have put together one explanation that seems to offer more than most.

"At the height of their power the Tar-Aiym came across a more primitive race far in toward the galactic center. This race was not quite the intellectual equal of the Tar-Aiym, and they'd had star travel for only a short time. But they were tremendously tenacious and multiplied at an extraordinary rate. They resisted, successfully, every effort to be forced into the Tar-Aiym hegemony. In fact, under the impetus provided by Tar-Aiym pressures, they began to make giant strides forward and to spread rapidly to other systems.

"Apparently the Tar-Aiym leadership did a most uncharacteristic thing. It panicked. They directed their war scientists to develop new and even more radical types of weaponry to combat this supposed new menace from the center. True to form, their great laboratories soon came up with several offerings. The one that was finally implemented was a form of mutated bacterium. It multiplied at a phenomenal rate, living off itself if no other host was available. To any creature with a nervous system more complex than that of the higher invertebrates it was completely and irrevocably lethal.

"The story from there," continued Truzenzuzex, "is a simple and straightforward one. The plague worked as the leadership had hoped, to the extent of utterly wiping out the Tar-Aiym enemies. It also set about totally eliminating the Tar-Aiym themselves and most of the intelligent and semi-intelligent life in that huge sector of space we know today as the Blight. You know it, Flinx?"

"Sure. It's a big section between here and the center. Hundreds of worlds on which nothing intelligent lives. They'll be filled again someday."

"No doubt. For now, though, they are filled only with the lower animals and the wreckage of past civilizations. Fortunately the surviving space-traversing worlds were informed of the nature of the plague by the last remnants of the dying Tar-Aiym. A strict quarantine must have been put into effect, because for centuries it appears that nothing was permitted in or out of the Blight. Otherwise it is probable that none of us would be sitting here now. It is only in recent times that the systems of the Blight have been rediscovered and somewhat hesitantly explored."

"The taboo lingers even if the reason behind it has gone," said Malaika quietly.

"Yes. Well, some of the quarantined races on the fringe of the epidemic died out rather slowly. By means of interspace relay or some similar device they managed to pass out some threads of fact describing the Armaggedon. Innocent and guilty alike died as the plague burned itself out. Thank Hive that all traces of the germ have long since departed the cycle of things!"

"Amen," murmured Malaika surprisingly. Then, louder, "But please, gentlesirs, to the point. And the point is—credit."

Tse-Mallory took over again. "Malaika, have you ever heard of the Krang?"

"*Nini*? No, I . . . no, wait a minute." The trader's thick brows furrowed in thought. "Yes. Yes, I believe I have. It forms part of the mythology of the, uh, the Branner folk, doesn't it?"

Tse-Mallory nodded approval. "That's right. The Branner, as you may or may not recall, occupy three star systems on the periphery of the Blight, facing Moth. According to a folk-legend of theirs passed down from the cataclysm, even though the Tar-Aiym were hard pressed to find a solution to the threat from the center, they had not yet given up all forms of nonmilitary development and experimentation. As we now know for a fact, the Tar-Aiym were inordinately fond of music."

"Marches, no doubt," murmured Truzenzuzex.

"Perhaps. Anyway, one of the last great works of artistic merit that their culture was supposed to have produced was a great musical instrument called the Krang. It was theoretically completed in the waning days of the Empire, just as the plague was beginning to make itself known on Empire planets as well as those of the enemy."

"*Ili*?" said Malaika. "So?"

"On the side of the Blight almost one hundred and

fifty parsecs from Branner lies the home world of a primitive race of hominids, little visited by the rest of the galaxy. They are far off the main trade routes and have little to offer in the way of value, either in produce or culture. They are pleasant, pastoral, and nonaggressive. Seemingly they once possessed star travel, but sank back into a preatomic civilization and are only just now beginning to show signs of a scientific renaissance. Interestingly enough, they also have a legend concerning something called the Krang. Only in their version it is not an artistic device, but a weapon of war. One which the Tar-Aiym scientists were developing parallel with the plague, before the latter was put into widespread use. According to the legend it was intended to be primarily a defensive and not an offensive weapon. If so, it would be the first time in the literature that the Tar-Aiym had been reduced to building a device for defensive purposes. This runs contrary to all we know of Tar-Aiym psychology and shows how severely they believed themselves pressed by their new enemy."

"Fascinating dichotomy," said Malaika. "And you have some indication as to where this weapon or lute or whatever might be? If either, it would be very valuable in Commonwealth markets."

"True, though we are only interested in its scientific and cultural properties."

"Of course, of course! While my accountants are estimating its net worth, you can draw theoretical rationalizations from its guts to your heart's content . . . provided that you remember how to put its pieces back together again. Now just where is this enigmatic little treasure trove, eh?" He leaned forward eagerly.

"Well, we know exactly, almost," said Tse-Mallory.

"Exactly? Almost? My weak mind again, gentlesirs. Forgive me, but I profess lack of comprehension."

Truzenzuzex made a very human-sounding sigh. Air made a soft *whoosh!* as it was forced out the breathing spicules of his b-thorax.

"The planet on which the Krang is supposedly located was discovered accidentally nearly a t-year ago by a prospector working independently in the Blight. He was hunting for heavy metals, and he found them. Only they weren't arranged in the ground the way he'd expected."

"This fellow, he must have had sponsors," said Malaika. "Why didn't he take this information to them?"

"The man owed a very great debt to my ship-brother. He knew of his interest in Tar-Aiym relics. Supplying Bran with this information was his way of paying off the debt. It was of a personal nature and going into it here can serve no purpose. It would have been a more than equitable reimbursement."

"Would have been?" Malaika's humor was degenerating visibly into irritation. "Come, come, gentlesirs, all this subtle evasion makes my mind sleepy and shortens my patience."

"No evasion intended, merchant. The man was to have met us in our rooms in the market section of the city, bringing with him a star map listing complete coordinates for the planet. As we had previously agreed on you as a likely sponsor, the three of us were then to proceed on to this house. When he did not arrive as scheduled we decided after some deliberation to seek you out anyway, in the hope that with your resources you might discover some hint as to his whereabouts. In any case, it would have been difficult to maintain our independence much longer.

Despite our best efforts, we do not look like tourists. Enterprising persons had already begun asking awkward questions."

"I will—" began Malaika, but Flinx interrupted.

"Did your friend by any chance have red hair?"

Tse-Mallory jerked around violently. For a second Flinx had a glimpse into something terrifying and bloody, which until now the sociologist had kept well buried beneath a placid exterior. It faded as rapidly as it had appeared, but a hint of it persisted in the crisp, military tones of the sociologist's voice.

"How did you know that?"

Flinx pulled the crumpled piece of plastic from his pocket and handed it to an astounded Truzenzuzex. Tse-Mallory recovered himself and glanced at the unfolded sheet. Flinx continued unperturbed.

"I have a hunch that's your star map. I was on my way to Small Symm's establishment when my attention was caught by a commotion in an alleyway. Ordinarily I would have ignored it. That is the way one lives in Drallar, if one wishes to live long. But for reasons unknown and thrice cursed my pet," he gestured at Pip, "got curious, and took it into his head to investigate. The occupants of the alley took exception to his presence. An unfunny fight was in progress, and in the situation which developed the only argument I had was my knife."

"Your friend had been attacked by two men. Professionals by their looks and actions. They weren't very good ones. I killed one, and Pip finished the other. Your friend was already dead. I'm sorry." He did not mention his earlier encounter with the three.

Tse-Mallory was looking from the map to Flinx. "Well, it was said before that it was a fortuitous

64

circumstance that brought you to our notice. Now it appears to have been doubly so."

He was interrupted by an intent Malaika, who snatched up the map and moved over to where a flexilamp was poised. Positioning the powerful beam he began to study the lines and symbols on the plastic with great deliberation. Dust motes danced drunken spirals in the subdued light.

"A most unusual and versatile pet," commented Truzenzuzex idly. "I've heard of them. The mortality rate from their venom is notoriously high, giving them a reputation all out of proportion to their numbers and disposition. Fortunately, as I understand it, they do not seem to attack without due provocation."

"That's right, sir," said Flinx, scratching the object under discussion on the side of its narrow head. "A ship's physician at the shuttleport once told me he'd met a scientist who'd actually been to Alaspin. The minidrag is native to there, you know. In his spare time, the man had done some limited research on them.

"He said they seemed standoffish, which struck me as kind of a funny way to describe a poisonous reptile. But harmless unless, as you said, provoked. Pip was already pretty tame when I found him. At least, I've never had any trouble with him. The people in my area have learned to tolerate him, mostly because they haven't any choice."

"Understandable attitude," murmured the philosoph.

"This doctor's friend was with an expedition to Alaspin to study the ruins of the ancient civilization there. He hypotha . . . hypothesized that the minidrag's ancestors might have been raised as pets by whoever had produced that culture. Selective breeding could account for some of their peculiar characteristics. Like, they have no natural enemies on the planet. Fortunately their birthrate is very low. And they are omnivorous as well as carnivorous. I found out early what that meant, when Pip started eating bread when he couldn't find meat. Oh yes, he also said they were suspected of being empathetic telepaths. You know, telepathic on the emotional but not the mental level. That's why I'm never cheated in the marketplace or at business or gambling. Pip's sensitive to such things."

"A fascinating creature, I say again," Truzenzuzex continued. "A subject I would like to pursue further. However as I am not an exoherpetologist, I don't think it would be worthwhile just now. Too many other things on my mind." The confession did not entirely ring true, as Flinx could read it. Not entirely.

Malaika was craning his neck over the map, tracing out lines in the plastic with his fingers and nodding occasionally to himself. "*Ndiyo, ndiyo* . . . yes." He looked up finally.

"The planet in question circles a GO, sol-type star. Four-fifths of the way toward GalCenter, straight through the Blight. Quite a trip, gentlesirs. He doesn't supply much information on the planet itself, no, not by an *ndege*-depositing, but it might be enough. Terratype, slightly smaller, marginally thinner atmosphere, higher proportion of certain gases . . . helium, for example. Also eighty-one point two percent water, so we should have little trouble finding the thing."

"Unless it happens to be submerged," said Truzenzuzex.

"So. I prefer not to consider possibilities upsetting to the liver. Besides, if that were the case I don't think your prospector friend would have found it. We'll have the same kind of heavy-metal detection instruments with us anyway, but I'd wager on its being above the water-line. If I recall, the information we do have on the Tar-Aiym suggests they were anything but aquatic in build."

"That's true," admitted the philosoph.

"We'll travel most of the way through unspaced areas, but then, one section of nothing is very much like any other, *kweli?* I foresee no problems. Which probably means a *mavuno* of them. At least we will be comfortable. The *Gloryhole* will not be crowded with all of us."

Flinx smiled but was careful to hide it from the merchant. The origin of the name of Malaika's private cargo-racer was a well-known joke among those in the know. Most thought it an ancient Terran word meaning a rich mineral strike. . . .

"Unless, of course, this gun or giant harp or whatever is going to crowd us. How big did you say it was?"

"I didn't," said Tse-Mallory. "We've no better idea than you. Only that it's . . . large."

"Hmph! Well, if it's too big to go up on the shuttle, we'll just have to send back for a regular transport. I'd rather sit on it once we've found it, but there are no relay stations in that area. If it's been there untouched for a few millenia it will wait a few days." He rolled up the map. "So then, sirs. If there are no objections, I see no reason why we cannot leave *kesho*, tomorrow."

There were none.

"*Ema*! A toast, then. To success and profit, not necessarily in that order! *Nazdrovia*!" He raised his tankard.

"Church and Commonwealth," murmured man and

thranx together, softly. They sipped down the remainder of their drinks.

Malaika burped once, glanced out through the crystal wall where the sun of Moth was sinking rapidly behind the fog-squalls.

"It is late. Tomorrow then, at the port. The dock stewards will direct you to my pit. The shuttle will take us all in one trip and I need little time to set my affairs in order."

Tse-Mallory rose and stretched. "If I may ask, who are 'us all'?"

"Those four of us here now, Wolf and Atha to run the ship, and, of course, Sissiph."

"Who?" asked Tse-Mallory.

"The Lynx, the Lynx," whispered Truzenzuzex, grinning and nudging his ship-brother in the ribs. "Have your eyes aged as much as your brain? The girl!" They were strolling to the hallway now.

"Ah yes." They paused by the shadowlike Wolf, who held the door open for them. The man grinned in what was obviously supposed to be a friendly gesture. It did not come off that way. "Yes, a very, ah, interesting and amusing personage."

"*Ndiyo,*" said Malaika amiably. "She does have quite a pair, doesn't she?"

As the others bid the spectral doorman goodeve, a hand came down on Flinx's shoulder. The merchant whispered. "Not you, *kijana*. I've a question for you yet. Stay a moment."

He shook hands with Tse-Mallory and touched olfactory organs with Truzenzuzex, waving them toward the elevator.

"Good rest to you, sirs, and tomorrow at first fog!"

Wolf closed the door, cutting off Flinx's view of the

scientists, and Malaika immediately bent to face him intently.

"Now, lad, that our ethical friends have left, a point of, um, business. The two hired corpses you left rotting so properly in that alley. Did they have any special insignia or marks on them or their clothing? *Think*, youth!"

Flinx tried to recall. "It was awfully dark . . . I'm not sure. . . ."

"And when did that ever bother you? Don't hedge with me, *kijana*. This is too important. Think . . . or whatever it is you do."

"All right. Yes. When I was trying to pry that map away from the dead man, I did notice the feet of the man Pip had killed. He'd fallen close by. The metal of his boots had a definite design etched on them. It looked to be some kind of bird . . . an abstract representation, I think."

"With teeth?" prompted Malaika.

"Yes . . . no . . . I don't know for sure. The questions you ask, merchant! It could have been. And for some reason, during the fight I got this picture of a woman, an old-young woman."

Malaika straightened and patted the boy on the back. His expression was jovial but his thoughts were grim—grim. Ordinarily Flinx would have resented the patronizing gesture, but this time, coming from the merchant, it seemed only complimentary.

"Thank the Mti of Miti for your powers of observation, lad. And for a good memory." Flinx saw another word: *uchawi*, witchcraft, but did not press the point. The big man changed the subject abruptly. "I'll see you *kesho*, on ship, then?"

"I would not miss it. Sir, may I ask the why of your question?"

"You may not. The ship tomorrow, then. Good rest." He ushered a puzzled Flinx to the elevator.

The merchant stood pondering silently awhile, curses bubbling like froth from the cauldron of his mouth. They constituted the only sounds in the now deserted room. He turned and walked over to an apparently blank section of wall. Striking a hidden switch he sent the deep-grained paneling sliding up into the ceiling to reveal a complex desk. The slim bulk of an interstellar transceiver dominated the other apparatus. Buttons were pushed, dials turned, meters adjusted. The screen lit up suddenly in a glorious fireball of chromatic static. Satisfied, he grunted and hefted a small mike.

"Channel six, please. Priority. I wish to speak straight-line direct person, to Madame Rashalleila Nuaman, on Nineveh, in the Sirius system."

A small voice floated out of a tiny speaker set to one side of the rainbow flux rippling on the screen. "Call is being placed, sir. One moment, please."

Despite the incredible distances involved, the slight delay was occasioned by the need to boost the call through half a hundred relay stations. Time of transit, due to the less-than-space concepts in use, was almost instantaneous.

The screen began to clear, and in a short while he was facing one of the ten wealthiest humanoid females in the universe.

She was lounging on some sort of couch. To one side he could easily make out the muscled, naked leg of whoever was holding the portable transceiver hookup for her. In the background he could see lush greenery, growing to fantastic size and shapes without the restraints of heavy gravity. Beyond that, he knew, was the dome which shut out the airless void that was the normal atmosphere of Nineveh.

Nature battled surgery as the woman pulled her face into a toothsome, slinky smile. This time, surgery won. It was intended to be sexy, but to one who knew, it only came out vicious.

"Why Maxy, darling! What a delightful surprise! It's always so delicious to hear from you. That lovely body of yours is well, I trust, and business equally?"

"I'm only well *when* business is good. At the moment it is passable, Rasha, just passable. However I have hopes it will take a sudden jump for the better very shortly. You see, I've just had a most interesting chat with two gentlemen . . . three, if you count the redhead."

Nuaman tried to project an aura of disinterest, but surgery couldn't hide the way the tendons tautened in her neck. "How interesting, I'm sure. I do hope it proves profitable for you. But your tone seems to imply that you believe I am somehow involved."

"It did? I don't recall saying anything that might lead you to that conclusion . . . darling. Oh, it isn't the redhead you're thinking of. Your bully-boys did get to that one . . . as per instructions, no doubt."

"Why Maxy, whatever are you thinking of? Why should any of my assistants be on Moth? My dealings on the planet are small, as you well know. You're the one who keeps blocking all my attempts to expand my interests there. Anyhow, I don't know many redheads altogether . . . certainly can't recall any I'd want killed. Messed up a little, perhaps, but not killed. No, darling, you're mistaken. What an odd conversation! There's nothing on that pitifully damp ball of dirt of yours, redheaded or otherwise, that I'd risk a murder for."

71

"Ummm. Not even this, *hasa*?" He held up the map. Folded, so that the interior would not show.

It didn't matter. She recognized it, all right! She sat bolt upright and leaned forward so that her face, witchlike, seemed to fill the whole screen.

"Where did you get that? That belongs to me!"

"Oh now Rasha, *bibi*, I do doubt that. And do sit back a little. Closeups are not your forte, you know." He made a pretense of examining it. "No name, I'm afraid. And besides, I got it from a *live* redhead. A boy, really. He happened along just as your 'assistants' happened to be performing acts of doubtful legality against the original owner. Either the youth is an extraordinary chap . . . which I am inclined to believe . . . or else the two assistants you assigned to this job were very low-grade morons . . . which, come to think of it, I am also inclined to believe. They *were* yours, I see. It had your typically brazen touch about it. I merely wanted to make certain. I've done that. Thank you, Rasha dear. *Sikuzuri*, now."

He cut her off in midcurse and went off to find Sissiph.

All in all, it had been rather a good day.

Chapter Three

On Nineveh, Rashalleila Nuaman, matriarch and head of one of the largest private concerns in the Commonwealth and one of the ten richest humanoid females in the known firmament, was howling mad. She booted the nearly nude male servant who held the portable transceiver in an indelicate place. The unfortunate machine fell into a pool of mutated goldfish. Startled, they scrambled for cover amidst pastel lily pads. A number of very rare and expensive opaline glasses were shattered on the stone pathway.

Her anger momentarily assuaged, she sat back down on the lounge and spent five minutes rearranging her hair. It was olive this week. At that point she felt sufficiently in control of herself to get up and walk to the main house.

How had that utter bastard Malaika found out about the map? And how had it found its way into his hands? Or possibly . . . possibly it had been the other way around? The two gentlemen he had so snidely referred to were undoubtedly that Tse-Mallory person and his pet bug. But who was this new "redhead"? Who had so rapidly and shockingly managed to wreck what had until a few minutes ago been a comparatively smooth, routine operation? And all this now, with Nikosos only two days out of Moth! It was insufferable! She took a clawed swipe in passing at a stand of priceless Yyrbittium trumpet-blooms, shredding the carmine leaves. The delicate tube-shaped petals sifted brokenly to the floor. Someone was definitely, yes definitely, going to be flayed!

She stomped into the lounge-room that doubled as her office and collapsed disconsolately in the white fur mouldchair. Her head dropped onto her right hand while the left made nervous clicking sounds on the pure corrundum table. The brilliant quicksilver flickering was the only movement in the wave-proofed room.

It *was* insufferable! He would not get away with it. It would be on his head, yes, on his, if a single killing operation devolved into a multiple one. It might even extend itself to his own exquisite carcass, and wouldn't that be sad. He *would* make a lovely corpse.

Don't just sit there, you slobbering bitch. Get cracking! She leaned over the desk and jabbed a button. A thin, weary face formed on the screen in front of her.

"Dryden, contact Nikosos and tell him that he is not to land at Drallar. He is instead to monitor all starships that are in parking orbit around the planet and stand off. Any which depart in the direction of the Blight he is to follow as closely as possible while at all times staying out of immediate detector range. If he complains, tell him I realize it's a difficult proposition and he's simply to do his best." I can always fire him later, she thought grimly. "If he presses you for an explanation, tell him plans have been changed due to unforeseen and unpreventable circumstances. He is to follow that ship! I guarantee there will be one, and probably shortly. It will be headed for the planet he was originally to have proceeded to by map. For now he'll have to do without his own set of coordinates. Is that all clear?"

"Yes, Madame."

She had cut him off before he reached the second "m". Well, she'd done what she could, but it seemed so goddamn *little*! Her feeling of comparative impotence magnified her rage and the corresponding desire to take out her frustration on someone else. Let's see. Who was handy? And deserving? Um. The idiot who had bungled with those two assassins? A fine choice! Her niece? That bubble-head. And to think, to think that one day she might have to take over the firm. When she couldn't even oversee a simple extraction. She pressed another button.

"Have Teleen auz Rudenuaman report to my office at, oh, five hours tomorrow morning."

"Yes Madame," the grid replied.

Now if there were only someone else. A budding career to squelch, perhaps. But in good faith there was no one else she could rake over the coals. Not that that should prove a consideration if she felt especially bitchy, but a loyal staff could be assured only through an equal mixture of fear and reward. No point in overdoing the former. No, face to it, what she really needed was relaxing. Hopefully that fop van Cleef would be in decent shape tonight. A smile suddenly sickled across her face. The unlucky button got jabbed again.

"Cancel that last. Have my niece report at five hours tomorrow . . . but to my sleeping quarters, not the office."

"Noted," said the grid compactly.

Rashalleila leaned back and stretched luxuriously. Definitely she felt better. She knew her niece was hopelessly in love with her current gigolo. Why, she couldn't for the life of her see, but it was a fact. It would be interesting to see if the girl could keep a straight face tomorrow as she was bawled out in front of him. While he stirred groggily in her aunt's bed. It would fortify her character, it would. She giggled at the thought and even in the empty room it was not a pleasant sound.

Chapter Four

Bran Tse-Mallory and Truzenzuzex were making their way casually back to their rooms via the routes of the marketplace. It was twice as noisy and confusing at night as it was during the day. The flashing lights of motorized handcarts and fluorescent vendors added much to the atmosphere of controlled anarchy. Still, they did not need the Flinx. No matter how tortuous or confused the route, a thranx could always retrace it once traveled.

"Well, brother," said Truzenzuzex, dodging a mobile seller of novelties, "what do you think of our friend the merchant?"

"I would feel much better if our friend the unusual youth were twenty years older and in his place. A partial telepath, for sure. I could sense it. But such wishes are useless. Chaos. Up the universe!" he muttered.

"Up the universe!" replied Truzenzuzex. Both smiled at the private joke, which had a deeper meaning than the surface humor implied. "The man seems as trustworthy a member of his type as we are likely to find, and he has the ship we need. I cannot be positive yet, of course, but under the circumstances I think we have done quite well. And the boy's presence on the vessel should serve as a moderating factor. He seems to trust the trader, too."

"Agreed. The lad's presence will inject an uncertainty element, if nothing else."

"A certain uncertainty factor. How apropos of this venture so far!" The insect shook its head in deliberate aping of the human gesture. "This has caused three deaths so far. I would hope there will be no more."

"So would I, brother, so would I. The two of us have seen too much death already." Truzenzuzex did not reply, as he was concentrating on a difficult forking of their path.

Tse-Mallory followed mechanically. The noise and lights had a tendency to hypnotize, he allowed his mind to drift. . . .

Chapter Five

The picture they were seeing in the viewscreen of the stingship was identical to the one being flashed to every member of the task force. It showed a tall, thin Ornithorphe with primarily black and yellow plumage. The being was possessed of a large amount of natural dignity, which it was at present being hard-pressed to retain. It is not easy to be dignified when one is begging.

Ensign Bran Tse-Mallory, aged twenty-six years, Fourth Battle Group, Sixth Corps of the Enforcement Arm of the United Church, watched the military governor of the blue planet below them crumble mentally as he pleaded with their own commander for aid. Anger and embarrassment mingled in his own throat, which was unaccountably dry, as he followed the conversation.

"Major Gonzalez," the Ornithorphe intoned, "I will ask you for a final time, and then I must go and do what I can to aid my people, even if it is only to die with them. *Will* you use the forces at your command to intercede and prevent a massacre?"

The voice of Task Force Commander Major Julio Gonzalez filtered through the small grid used for interfleet frequencies. It was cool and controlled. Bran wanted to smash the grid and the sickly smug face that sat behind it.

"And I am forced to remind you once again, Governor Bolo, that much as I sympathize with your plight there is nothing I can do. It is, after all, only by pure coincidence that my force is here at all. We are on a peaceful patrol and stopped by your planet only to pay the customary courtesy call. Had we been a week earlier or later we would not even be witness to this unfortunate situation."

"But you *are* here and you *are* witness, Jaor," began the governor for the seventeenth time," and. . . ."

"Please, sir, I've listened quite too long as it is. The Church and the Commonwealth have been at peace with the AAnn Empire for years now. . . ."

"Some peace!" muttered an indiscreet voice elsewhere on the network. If Gonzalez heard it, he gave no sign.

". . . and I refuse to jeopardize that peace by interceding in an affair that is none of my business. To intervene on either side would be tantamount to an act of war. Also, I should be acting directly contrary to my orders and to the purpose of this patrol. I must refuse to do so, sir. I hope you can understand my position."

"Your *position*!" the governor gasped. His voice was breaking noticeably under the strain of the last few days and he had to fight to keep his thoughts framed in symbospeech. "What of those AAnn-*ghijipps* out there? An open attack on a helpless colony. 'Act of war' you say! Isn't that a direct violation of your precious Convention? The one that 'your' patrol is supposed to be upholding?"

"If your claim is just, I am sure the Convention arbiters will decide in your favor."

"*Whose* favor!" roared the Governor. "Surely you know what the AAnn do to subject planets! Especially those who have the impertinence to resist. If there are none of us left alive to accept the favorable decision of the arbiting board, what use your damned Convention! Will our memories receive pensions?"

"I *am* sorry, governor. I wish I could help you, but. . . ."

"Send just *one* of your ships, a token showing," he cried. "They might hesitate. . . ."

"I said I was sorry, governor. I am distraught. Goodbye, sir." Gonzalez had broken the connection.

From above and behind him, Bran heard the voice of his young ship-brother. The insect's deep blue-green chiton was rendered even more resplendent by the silver battle harness that enclosed its cylindrical body.

"That," said Truzenzuzex in cool, even tones, "was just possibly the most nauseating bit of rhetorical doggerel it has ever been my misfortune to overhear."

Bran agreed. He was finding it more and more difficult to restrain himself. Even without the heightened-instinct-perception drugs, the killing urge was beginning to steal warmly over him. It had the powerful push of righteous indignation behind it.

"Isn't it possible that maybe the locals . . .?"

". . . haven't got a chance," finished Truzenzuzex. "They're outnumbered and outgunned, and not a regular armed force among them in the first place. As the AAnn doubtlessly surmised well in advance. I doubt if their ships even have doublekay drives. Theirs is only a colony and they wouldn't have need of many."

"Typical AAnn maneuver. Damn those anthropomorphic bastards! Always sniping and chipping at edges. I wish they'd come right out and say they're going to contest us for this part of the galaxy. Let 'em stand up and fight like men!"

"No can do, brother, because they obviously aren't. And I refer not to their physiologies alone. According to the AAnn standards set down by their philosophy of 'perpetual warfare as the natural state of things,' any advantage you can get over your opponent is by definition of success ethical. They're not immoral, just amoral. Sneak attacks are like sugar—pardon, like bread—to them."

"If the major agreed to step in I'm sure headquarters would give retroactive approval to the action," Bran said. "They'd offer obeisance in public, sure, but privately I'll bet Marshal N'Gara would approve."

"He might. Might not. As soldiers grow older and more powerful their personalities tend more and more to the mercurial. I can't see dear sweet Gonzalez risking a chance to help a bunch of aliens, especially non-Commonwealth. He's far too fond of his scotch and imported Terran cigars. Besides, to undertake such an action would require at least a modicum of imagination, a commodity in which our commander is sadly deficient. Look. It's starting already."

Bran glanced up above the communications equipment to the huge battle screen. Out in the void a number of ships represented only by ghostly dots were maneuvering across thousands of kilometers for position in a battle which would prove notable only for its brevity. Somehow the locals had mustered six spaceworthy ships. He'd bet a year's credit not one of them was a regular warship. Police launches, most likely. Opposite, the well-drilled, superbly disciplined AAnn force was forming one of its characteristic tetrahedrons. Fifteen or so attack ships, a couple of destroyers, and two bloated pips that in a normal

battle situation he would have interpreted as dread-
noughts. The finer instruments on the big board told
the true story: same mass, small gravity wells. Troop
carriers, nursing dozens of small, heavily screened
troop shuttles.

He'd observed AAnn occupation forces in action
before. No doubt by now the members of the first
assault wave were resting comfortably in their respective holds, humming softly to themselves and waiting
for the "battle" to begin, making sure their armor was
highly polished, their nerve-prods fully charged. . . .

He slammed a fist down on the duralloy board,
scraping the skin on the soft underside of his wrist.
There were ten stingers and a cruiser in the humanx
force . . . more than a match for the AAnn, even
without the dubious "help" of the locals. But he knew
even before the pathetic debate of a few moments
ago that Major Gonzalez would never stir from his
wood-paneled cabin on the *Altair* to intervene in any
conflict where humanx interests weren't directly
threatened. He paused at a sudden thought. Of course,
if a confrontation could be forced to the point that
such a threat occurred . . . still no certain guarantee
. . . definite court-martial . . . dismissal from the Corps
. . . 300,000 sentient beings . . . processing camps . . . .
He suddenly wasn't so sure that he wanted to make
captain after all. Still, he'd need the concurrance
of. . . .

"Bran, our drive appears to be malfunctioning."

"Wha? I don't. . . ."

"Yes, there is no question about it. We appear to be
drifting unavoidably into the area of incipient combat. At top speed, no less. A most unusual awkwardness, wouldn't you agree?"

"Oh. Oh, yes." A pseudo-smile sharp as a scimitar

cut his face. "I can see that we're helpless to prevent it. Goddamn unfortunate situation. Naturally we'll have to make emergency preparations to defend ourselves. I don't think the AAnn computers will be overly discerning about ships which float into their target area."

"Correct. I was just about to commence my own injections."

"Myself also." He snuggled back into the reaction seat, felt the field that enabled them to maneuver at high speed and still live take hold gently. "Best hurry about it."

He followed accepted procedure and did his best to ignore the barely perceptible pressures of the needles as they slipped efficiently into the veins on his legs. The special drugs that heightened his perceptions and released the artificial inhibitions his mind raised to constrain the killer instinct immediately began to take effect. A beautiful rose-tinted glow of freedom slipped over his thoughts. This was proper. This was *right*! This was what he'd been created for. Above and behind him he knew that Truzenzuzex was undergoing a similar treatment, with different drugs. They would stimulate his natural ability to make split-second decisions and logical evaluations without regard to such distractions as Hive rulings and elaborate moral considerations.

Shortly after the Amalgamation, when human and thranx scientists were discovering one surprising thing after another about each other, thranx psychologists unearthed what some humans had long suspected. The mind of *Homo sapiens* was in a perpetual state of uneasy balance between total emotionalism and computerlike control. When the vestiges of the latter, both natural and artificial, were removed, man reverted to a kind of controlled animalism. He became the universe's most astute and efficient killing machine. If the reverse was induced he turned into a vegetable. No use had been found for that state, but for the former. . . .

It was kept fairly quiet. After a number of gruesome but honest demonstrations put on by the thranx and their human aides, mankind acknowledged the truth of the discovery, with not a small sigh of relief. But they didn't like to be reminded of it. Of course a certain segment of humanity had known it all along and wasn't affected by the news. Others began to read the works of ancients like Donatien Francois de Sade with a different eye. For their part human psychologists brought into clearer light the marvelous thranx ability to make rapid and correct decisions with an utter lack of emotional distraction and a high level of practicality. Only, the thranx didn't think it so marvelous. Their Hive rulings and complicated systems of ethics had long kept that very same ability tied down in the same ways humanity had its killer desires.

The end result of all the research and experimentation was this: in combination with a ballistics computer to select and gauge targets, a thranx-human-machine triumvirate was an unbeatable combination in space warfare. Thranx acted as a check on human and human as a goad to thranx. It was efficient and ruthless. Human notions of a "gentleman's" war disappeared forever. Only the AAnn had ever dared to challenge the system more than once, and they were tough enough and smart enough to do it sporadically and only when they felt the odds to be highly in their favor.

It was fortunate that thranx and human proved even

more compatible than the designers of the system had dared hope—because the nature of the drug-machine tie-up resulted in a merging of the two minds on a conscious level. It was as if the two lobes of a brain were to fight out a decision between themselves, with the compromise then being passed on to the spinal cord and the rest of the body for actual implementation. Some stingship pilots likened it more closely to two twins in the womb. It was that intimate a relationship. Only in that way would the resultant fighting machine operate at 100 percent effectiveness. A man's partner was his ship-brother. Few stinger operators stayed married long, except those who were able to find highly understanding wives.

The tingling mist flowed over his eyes, dimming and yet enhancing his vision. The tiniest things became obvious to his perception. Specks of dust in the cabin atmosphere became clear as boulders. His eyes fastened on the white diamonds on the battle screen with all the concentration of a starving cobra. All stinger pilots admitted to a slight but comforting sense of euphoria when under battle drugs. Bran was experiencing it now. For public relations purposes the enforcement posters insisted it was a beneficial by-product of the HIP drugs. The pilots knew it for what it was: the natural excitement that overtakes most completely uninhibited humans as they anticipate the thrill of the kill. His feelings whirled within, but his thoughts stayed focused.

"Up the universe, oh squishy bug!" he yelled drunkenly. Off from never-never land Truzenzuzex's voice floated down to him.

"Up the universe, oh smelly primate!"

The ship plunged toward one corner of the AAnn tetrahedron.

The enemy force stood it as long as possible. Then three ships broke out to intercept their reckless charge. The rest of the formation continued to form, undaunted. Undoubtedly no one in a position of command had yet noticed that this suicidal charge did not come from the region of the pitiful planetary defense force circling below. And having all heard the interfleet broadcast they *knew* it couldn't possibly be a Commonwealth vessel. Bran centered their one medium SCCAM on the nearest of the three attackers, the pointer. Dimly, through the now solid perfumed fog, he could make out the outraged voice of Major Gonzalez on intership frequency. It impinged irritatingly on his wholly occupied conscious. Obviously Command hadn't bought their coded message of engine trouble.

"You there, what do you think you're doing! Get back in formation! Ship number . . . ship number twenty-five return to formation! Acknowledge, uh . . . by heaven! Braunschweiger, whose ship is that? Someone get me some information, there!

It was decidedly too noisy in the pod. He shut off the grid and they drove on in comparative silence. He conjured up a picture of the AAnn admiral. Comfortably seated in his cabin on one of the troop carriers, chewing lightly on a narco-stick . . . one eye cocked on the Commonwealth force floating nearby. Undoubtedly he'd also been monitoring the conversation between the planetary governor and Major Gonzalez. Had a good laugh, no doubt. Expecting a nice, routine massacre. His thoughts must now be fuzzing a bit, especially if he'd noticed the single stinger blasting crazily toward the center of his formation. Bran hoped he'd split an ear-sac listening to his trackers.

His hand drifted down to the firing studs. The calm

voice of Truzenzuzex insinuated itself maddeningly in his mind. No, it was already *in* his mind.

"Hold. Not yet." Pause. "Probability."

He tried angrily to force the thought out and away. It wouldn't go. It was too much like trying to cut away part of one's own ego. His hand stayed off the firing stud as the cream-colored dot grew maddeningly large in the screen.

Again the calm, infuriating voice. "Changing course ten degrees minus y, plus x two degrees achieve optimum intercept tangent."

Bran knew they were going to die, but in his detached haze of consciousness it seemed an item of only peripheral importance. The problem at hand and the sole reason for existence was to kill as many of *them* as possible. That their own selves would also be destroyed was a certainty, given the numbers arrayed against them, but they might at least blunt the effect of the AAnn invasion. A tiny portion of him offered thanks for Truzenzuzex's quiet presence. He'd once seen films of a force of stingships in action with only human operators. It had resembled very much a tridee pix he'd seen on Terra showing sharks in a feeding frenzy.

The moment notified him of itself. "Firing one!" There were no conflicting suggestions from the insectoid half of his mind. He felt the gentle lurch of his body field as the ship immediately executed an intricate, alloy-tearing maneuver that would confuse any return fire and at the same time allow them to take the remaining two enemy vessels between them. Without the field he would have been jellied.

The disappearance of a gravity well from the screen told him that the SCCAM projectile had taken the AAnn ship, piercing its defenses. A violent explosion flared silently in space. A SCCAM was incapable of a "near-miss."

The SCCAM system itself was a modification of the doublekay drive that powered the ships of most space-going races. When human and thranx met it was found that the human version was more powerful and efficient than the thranx posigravity drive. It also possessed a higher power-conservation ratio, which made it more reasonable to operate. Working with their human counterparts after the Amalgamation, thranx scientists soon developed a number of improvements in the already remarkable system. This modified propulsive drive was immediately installed in all humanx ships, and other races began to order the components which would enable them to make their own modifications.

A wholly thranx innovation, however, had been the adaptation of the gravity drive as a weapon of irresistable power. The SCCAM projectiles were in actuality thermonuclear devices mounted on small ship drives, with the exception that all their parts other than those requiring melting points over 2400 degrees were made of alloyed osmium. Using the launching vessel's own gravity well as the initial propelling force, the projectile would be dispatched toward a target. At a predetermined safe distance from the ship, the shell's own drive would kick in. Instantly the drive would go into deliberate overload. Impossible to dodge, the overloaded field would be attracted to the nearest large gravity well—in this case, the drive system of an enemy ship. Coupled with the uncontrolled energy of a fusion reaction, the two intersecting drive fields would irrevocably eliminate any trace of the target. And it would be useless for an enemy vessel to try to escape by turning off its own field, for while it might survive impact with the small projectile field, the ship had not yet been constructed that could take the force of a fusion explosion unscreened. And as the defensive screens were powered by the posigravity drives. . . .

He felt the ship lurch again, not as violently this time. Another target swung into effective range. He fired again. Truzenzuzex had offered a level-four objection and Bran had countered with a level-two objective veto. The computer agreed with Bran and released the shell. Both halves of the ship-mind had been partially correct. The result was another hit . . . but just barely.

The AAnn formation seemed to waver. Then the left half of the Tetrahedron collapsed as the ships on that side sought to counter this alarming attack on their flank. More likely than not the AAnn commander had ordered the dissolution. Penned up in a slow, clumsy troop carrier he was by now likely becoming alarmed for his own precious skin. Heartened by this unstrategic move on the part of their opponents the native defensive force was diving on the broken formation from the front, magnifying the confusion if not the destruction and trying to avert the attention of the AAnn warships from their unexpected ally.

Bran had just gotten off a third shot—a miss—when a violent concussion rocked the stinger. Even in his protective field he was jerked violently forward. The lights flickered, dimmed, and went off, to be replaced a moment later by the eerie blue of the emergency system. He checked his instruments and made a matter-of-course report upward.

"Tru, this time the drive is off for real. We're going to go into loosedrift only . . . he paused. A typically ironic reply was not forthcoming.

"Tru? How are things at your end?" The speaker gave back only a muted hiss. He jiggled the knob several times. It seemed operative. "Tru? Say something, you slug! Old snail, termite, boozer . . . goddamn it, say *some*thing!"

With the cessation of the ship's capacity for battle the HIP antidotes had automatically been shot into his system. Thank Limbo the automedics were still intact! He felt the killing urge flow out of him, heavily, to be replaced by the dull aftertaste and temporary lethargy that inevitably followed battle action.

Cursing and crying all at once he began fighting with his harness. He turned off the body field, not caring if the ship suddenly decided to leap into wardrive and spatter him all over the bulkhead. Redfaced, he started scrambling over broken tubing and sparkling short-circuits up to where Truzenzuzex lay in his own battle couch. His own muscles refused to respond and he damned his arms which persisted in slipping off grips like damp hemp. He hadn't realized, in the comfort of HIPnosis, how badly the little vessel had been damaged. Torn sheeting and wavering filaments floated everywhere, indicating a loss of shipboard gravity. But the pod had remained intact and he could breathe without his hoses.

The thranx's position was longer and lower than his own, since the insect's working posture was lying prone and facing forward. Therefore the first portion of his fellow ensign's body that Bran encountered was the valentine-shaped head with its brilliant, multifaceted compound eyes. The familiar glow in them had dimmed but not disappeared. Furiously he began to massage the b-thorax above the neck joint in an operation designed to stimulate the thranx's open circulatory system. He kept at it despite the cloying wetness that insisted on floating into his eyes. Throwing his head back at least made the blood from the gash on his forehead drift temporarily backwards.

"Tru! C'mon, mate! Move, curse you! Throw up, do something, dammit!" The irony of trying to rouse his companion so that he could then be conscious when the AAnn disruption beams scattered their component parts over the cosmos did not interrupt his movements.

Truzenzuzex began to stir feebly, the hissing from the breathing spicules below Bran's ministering hands pulsing raggedly and unevenly.

"Mmmfff! Ooooo! My friend, I hereby inform all and sundry that a blow on the cranium is decidedly not conducive to literate cogitation! A little lower and to the right, please, is where it itches. Alas, I fear I am in for a touch of the headache."

He raised a truehand slowly to his head and Bran could see where a loose bar of something had struck hard after the body-field had lapsed. There was an ugly dark streak in the insect's azure exoskeleton. The thranx organism was exceptionally tough, but very vulnerable to deep cuts and punctures because of their open circulatory system. When their armor remained intact they were well-nigh invulnerable. Much more so than their human counterparts. The same blow probably would have crushed Bran's skull like eggshell. The great eyes turned to face him.

"Ship-brother, I notice mild precipitation at the corners of your oculars, differing in composition from the fluid which even yet is leaking from your head. I know the meaning of such a production and assure you it is not necessary. Other than injury to my immaculate and irresistable beauty, I am quite all right . . . I think.

92

"Incidentally, it occurs to me that we both have been alive entirely too long. As I appear to be at least momentarily incapacitated I would appreciate it if you would cease your face-raining, get back to your position, and find out just what the hell is going on."

Bran wiped the tears from the corners of his eyes. What Tru said was perfectly correct. He had been so absorbed in reviving the insect he had failed to notice that by all reasonable standards of warfare they should both have been dead several minutes now. The AAnn might be unimaginative fighters, but they were efficient. He scrambled back to his seat and flipped emergency power to the battle screen. What he saw there stunned his mind if not his voice.

"Oooo-wowwww! Fibbixxx! Go get 'em Sixth, bay-bee!"

"Will you cease making incomprehensible mouth-noises and tell me what's taking place? My eyes are not fully focused yet, but I can see that you are bouncing around in your seat in a manner that is in no way related to ship actions."

Bran was too far gone to hear. The scene on the screen was correspondingly weak, but fully visible nonetheless. It resembled a ping-pong game being played in zero gravity by two high-speed computers. The AAnn force was in full retreat, or rather, the remainder of it was. The bright darts of Common-wealth stingships were weaving in and out of the retreating pattern with characteristic unpredictabili-ty. Occasionally a brief, terse flare would denote the spot where another ship had departed the plane of material existence. And a voice drifted somehow over the roaring, screaming babble on the communicator, a voice that could belong to no one but Major Gonzalez. Over and over and over it repeated the same essential fact in differing words.

"What happened what happened what happened what. . . ?"

Bran at this time suffered his second injury of the action. He sprained a lattisimus, laughing.

It was all made very clear later, at the court martial. The other members of the Task Force had seen one of their members break position and dive on the AAnn formation. Their pilot-pairings had stood the resultant engagement as long as possible. Then they began to peel off and follow. Only the cruiser *Altair* had taken no part in the battle. Her crew had a hard time living it down, even though it wasn't their fault.

Not so much as a tree on the planet had been scorched.

The presiding officer at the trial was an elderly thranx general officer from the Hiveworld itself. His ramrod stiffness combined with fading exoskeleton and an acid voice to make him a formidable figure indeed. As for the majority of the Task Force, its members were exonerated of wrongdoing. It was ruled that they had acted within Commonwealth dictates in acting "under a justifiable circumstance where an act of violence against Commonwealth or Church property or persons shall be met with all force necessary to negate the effects of such violence." This provision was ruled to have taken effect when the AAnn ships had engaged stingship number twenty-five in combat. That ship number twenty-five had provoked the encounter was a point that the court would "take under careful study . . . at length."

Ensigns Bran Tse-Mallory and Truzenzu of the Zex were ordered stripped of all rank and dismissed from the service. As a preliminary, however, they were to be awarded the Church Order of Merit, one star cluster. This was done. Unofficially, each was also presented with a scroll on which those citizens of the colony-planet known as Goodhunting had inscribed their names and thanks . . . all two hundred and ninety-five thousand of them.

Major Julio Gonzalez was promoted to commander and transferred immediately to a quiet desk post in an obscure system populated by semi-intelligent amphibians.

After first being formally inducted into his ship-brother's clan, the Zex, Bran had entered the Church and had become deeply absorbed in the Chancellory of Alien Sociology, winning degrees and honors there. Truzenzuzex remained on his home planet of Willow-Wane and resumed his preservice studies in psychology and theoretical history. The title of Eint was granted shortly after. Their interests converged independently until both were immersed in the study of the ancient Tar-Aiym civilization-empire. Ten years had passed before they had remet, and they had been together ever since, an arrangement which neither had had cause to regret.

"Buy a winter suit, sir? The season is fast nearing, and the astrologers forecast cold and sleet. The finest *Pyrrm* pelts, good sir!"

"*Pas*? No. No thank you, vendor." The turnout to their little inn loomed just ahead, by the seller of prayer-bells.

Bran felt an uncommonly strong need of sleep.

Chapter Six

Flinx returned to his apartment to set himself in order for the trip. On the way back from the inurb he had stopped at a shop he knew well and purchased a small ship-bag. It was of a type he'd often seen carried by crewmen at the port and would do equally as well for him. It was light, had a built-in sensor lock on the seal, and was well-nigh indestructible. They haggled formally over the price, finally settling on the sum of nine-six point twenty credits. He could probably have cut the price another credit, but was too occupied by thoughts of the trip, so much so that the vendor inquired as to his health.

At the apartment he wasn't too surprised to find that all his possessions of value or usefulness fit easily into the one bag. He felt only a slight twinge of regret. He looked around for something else to take, but the bed wouldn't fit, nor would the portikitchen, and he doubted there'd be a shortage of either on the ship anyway. Memories were stored comfortably elsewhere. He shouldered the bag and left the empty room.

The concierge looked at him warily as he prepared to leave her the keys. She was generally a good woman, but inordinately suspicious. In reply to her persistent questioning he said only that he was departing on a journey of some length and had no idea when he would return. No, he wasn't "running from the law." He could see that the woman was suffering from a malady known as tri-dee addiction, and her imagination had been drugged in proportion. Would she hold the room for his return? She would . . . for four months' rent, in advance if you please. He paid it rather than stand and argue. It took a large slice out of the hundred credits he'd made so recently, but he found that he was in a hurry to spend the money as quickly as possible.

He strolled out into the night. His mind considered sleep but his body, tense with the speed at which events had been moving around him, vehemently disagreed. Sleep was impossible. And it was pleasant out. He moved out into the lights and noise, submerging himself in the familiar frenzy of the marketplace. He savored the night-smells of the food crescent, the raucous hooting of the barkers and sellers and vendors, greeting those he knew and smiling wistfully at an occasional delicate face peeping out from the pastel-lit windows of the less reputable saloons.

Sometimes he would spot an especially familiar face. Then he would saunter over and the two would chat amiably for a while, swapping the stories and gossip of which Flinx always had a plentiful supply. Then the rich trader or poor beggar would rub his red hair for luck and they'd part—this time, at least, for longer than the night.

If a jungle could be organized and taxed, it would be called Drallar.

He had walked nearly a mile when he noticed the slight lightening of the western sky that signified the approach of first-fog (there being no true dawn on Moth). The time had run faster than expected. He should be at the port shortly, but there remained one last thing to do.

He turned sharply to his right and hurried down several alleys and backways he knew well. Nearer the center of the marketplace, which was quieter at night than the outskirts, he came on a sturdy if small frame building. It advertised on its walls metal products of all kinds for sale. There was a combination lock, a relic, on the inside of the door, but he knew how to circumvent that. He was careful to close it quietly behind him.

It was dark in the little building but light seeped in around the open edges of the roof, admitting air but not thieves. He stole softly to a back room, not needing even the dim light. An old woman lay there, snoring softly on a simple but luxuriously blanketed bed. Her breathing was shallow but steady, and there was what might have been a knowing smile on the ancient face. That was nonsense, of course. He stood staring silently at the wrinkled parchment visage for several long moments. Then he bent. Gently shifting the well-combed white hair to one side he planted a single kiss on the bony cheek. The woman stirred but did not awaken. He backed out of the room as quietly as he had entered, remembering to lock the main door behind him.

Then he turned and set off at a brisk jog in the direction of the shuttleport, Pip dozing stonelike on one shoulder.

Chapter Seven

The great port lay a considerable distance from the city, so that its noise, fumes, and bustling commerce would not interfere with the business of the people or the sleep of the king. It was too far to walk. He hailed a *Meepah*-beast rickshaw and the driver sent the fleet-footed creature racing for the port. The *Meepahs* were fast and could dodge jams of more modern traffic. It was a sporting way to travel, and the moist wind whistling past his face wiped away the slight vestiges of sleepiness which had begun to overtake him. As the animals were pure sprinters and good for only one long run an hour they were also expensive. They flew past slower vehicles and great hoverloaders bringing tons of goods to and from the port. As they had for centuries and doubtless would for centuries to come, the poor of Moth walked along the sides of the highway. There were none of the public moving walkways on Moth that could be found in profusion in the capitals of more civilized planets. Besides being expensive, the nomad populace tended to cut them up for the metal.

When he reached an area away from the bustling commercial pits that he thought would be close to the private docks, he paid off the driver, debarked, and hurried off into the geat tubular buildings. He knew more than a little of the layout of the great port from his numerous trips here as a child. Where his interest in the place had sprung from he couldn't guess. Certainly not from Mother Mastiff! But ever since an early age he'd been fascinated by the port for the link it provided with other worlds and races. When he had been able to steal away from that watchful parental eye he'd come here, often walking the entire distance on short, unsteady legs. He'd sit for hours at the feet of grizzled old crewmen who chuckled at his interest and spun their even older tales of the void and the pinpricks of life and consciousness scattered through it for his eager mind and the fawning attention he gave freely. There were times when he'd stay till after dark. Then he'd sneak ever so carefully home, always into the waiting, scolding arms of Mother Mastiff. But at the port he was all but mesmerized. His favorites had been the stories of the interstellar freighters, those huge, balloonlike vessels that plied the distances between the inhabited worlds, transporting strange cargoes and stranger passengers. Why sonny, they'd tell him, if'n it weren't fer the freighters, the hull damn uneeverse 'ud collapse, 'an Chaos himself 'ud return t' rule!

Now maybe he'd have a chance to see one of those fabulous vessels in person.

A muted growl went audible behind him and he turned to see the bulky shape of a cargo shuttle leap spaceward, trailing its familiar tail of cream and crimson. The sound-absorbing material in its pit was further abetted by the layered glass of the building itself in muffling the scream of the rockets and ramjets. It was a sight he'd seen many times before, but a little piece of him still seemed to go spaceward with each flight. He hurried on, searching for a dock steward.

Approximately every fifteen minutes a shuttle landed

or took off from Drallar port. And it was by no means the only one on the planet. Some of the private ports managed by the lumbering companies were almost as big. The shuttles took out woods, wood products, furs, light metals, foodstuffs; brought in machinery, luxury goods, traders, and *touristas*. There! Checking bales of plastic panels was the white and black checkered uniform of a steward. He hurried over.

The man took in Flinx's clothing, age, and ship-bag and balanced these factors against the obviously dangerous reptile coiled alertly now about the boy's shoulder. He debated whether or not to answer the brief question Flinx put to him. Another, senior steward pulled up on a scoot, slowed and stopped.

"Trouble, Prin?"

The steward looked gratefully to his superior. "This . . . person . . . wishes directions to the House of Malaika's private docks."

"Um." The older man considered Flinx, who waited patiently. He'd expected something of this sort, but read only good intentions on the elder's part. "Tell him, then. 'Twill do no harm to let him have a gander at the ships, and mayhap he has real reason for being there. I've seen queerer board Malaika's craft." The man revved his scoot and darted off down the vaulting hallway.

"Pit five, second transverse tube on your left," the man said reluctantly. "And mind you go nowhere else!"

But Flinx had already started off in the indicated direction.

It wasn't hard to find, but the telescoping rampway seemed endless. It was a relief to see the tall figure of the merchant waiting for him.

"Glad to see you show, *kijana*!" he bellowed, slapping Flinx on the back. Fortunately, he managed to avoid most of the blow. Pip stirred slightly, startled. "You're the last to arrive. Everyone else is already aboard and safely tucked away. Give your pack to the steward and strap in. We're just ready to cut."

Malaika disappeared forward and Flinx gave his bag to the officious-looking young fellow who wore the House of Malaika arms (crossed starship and credit slip) on his cap and jacket. The man ducked into a low door to the rear, leaving Flinx alone in the small lock. Rather than stand by himself until the man returned to check him off, he moved forward to the passenger cabin and found himself an empty seat.

Since this was a private and not a commercial shuttle, it was smaller than most. There were only ten seats in the low, slim compartment. The craft was obviously not designed for extended journeys. The decoration verged on the baroque. He peered down the narrow aisle.

The first two seats were occupied by Malaika and his Lynx, Sissiph. She was clad in a bulky jumpsuit for a change, but it served only to emphasize the beauty of her face. In the second row Bran Tse-Mallory and Truzenzuzex were leaning into the aisle, arguing animatedly but amiably on some subject which remained incomprehensible to Flinx on every level of perception. Then came their two starship pilots, Atha Moon and the shadow man, Wolf. Both were staring intently, but at different things. Atha was gazing out the port, observing what she could of their normal preparations for lift. The man's eyes were focused unwaveringly on an invisible point six inches in front of his nose. His face was, as usual, utterly devoid of expression. He remained unreadable.

Atha's attention seemed to vary awkwardly between the outside of their tiny vessel and the front of the cabin. She was continually darting her head into the aisle or poking it above the back of the seat in front of her. Especially whenever an unusually loud giggle or chuckle came from that vicinity. Probably she thought herself inconspicuous. Perhaps she hadn't noticed him come aboard behind her. In any event she seemed unconcerned about Wolf's presence. Even from here he could see the way the muscles in her neck and cheeks tightened, the way her blood pressure changed and her breathing increased, in response to the by-play from up front. It was mild, but still. . . . He shook his head. They hadn't even reached their ship yet and already an explosive situation was building. He could not tell how long it had been forming, but he did know one thing. He personally had no wish to be around when it finally came to a head.

He wondered if Malaika had the slightest inkling that his personal pilot of six years was hopelessly in love with him.

There were several empty seats, so he chose the one behind Atha. Not that he preferred it so much to any other, but he preferred to stay as far away as possible from the enigmatic Wolf. He couldn't read the man, so he was still unsure of him. As he had on numerous other occasions, he wished his peculiar talents wouldn't be so capricious in their operation. But when he directed his attention to Wolf there was only an oddly diffuse blank. It was like trying to fathom a heavy mist. Dew did not hold the symbols well.

A brief admonition came over the cabin speaker and Flinx felt the ship tilt under him. It was being raised hydraulically. Shortly it had settled steady at its liftoff angle of seventy degrees.

Another problem brought itself to his notice as he was strapping himself in. Pip was still coiled comfortably about his left shoulder. This definitely was not going to work! How were they going to handle the minidrag? He motioned the steward over. The man struggled up the aisle by means of handles set into the sides of the chairs. He eyed the snake warily and became a bit more polite.

"Well, sir, it seems to be capable of keeping a pretty firm grip with that tail. It can't stay like it is, though, because on lift it'd be crushed between your shoulder and the chair." The way he said it made it plain that he wouldn't mind observing that eventuality. He went back down the aisle.

Flinx looked around and finally managed to urge the snake onto the thick arm of the seat opposite his. Since Pip was an arboreal creature, Flinx was much more concerned about how it would react to the pressure of liftoff than to the condition of weightlessness. Not to mention how he'd manage himself.

He needn't have worried. The luxurious little craft lifted so smoothly that pressure was practically nonexistent, even when the rockets took over from the ramjets. It was no worse than a heavy blanket on his chest, pressing him gently back into the padded seat. The muted hum of the rockets barely penetrated the well-shielded cabin. Overall, he felt only a mild sense of disorientation. By contrast, Pip appeared positively ecstatic. Then he remembered that Pip had been brought to Moth by spaceship and had therefore undergone this same experience at least twice before. His apprehensions had been groundless. But they had served to take his mind off the flight. Another glance at the minidrag showed the narrow head weaving from side to side while the single-tipped tongue darted rapidly to and fro, touching everything within reach. The pleated wings were unfurled and flapping in sheer pleasure.

After the rockets cut off and the little ship drifted weightlessly, Flinx felt acclimated enough to reach over and pick up the snake. He replaced it on its familiar spot on his shoulder. The confident pressure on his arm and back was, as ever, reassuring. Besides, the darn thing was having entirely too much fun. And the one thing they definitely did not need at the outset of their expedition was the venomous reptile flapping crazily in free fall about the confined space of the cabin.

They passed several vessels in parking orbit around the planet, including one of the great fueling stations for the shuttles. Some of the giant craft were in the process of loading or unloading, and men in suits floated about them sparkling like diamond dust. The boy's eyes drank in everything and hungered for more. Once, when the shuttle turned ninety degrees on its side and moved to line up for conjunction with their starship, the planet itself rolled majestically into view beneath them.

From this angle the famous ring-wings were clearly visible. The radiant butter-gold layers of rock and gas combined with the lakes which glistened sapphirelike through breaks in the cloud cover to make the planet more than ever resemble the Terran insect for which it had been named.

He got only the slightest glimpse of their ship, the *Gloryhole*. That was enough. Sandwiched in among bloated freighters and pudgy transports she looked like a thoroughbred in a barnyard. She still had the inevitable shape of a doublekay drive ship, a balloon stuck onto the end of a plumber's helper, but the lines were different from most. The balloon at one end was the passenger and cargo space, and the plunger at the other the generating fan for the posigravity field. Instead of being wide and shallow, like a plate, the *Gloryhole*'s generating fan was narrower and deep, chalicelike. The passenger-cargo area was still balloon-shaped, but it was a streamlined, tapered balloon. Simply on looks alone one could tell that the *Gloryhole* was faster than any regular freighter or liner aspace. It was one of the most beautiful things he'd ever seen.

He felt a slight jolt through his harness as the shuttle clicked into the transfer lock of the big ship. Following the steward's instructions he released himself from the restraining straps and drifted after the others into the umbilical tube, pulling himself hand over hand along the portable pullway. The luxury of the *Gloryhole* in comparison to the freighters he'd had described to him made itself quickly apparent. The starship's airlock was furlined.

The steward and Malaika exchanged brief orders and the uniformed young man drifted out of the tube, pulling in the line behind him. After a bit the door whirred shut, and they were effectively separated from the shuttle.

"*Je*? If you'll all follow me—use the handholds—we'll adjourn to the salon." Malaika started off through the lock exit. "Atha, you and Wolf get up to Control and start up the drive. Let's have some decent gravity around here. A *buibui* I'm not, to spin my own web! The two of you know where your cabins are." Atha and the skull-face moved off through a side passage. Malaika swiveled to face them. "The rest of you I'll show to your rooms myself."

The salon was a fairyland of glass, wood, and plastics. Bubbles of crystal containing brilliantly colored forms of aquatic life were suspended throughout the big room by a thin but unbreakable network of plastic webbing. Real trees grew through the green-fur floor, each representing a different species native to Moth. Metal sculptures layered with gem dust hung cloudlike from the ceiling, which was a tri-dee soloid depicting an open sky complete to clouds and sun. It began to darken, effectively simulating the sunset taking place on the planet's side below. It was an odd simile to come to mind, but for some reason Flinx could best liken the sensation to walking through an especially fine beer.

The ship shuddered once, twice, ever so imperceptibly, and he could feel the weight beginning to return to his body. He started to float toward a side door and then began flailing frantically so that he would land on his feet and not his head. A glance showed that none of the other passengers were experiencing similar difficulties. Sissiph was being steadied by Malaika, and Tse-Mallory and Truzenzuzex hadn't even bothered to pause in their argument. Angrily he got his errant legs under him. No one commented on his obvious difficulty, for which he was grateful. Full gravity returned after a very short interval.

Malaika walked over to what looked like a cactus but was actually a bar. "We'll remain at point nine five gravity for the duration of the trip. Possibly most of you aren't used to keeping up muscle tone in space" (Flinx took a quick sensing of the two scientist's compositions and doubted the accuracy of Malaika's remark) "and so I'd hesitate to set it lower than that.

The slight difference should be just enough to be exhilarating, and it approximates what we'll encounter on our objective planetfall."

"This will serve as a regular gathering place. Meals will be served here by the autochef, unless you prefer to eat in your cabin. *Njoo*, I will show you your own. . . ."

Flinx spent three days just examining his "own." It was packed with fantastic devices that sprang at you out of floor, ceiling, and walls. You had to watch your step. Press the wrong switch and you were liable to be doused with warm water . . . irrespective of your attire of the moment. That had been a disheartening experience, especially as he had been trying for a haircut. Fortunately no one but Pip had been around to witness it.

He had been concerned to see how his pet would take to the confinements of shipboard life. Everyone else, excepting possibly Sissiph, had adjusted to the reptile's presence. So that didn't give him cause for worry. As it happened, there were no others. The minidrag would go swooping in and out among the pylons and plastic tapestries of the salon as if he owned them, frightening the devil out of the inhabitants of the glass bubbles. Occasionally it would hang batlike from a particularly inviting artificial branch or real one. When it was discovered that the food selector in their cabin could deliver fresh bits of raw *Wiodor* meat, the snake's contentment was assured.

They had been moving out of Moth's system at a slow but continually building speed for several days now. Malaika was in an expansive mood, and so when Flinx requested permission to stand by in Control during changeover, the merchant acceded gracefully. Once they made the initial jump past lightspeed at changeover their rate of acceleration would go up tremendously.

Apparently no one else shared his curiosity. Malaika remained secluded in his cabin with his Lynx. Tse-Mallory and Truzenzuzex spent most of their time in the salon, playing personality chess and conversing in languages and on subjects Flinx could grasp only an occasional bit of. Once more he reflected on their complete ease and familiarity with starship travel.

Malaika had half-promised to come up to Control for changeover to explain the workings to Flinx. But when the time came, Sissiph was pouting over some incomprehensible slighting and the merchant was compelled to remain in the cabin with her. In his place he instructed Atha to answer any questions Flinx might have regarding the workings of the ship or drive. She had acknowledged the order with obvious distaste.

Flinx had come to the conclusion that he was going to have to be the one to break the silence that their unceremonious first meeting had produced. Otherwise they might not exchange a word the entire trip, and even a large spaceship is too small an area in which to retain animosities.

He entered Control and strolled up behind her seat. Wolf was off on the opposite side of the room. She said nothing, but he knew she had noticed his entrance.

He read directness and decided to counter with same.

"Look, I didn't mean to kick you back there in the tower, that time." She swiveled to eye him questioningly. "That is, I didn't mean to kick *you*, I meant to kick . . . oh, hell!" The explanation hadn't seemed this complicated when he'd rehearsed it in his mind. Of course, then, he hadn't had to contend with the rich red-brown in those eyes. "I thought you were a spy . . . or an assassin, or something. You certainly didn't look as though you belonged where you were, so I took the least bloody route I could think of at the time of forcing you into the open. It worked, you turned out to be not what I expected, and I apologize. There! Truce?"

She hesitated, and then her face softened into an abashed grin. She put out a hand. "Truce!" He kissed it instead of shaking it, and she turned, pleased, back to her instruments. "You know, you were right, actually. I had no business at all being where I was. Nor doing what I was doing. Do I look that much like an assassin from the back?"

"The contrary, the contrary." Then, abruptly, "You're quite attracted to your boss, aren't you?"

Her face jerked up, surprised. One would have thought he'd just revealed one of the great secrets of the universe. He had to work to keep from grinning. Tree, was she that naive?

"Why . . . why, what a thing to say! What a perfectly *absurd* thought! Maxim Malaika is my employer, and a good one. Nothing more. What makes . . . ? Uh, do you have any questions about the ship? If not, I *am* bus. . . ."

Hastily, he said, "Why is it that while this ship is infinitely more complicated than the shuttle, both require the same crew of two?" He knew the answer, but wanted to keep her talking.

"That's the reason, right there." She indicated the panoply of ranked lights and instruments around them. "Because it is so complex, it requires a lot more automation just to operate. Actually, the *Gloryhole*

110

pretty well runs herself most of the time. Except for providing instructions and handling decisions, we're here just in case of the unforeseen situation. Interstellar navigation, for example, is much too complex for human or thranx minds to manage on any really practical level. Starships *have* to be run by machines or they'd be impossible altogether."

"I see. By minor situations and unforeseen things, do you mean like at changeover?"

"Oh, there's no real danger from changeover. The companies like to make a big thing of it to give their passengers a slight thrill. Sure, once in a while you'll hear about something happening. A meteor will make a millions-to-one infringement on the gravity well of a ship at the moment of shift and the ship will turn inside out, or something equally weird. Those are real exceptions. The tri-dee and faxcax blow those incidents all out of proportion for their ratings value. Usually it's no more trouble than stepping from land onto a floating boat."

"Glad to hear it. I don't think I'd enjoy being turned inside out. That was the old *Curryon,* wasn't it?"

"Why, yes. It was twenty-four thirty-three, old calendar. Actually, we have to worry only about keeping the center of the field positioned constant with respect to the fan and generator. The computers take care of most of that. Once it falls too far ahead or drops too close, you have to stop the ship, then start up all over again. That takes a lot of time, for deceleration and acceleration, and it's expensive as well as tricky. If the field should start to oscillate, the ship could be shaken to pieces. But as I said, the computers handle all that worry for us. Barring those unforeseen circumstances, of course."

111

"I've never been on a doublekay drive ship before. I'm no physicist, but could you maybe give me a quickee explanation of how the thing works? One that even my simple mind could understand?"

She sighed. "Okay. What the Caplis generator does ... that's what we hold in the 'fan' up ahead ... is in effect produce a powerful but concentrated gravitational field at the nose of the ship. As soon as the field exceeds the natural one of the ship, the ship moves toward it, naturally attracted by a 'body' of greater 'mass' than itself. Being part of the ship, the doublekay drive unit naturally goes along with it. But the unit, having moved forward, is set to keep the field at a constant distance from the hull of the craft. Therefore the field is moved forward also. The ship will try to catch up to it again, and so on, ad infinitum. The field is in effect pulling the ship instead of pushing it, as the shuttle rockets do. Doublekay vessels actually move in a series of continuous jerks, so rapid and close together that they seem to be one smooth, unbroken pull. The increase or decrease in the size of the field determines the speed of the ship.

"Being a wave and not a particle form of energy, gravity isn't affected in the same way that mass is on approaching the speed of light. The doublekay field creates a cone-shaped zone of stress behind it, in which mass acts differently than it does under normal circumstances. That's why when we exceed the speed of light I don't see through you, or something. Once we've made that initial breakthrough, or 'changeover,' our rate of travel goes up enormously. It's something like riding the back of a very tame SCCAM shell.

"Our initial power comes from a small hydrogen 'sparkplug' ... I wonder sometimes where that word

112

came from . . . up near the generator housing in the tube section of the ship. Once started up, the field can be 'channeled' to a certain extent. That's where we get our gravity for the ship and power to run the lights and autobar and things."

"In the event of a drive failure there are provisions for converting the fan to an old ion-type drive, powered by the hydrogen plug. It would take twelve years at its best speed to get from Moth to Powerline, the nearest inhabited planet. Farther out where the stars are more scattered it's even worse. But twelve years or so is better than never. Stranded ships *have* been saved that way . . . those that managed to overcome problems like lack of food and insanity. But the rate of failure for doublekay drives is miniscule. Only rarely can a mere human manage to screw one up."

"Thanks," said Flinx. "That helps . . . sort of." He glanced over at Wolf and saw that the man was totally immersed in his work. He lowered his voice. "Incidentally, I think maybe you've got the wrong idea of what a Lynx is."

"A prostitute," she replied automatically.

"Uh-uh. The Lynx are a group of very beautiful and ambitious women who don't regard lifemating as the end-all of civilization. They prefer to move from one fascinating man to another."

"So I've been told. And seen. That's still a matter of opinion." She sniffed calculatingly.

He started for the exit. "So I don't think you need worry about Sissiph or any of the others settling down with your merchant, permanent-like."

"Listen!" she shouted, "For the last time, I . . . !" She dropped her voice as Wolf looked over curiously. "I am *not* in love with Maxim Malaika!"

"Sure, sure," said Flinx from the doorway. "I can see that."

It was only a short while later, while watching a viewtape in his cabin, that he realized he'd missed changeover.

Chapter Eight

Teleen auz Rudenuaman was resting easily in her rooms on the great estate complex of her aunt. She was scantily clad. That is, she wore at least as little as the huge male form which stood admiring the play of its muscles in the wall-length mirror across from the bed-desk.

"Rory," she said to the ceiling, "you do love me, don't you?"

"Um-hmm," said the figure, bending on one knee and flexing a forearm.

"And you'd do anything for me, wouldn't you?"

"Um-hmm."

"Then why," she said, sitting up abruptly and shouting, "the hell didn't you do anything when the old witch started in on me this morning?"

The figure sighed and turned regretfully from the mirror to face her. Its body was hard, but the face was curiously soft, almost childlike. Beautiful and soft. The expression it wore was amiable and best described as intensely vacuous.

"I *could* have said something, Teleen, dear, but what would it have accomplished? Besides making her even more suspicious of *us*. She had it in for you anyway, and nothing I could have said would likely have turned her off. Besides, she was right, you know. You *did* foul up that. . . ."

"I'm not interested. I had enough of that from *her* this morning. Surely she can't reasonably expect me to be responsible for the ineptitude of men *her* people hired in the first place?"

Rory Mallap van Cleef sighed again and began pulling on a gold dressing gown. "I suppose not, dear. But then when has she ever been reasonable about anything? I really don't understand the intricacies of such dealings. She was awfully bitchy, wasn't she?"

Teleen slid out of the bed and moved to sit next to him. She put her arms possessively around the massive shoulders, resting her head against one bulging dorsal.

"Look, Rory, I've told you before. The only way we're ever going to have any happiness is to eliminate the old bag once and for all."

Rory grinned. He was not without a sense of humor, even if it did tend more than a bit to the primitive.

"Now is that any way to talk about your beloved aunt?"

"No. It's the *only* way to talk about her! And at that I'm flattering her. Every time we discuss her elimination my charitable instincts get the better of me. But to be specific. . . ."

"Please, darling, I'm not in the mood now."

"Rory," she said, sitting back, "are you in love with me . . . or with her?"

"Don't be obscene, dear! You have no idea, no *idea*, what a task it is constantly to have to feign interest in that sack of surgical miracles. Especially," and he drew her onto his lap and kissed her, "after you."

"Mmmmm. That's the way I like to hear you talk!" He had her purring again. "You'll go along with me, then?"

"As I've said before, if you come up with a reasonably sensible plan. Love or not, I'm not going to take a chance on spending the rest of my life on some prison moon because some scheme is only half worked out. I'm no genius, but I'm smart enough to know it. So you manage the brains for both of us. I'll supply any needed muscle. Of which," he added, flexing a tricep lovingly, "I have more than sufficient."

She slipped out of his grasp and stamped angrily on the deep fur floor. It did interesting things to the rest of her body. "Stop admiring yourself for a minute and try to be serious. Murder is not a funny business!"

"It is when it involves your aunt."

"Oh, you're impossible! All right; look, you know how fond she is of bathing in that pool, the little one with all those lovely fish and snails and things?" Her eyes were slitted. "How she never misses a daily swim?"

"Yes, I know the place. So?"

"Would it be a simple matter to wire the thing, do you think?"

He shook his head, doubtfully. "Her people would notice that sort of thing. You know how careful she is."

"Not if we disguised it as one of those censored frogs, or something!" She glowed. "Yes, a frog. I'm sure such a device could be made. Waterproof, small, but still capable of delivering a lethal charge, yes. And you could, um, put the guard 'to sleep' for the minute necessary to slip the thing into the water."

"That does sound good, darling. Yes, Teleen, I do think so too!" He lifted her off the floor and kissed her gently. "One thing, though. Why haven't you thought of something like this before?"

Her mouth twisted in a feral smile that, had she known it, was almost a carbon copy of her aunt's. "Oh, I have, I have, sort of. But until this morning, I really hadn't been sufficiently inspired! Today I was finally convinced she is quite mad. It will be only a kindness to gift her with a long sleep."

Rashalleila Nuaman switched off the spy-screen and smiled kittenishly to herself. Her niece's generosity and concern was . . . well, appalling. So she had finally dug up enough courage to actually plan the thing! About time, yes. But to trust that side of beef van Cleef with such knowledge! Tsk. Poor judgment, poor. How anyone could actually fall in *love* with an automaton, an utter nonentity, like that! Oh sure, he was great between the sheets. But beyond that he was a nothing, a void, a null factor. Well-meaning and affectionate, to be sure. Like a large puppy-dog. Ah, well. Let them enjoy their private games. It would be good practice for Teleen. Buoy her self-confidence, and all that. Eventually, though, the poor thing would have to be jolted back to her senses. She giggled at the small witticism. Such folderol was fine, but not on company time. Which reminds. Must have the ground keeper get rid of all those nice froggies. Temporarily, at least. No use wasting. Dinner tomorrow, perhaps.

She had turned off the spy-screen a few moments too early. Downstairs, her niece's stimulated mind had come up with another thought.

"We also ought to keep the old bitch off balance, Rory. While we're trying to hammer this thing out. She's not a complete idiot, you know."

"I suppose that's a good idea," said van Cleef, flexing his quadriceps. "You'll think of something."

Her face was alight. "I have. Oh, *have* I!" She

turned away and walked over to the china desk. A hidden switch revealed a comm-screen she *knew* wasn't being tapped by any of her dear auntie's automatic spy monitors. It was the one machine on the estate whose circuitry she'd checked over herself. She tapped out a rapid, high-speed series of numbers that sped her call over a very special and very secret relay system to a little-contacted section of space.

Eventually the screen cleared and a face began to take shape.

"Well, good light to you, Amuven DE, and may your house always be filled with dust."

The face of the AAnn businessman crinkled in a toothy smile. "As always, as always. So good to hear from you again, Mistress Rude!"

Chapter Nine

Flinx had been staring silently out through the main viewport of the salon for some time, well aware that there was someone behind him. But to have turned immediately would have engendered unnecessary awkwardness. Now he turned to see the two scientists and became aware that he needn't have been concerned. Neither was paying the slightest attention to him. They had drawn over lounges and were staring out at the magnificent chaos of the drive-distorted heavens. Taking no notice of their scrutiny, the prismatic panoply flowed on unchanged.

"Don't mind us, Flinx. We're here for the same thing. To enjoy the view." The philosoph returned his attention to the great port and the doppler-distorted suns which glowed far more sharply than they ever could in their natural state.

But Flinx's concentration and mood had been broken. He continued facing the two scientists.

"Sirs, doesn't it strike you as odd that in a time when so many folk have so much trouble getting along with one another, you two, of two utterly different races, manage to get along so well?"

"Your questions, I fear, will never carry the burden of subtlety, lad." Tse-Mallory turned to the thranx. "At times in the past my friend and I existed in a rather close—one could say intimate—association. Our work necessitated it. And we are not so very different as you might think."

"I remember your calling each other ship-brother several times."

"Yes? I suppose we did. We've never gotten used to the idea that other people might find it unusual. It's so very natural to us."

"You were a gunnery team?"

"No," said Truzenzuzex. "We flew a stingship. Small, fast, a single medium SCCAM projector."

"As to our relationship irrespective of ship life, Flinx, I'm not sure Tru and I could give you an objective answer. Our personalities just seem to compliment one another. Always have. The attraction between human and thranx is something that psychologists of both races have sweated over for years, without ever coming up with a satisfactory explanation. There are even some pairs and groupings that become physically ill if one is separated long from its alien counterpart. And it seems to work on both sides. A kind of mental symbiosis. Subjectively, we just feel supremely comfortable with each other.

"You know the events leading up to the Amalgamation, the Pitar-humanx war, and such?"

"Only bits and pieces, I'm afraid. Regular schooling is something that eluded me early."

"Umm. Or vice versa, I suspect. Tru?"

"You tell the lad. I'm certain he'd find the human version of the story more palatable."

"All right."

"Human and thranx have known each other for a comparatively short period of time. Hard to believe today, but true. A little over two t-centuries ago, scoutships of both races first encountered each other's civilizations. By that time, mankind had been in space for several previous t-centuries. In that time, while engaged in exploration and colonization, he had encountered many other alien life-forms. Intelligent and otherwise. This was also true of the thranx, who had been in space even longer than humanity."

"There was an indefinable attraction between the two races from the very outset. The favorable reactions on both sides far outweighed the expected prejudice and aversions."

"Such existed on the thranx planets as well," put in Truzenzuzex.

"I thought I was going to tell this?"

"Apologies, oh omnipotent one!"

Tse-Mallory grinned, and continued. "The thranx were as alien as any race man had yet encountered. A hundred-percent insectoid, hard-shelled, open circulatory system, compound eyes, rigid, inflexible joints . . . and eight limbs. *And* they were egg-layers. As a news commentator of the time put it, 'they were completely and delightfully weird.'"

"If I recall aright, your people laid a few eggs at that time too," piped the philosoph. Tse-Mallory shut him up with an exasperated glance.

"From past experiences one would have expected the human reaction to the discovery of a race of giant sentient insects to be hostile or at least mildly paranoid. That had proved the pattern in too many previous contacts. And man had been fighting smaller and much more primitive cousins of the thranx for thousands of years on the home planet. In fact, if you can believe it, the term 'bug' originally had a derogatory connotation.

"But by now mankind had learned it was going to have to live in peace and harmony with beings whose appearance might be personally repulsive. It didn't

help things to know that many of those same beings
considered man at least as repulsive-looking as he
considered them." He glanced expectantly at
Truzenzuzex, but that worthy was at least temporarily subdued. "So the actual reaction between human
and thranx was doubly unexpected. The two races
took to each other like a pair of long-separated twins.
The thranx traits of calmness, cool decision-making
ability, politeness, and wry humor were admired
tremendously by humans who'd sought such qualities
in themselves. By the same token there was a reck-
lessness combined with brains, an impossible self-
confidence, and a sensitivity to surroundings that
thranx found appealing in man.

"Once it had been voted on by both races and
approved by considerable margins despite the expected opposition from moneyed chauvinists, Amalgamation proved to be even less trouble than the op-
timists had anticipated. Thranx click-speech, with its
attendant whistling, actually had a reasonable phonet-
ic counterpart among the thousands of Terran languages and dialects."

"African sub-divisions," mused Truzenzuzex.
"Xhosa."

"Yes. For their part thranx could, with difficulty,
manage the major human language system of Terranglo. The eventual outgrowth of much work by phonet-
icists, semanticists, and linguists on both sides was a
language that hopefully combined the better aspects
of both. The clicks and whistles and some of the
rough rasps of Hive-speech major were kept in, intact,
along with most of the smoother sounds and vowels of
Terranglo. The result was probably the closest thing
to a universal language, barring telepathy, we'll ever
have: symbospeech. Fortunately for business pur-

poses, most other races with vocal apparatus can also manhandle at least enough of it to get by with. Even the AAnn, who turned out to be better at it than most.

"The mutual admiration society was off and winging. Pretty soon it had extended itself to other aspects of the new humanx life-system. Our politicians, judges, and law-makers couldn't help but admire the beauty and simplicity with which thranx law and government had been put together. It was practically an art-form, built up as it had been from the old Hive structure itself. Not that it was that different from the oldest human municipalities and nation-states. Just much more sensible. Thranx lawyers and magistrates soon cleared away a lot of the backlog that had been clogging human courts. Besides their superlative natural sense of jurisprudence, they could not possibly be accused by anyone of partiality.

"Terran-derived sports, on the other hand, completely revolutionized the thranx's biggest problem— that of leisure. They simply hadn't realized that there were so many organized ways of having fun. When they discovered chess and judo, it was all over with flip-the-rock and that ilk."

"Third-degree black belt," noted Truzenzuzex proudly. "Although I'm getting a bit creaky for such activity."

"So I've noticed. I could go on and on, lad. Human planets were deluged with exquisite examples of thranx workmanship. Machinery, handicrafts, personal gadgetry, delicate electrical products, and so on. Even the body coloring of each was pleasing to the other, although thranx odor had a decided advantage over the human."

"No argument there," puffed the philosoph. That earned him another sharp glance.

"When the thranx got hold of Terran literature, paintings, sculpture, and such seemingly unrelated things as ice-cream and children's toys . . . in short, the two races just seemed to merge amazingly well. And the greatest of humanx achievements, the modified doublekay drive, you must know about.

"But by far the greatest impetus toward amalgamation—along with the Pitar-humanx war—was the formation of the United Church. Powerful, relatively new groups existed among both races with similar beliefs. When they learned of one another's existence, an alien organization with practically identical theologies and desires, they soon had formed a combine which rapidly overwhelmed all but the most die-hard members of the older established churches. Not the least of its strengths was that it insisted on being called a nonreligious organization. For the first time, people could get top-level spiritual guidance without having to profess a belief in God. Back when, it was a real revolution."

"As near as we can tell, put in Truzenzuzex, "it is still unique in being the only multiracial spiritual institution in the galaxy. And other races have members."

"I'm afraid I don't belong," said Flinx.

"Doesn't bother me. The Church really couldn't care less. They don't proselytize, you know. They're much too busy with the important things. Sure, they'd be glad to have you or anyone else as a new member, but you have to go to them. The mountain will have to go to Mohammed, because Mohammed is busy enough in *his* neighborhood!"

"What?" said Flinx.

"Forget it. Archaic reference. Even our materialistic captain is a member."

"I guessed that. Does he believe in God, too?"

"Difficult to tell," said Tse-Mallory thoughtfully. "That's only incidental, anyway. I'm more concerned about whether or not God believes in him, because I've a hunch we're going to need any outside help we can get before this trip is over."

"How about the Pitar-humanx war?" Flinx prompted.

"Oh that. Tomorrow, hmm? I could use a drink right now. Haven't done that much lecturing since . . . a long time."

True to his word he picked up the narrative the following morning, over tea and sweetcakes. Besides, one gets bored quickly in space. His audience had grown, however, since everyone was now in the salon except Wolf. It was his turn on duty watch.

"I too am familiar with the details," put in Malaika, an arm curled possessively around Sissiph's waist. "But I think I'd enjoy hearing you tell it, *juu ya*. I *know* my versions are wrong!" He laughed uproariously.

"So," said Tse-Mallory, unconsciously aping their host. "Some five t-decades after the initial Terran-thranx contact, relations between the two civilizations were growing at a geometric pace. Both sides, however, were still wary of each other. Contact between the two religious groups was still in a formative stage, and amalgamation was a dream in the minds of a few outstanding visionaries of both races. These were still greatly outnumbered by the 'patriots' on both sides."

"Then came the first Terran contact with the Pitar. That race occupied two densely populated planets in the Orion sector. They were a totally unexpected factor, an alien race human to point nine six three places. Really a remarkable and as yet unequaled coincidence of form. Externally they were for all practical purposes identical with humankind. In looks, as a race, they came pretty close to the Terran ideal. The males were tall, muscular, handsome, and exceptionally structured. The women were one hundred percent feminine and at least as attractive as the men. Humanity went through a brief, hysterical phase in which anything even remotely Pitarian was the subject of slavish imitation. The Pitar themselves seemed cordial enough, if a bit nervous and self-centered. Limitless professions of mutual aid and undying friendship were exchanged between the two races.

"The Pitar were highly scientific, and in a few phases of research came surprisingly close to matching Terra. Weaponry, for example. The reasons for this obvious dichotomy in their seemingly peace-loving civilization became apparent later. Too much later. It also appeared to have a disproportionate influence in their social setup.

"Human-Pitar friendship was progressing at a rate comparable to human-thranx. Several years after first contact, a tramp freighter happened to put in at a large but out-of-the-way humanoid colony. Tree-trunk, or Argus V, as it's better known now. Apparently the entire colony, some six hundred thousand souls, had been utterly and ruthlessly wiped out by an unknown lifeform. Not a man, woman, or child had been left alive on the entire planet. Corpses of women seemed to be especially lacking. The reason for this was discovered later also. Well, expressions of sympathy poured in from the other intelligent races, including the Pitar. They were at least as outraged as any of the others. Most races then sent out scouts to try to locate this new and virulent alien race before they themselves could become the victims of a similar atrocity.

"Two months later a man was found orbiting one of the devastated planet's two moons in an antique, jury-rigged lifeboat. A cruiser of the *Unop-Patha*—you know that race?—was on courtesy patrol at the time and happened to drift within range of the boat's feeble transmitter. They had never encountered an insane human before and were pretty much at a loss as to what to do with him until they could finally turn him over to the nearest human authorities. That happened to be the big research group which was sifting Treetrunk for clues. A month of intensive treatment succeeded in restoring the fellow to partial coherency.

"It took them some time to make sense of his story. His mind had been badly unhinged by months of helpless drifting in space, fears of meeting an enemy ship—and, after a while, of not meeting one—and by what he had seen on the planet itself. It was fortunate that he didn't have the courage to commit suicide. The ugly story he told has been documented many times over and I find it personally distasteful, so I will skip over the gory parts.

"The enemy had struck without warning, raining death on the unprepared populace. Being without a regular military force—or need of one—the planet was quite helpless. The police skiffs tried and, as might have been expected, proved useless. All appeals for mercy, negotiations, or surrender were met with the same response as ferocious resistance. When all opposition had been crushed and all interstellar communications completely destroyed or blanketed out, the invaders came down in ships of vaguely familiar design to inspect what remained of the battered colony.

"Our single survivor had been as surprised as anyone when the sneak tri-dee screens had focused on the locks of the landing shuttles and armed Pitarian troops had come pouring out. They were remorseless in their destruction of the surviving human population, treating it as if they were the lowest, filthiest organisms in the universe. They helped themselves to a few valuables and such, but for the most part they seemed to enjoy killing for the love of it. Like weasels on Terra. At this point the man's mind started to shrink away again. The psychiatrists who attended him felt that if he'd remained sane he never would have been able to cope with the other stresses that his escape put on his mind. Like not eating for four days, and such. The Pitar were thorough. They carried life detectors to search out survivors no matter how well they were hidden.

"Our informant had lived in a small town near the planet's equator. He had once been a ship's engineer and had bought a small, obsolete lifeboat which he enjoyed tinkering with in his spare time. Again, it took a madman to suppose that that wreck could ever make it to the nearest moon. Before the enemy troops had reached his area he had managed to provision the tiny ship and perform a successful liftoff. Obviously the orbiting warships were no longer expecting a vessel from the planet's surface. All spaceports had been destroyed, and all the commercial doublekay drive ships in parking orbit had been vaporized while trying to escape or taken over by Pitarian prize crews. No one thought of an attempt to escape simply to space. The moons are uninhabitable and there are no other planets in the system capable of supporting human life. Or possibly they weren't geared to the detection of a propulsive system as tiny and outmoded as his. Anyway, he made it safely through their outward-turned screens and into a closed orbit around the first moon. He never really expected to be picked up. All his addled mind could think of was getting away from the abomination below. It was pure chance that he was rescued.

"That was the gist of his story. Among the nauseating details the probes pumped out of him was what the Pitar did with the bodies of all those missing women. That was so disgusting the authorities tried to keep it from the general public, but as usually happens in such cases, the word got out. The resultant uproar was violent and widespread. War was never even formally declared because most of the members of the Terran Congress held reserve commissions and rushed to get aboard their ships.

"The gigantic armada that was assembled hurled itself into the Pitarian system. Much to everyone's surprise, the Pitarians held their own from their planetary and satellite bases. In space their ships were no match for the human fleet, in addition to being heavily outnumbered, but the possibility of such an eventuality had been considered by the Pitarians and their scientists had put up an offensive-defensive network which the starship weaponry was unable to batter through. It settled down to a war of attrition which the Pitarians hoped to win by making it too expensive to bear. As a result they were effectively blockaded from the rest of the universe, or, as the more polite were wont to put it, were placed in a state of 'enforced quarantine.'

"It appeared as though the situation might stay that way indefinitely. That is, until the thranx stepped in. Like most of the rest of the intelligent races the thranx had heard the details of the Argus V massacre. Unlike most of them, however, they were determined to do something more effective than blockading. As far as the thranx were concerned the final straw was the use to which the Pitar had put human females. The female is considered even more an object of veneration and helplessness on thranx worlds than on the most gallant of humanoid ones. This is a legacy from their early ancestors, when there was one egg-laying queen to protect and nurture. When this hereditary attitude was translated into manners, it was one reason why Terran and other humanoid females who had had contact with the thranx were among the first vociferous boosters of the idea of amalgamation.

"So the thranx added their fleets to the human. At first this had no effect other than to intensify an already near-perfect blockade. Then the human-thranx teams made their first big breakthroughs on the doublekay drive systems, the SCCAM weapons complex, and more. A device had finally been found which could successfully penetrate the Pitarian battle network. It was used. There was at this time some desire among humanx scientists to make an attempt to preserve at least a portion of Pitarian civilization intact, for study. They hoped to find an explanation for their extreme racial paranoia. Sentiment being what it was on the human planets, however, this proved impossible. There is also some reason to believe that the Pitarians themselves would not have permitted this. Their affliction was that strong. Anyway, they fought to the last city.

"The three planets remain, blasted and empty.

131

One human, two Pitarian. They are not often visited, except by the curious and the morbid.

"The scientific teams that worked on the ruins of the Pitarian civilization came to the conclusion that the race was totally unable to accept or understand terms like mercy, compassion, openness, and equality, and similar abstract concepts. They believed themselves to be the only race worthy of existence in the universe. Once they had managed to steal all the knowledge they would stoop to borrow from the barbaric humans, they set out to destroy them. The other intelligent races of the galaxy would have been next on their program of extermination, including the thranx. Compared to them our erstwhile modern competitors, the AAnn, are positively pacific.

"Fortunately, in most respects the Pitarians were nowhere near as sharp as the AAnn. Their weapons development far exceeded their racial maturity, and their conceit their cleverness. I've often wondered whether the Pitar-humanx war was a single boost to amalgamation or a multiple one. There was mutual hatred of the Pitarians, the gratitude mankind felt for the thranx aid, and the fear that somewhere out among the stars there might exist another bunch of psychopathic killers like the Pitar."

It was very quiet in the elegant room when Tse-Mallory had finished.

"Well," said Atha finally, breaking the thought-heavy silence, "it's my turn up front. I'd better go and relieve Wolf." She uncurled herself from the lounge and departed forward.

"*Ndiye, ndiye.*" The merchant leaned over and leered at Sissiph. "Come, my *pakadoge*, little pussy. We are only halfway through that delightful book of yours, and I can't wait to see how it turns out. Even if it is mostly pictures. You'll excuse us, gentlesirs?"

Giggling, the girl led him out of the salon.

Tse-Mallory began setting up the levels for the personality-chess board, while Truzenzuzex began shuffling the cards and lining up the blue and red and black pieces.

Flinx looked up at the sociologist. "Sir, *you* didn't participate in the Pitar-humanx war, did you?"

"Pure Flux, youth, no! I'll admit to being aged, and rarely even to old, but archaic—never! I did have a grandfather who participated, though. As I suppose all of our ancestors of that time did, one way or another. Didn't yours?"

Flinx rose and idly brushed off his pants. The fur from the carpet had a tendency to cling. "Excuse me, please, sirs. I recall that I haven't fed Pip his evening meal, and I wouldn't want him to get irritated and start nibbling on my arm."

He turned and headed for the passageway. Tse-Mallory looked after him curiously, then shrugged and turned back to the game. It was his move.

Chapter Ten

Thus far there had been no trouble. The first sign of it came three ship-days later.

Malaika was in Control, checking out coordinates with Wolf. In his cabin Truzenzuzex was rigid in a meditation trance. He utilized that technique whenever he wished to consider a problem involving extreme concentration. And sometimes just to relax. In that state he required less body energy. In the salon, Tse-Mallory was trying to explain the workings of a semantic puzzle to Flinx. Atha was nearby, attempting somewhat boredly to beat herself at the ancient and timeworn game of Mono-Poly. She moved the obscure little idols and symbols in ways that Flinx had always found dully repetitive. Everything continued normally until Sissiph, bored and ejected from Control by the busy Malaika, stomped crankily into the room, a trail of translucent pseudolace flowing behind her.

"This is a *dull* place! Dull, dull, *dull!* Like—like living in a coffin!" She fumed quietly for a few minutes. As no one deigned to notice her, she moved to a more central location. "What a collection! Two pilots, two braincases, and a kid with a poisonous worm for a pet!"

Pip's head lifted abruptly and the minidrag made an unfriendly motion in the girl's direction. Flinx stroked the back of its head until it had relaxed sufficiently for some of the tightness to leave the long muscles. His own response was mild as he considered the self-uncertainty/anger/confusion in the girl's mind.

"It is a reptile, and bears no relation to. . . ."

"Reptile! *Worm*! What difference does it make?" She pouted. "And Maxy won't even let me *watch* while he plays with all those *darling* coordinates and standards and things! He says I 'distract' him. Can you imagine? *Distract* him?"

"I can't imagine why it should either, my dear," murmured Atha without looking up from her game.

Ordinarily Sissiph probably wouldn't have made anything of it. Back in Drallar she'd had more than ample opportunity to inure herself to Atha's sarcasm. But the combination of the long flight and her frustrations of the moment combined to make her turn. Her voice was tight.

"Is that supposed to be some kind of crack?"

Still Atha did not look up from her game. No doubt she expected Sissiph to brush off the remark as she usually did and go flouncing from the room in a dignified huff. She returned with a slang phrase.

" 'Tis truth, forsooth."

"And your mouth," rejoined Sissiph, parodying the words terribly, "is a bit too 'looth'!" She gave the game table a quick shove with a knee. Being portable and not bolted to the fabric of the ship, it toppled easily. Small metal objects and plastic cards sailed in all directions.

Atha closed her eyes tightly, not moving, and then slowly opened them again. She turned easily to stare at the Lynx, her eyes even with the other girl's knees.

"I think, honey, that if we're going to pursue this

conversation, we'd do it better on a more equal level."

Her forearm shot out and caught the surprised Sissiph behind the knees. She let out a startled squeak and sat down hard.

From there on, their bodies seemed to merge so closely that Flinx was hard put to tell them apart. Their thoughts were indecipherable. Scientific combat went out the port, so to speak. Tse-Mallory left his puzzle and made a laudable, if foolhardy, attempt to stop it. All he received for his efforts was a long scratch on one cheek. At that moment Malaika, summoned hastily by Flinx with a gentle probe, appeared in the fore doorway. He took in the whole scene at a half-glance.

"What in the name of the obscenity seven hells is going on here?"

Even his familiar bellow had no effect on the two combatants, who were by now too deeply engrossed in their work to notice mere mortal entreaties. The merchant moved forward and made an attempt to separate the two. Several, in fact. It was like dipping one's hands into a whirlwind. Frustrated, he backed off.

The longer one lived in the lower levels of Drallar, the greater one's acquired knowledge of elementary human psychology. Flinx said loudly but evenly, putting as much disgust into his voice as he could muster, "My, if you two only knew how funny you look!" He also risked a brief mental projection of the two combatants, suitably embellished.

There was immediate peace in the room. The cloud of hair, teeth, nails, and shredded clothing ground to an abrupt halt, resolving itself into two distinct

bodies. Both stared blankly at Flinx, then uncertainly
at each other.

"Thanks, *kijana*. I'd thought you might help out
here and there, but apparently there's no end to your
talents." Malaika reached down and grasped each girl
by the remaining material at the scruff of her neck,
lifting them much as one would a pair of obstinate
kittens. The two glared silently at one another and
seemed more than willing to start in all over again.
Perceiving this, he shook them so hard that their
teeth rattled and their slippers fell off.

"We're on a billion-credit hunt in rarely spaced
territory after something which any other company in
the galaxy would gladly slit my throat for an inkling
of, and you two *mwanamkewivu*, cretins, idiots, can't
live in peace for a month!" He shook them again,
although not as furiously. Neither of them looked in
the mood for fighting now. "If this happens again,
and I'll warn you only once, I will cheerfully chuck
the both of you, biting and scratching if that's the
way you want it, out the nearest airlock! *Is that
understood?*"

The two women stared silently at the floor.

"*Au ndiyo au la!* Tell me now!" The voice reverber-
ated around the salon.

Finally Sissiph murmured, almost inaudibly, "Yes,
Maxy." He turned to glare murderously at Atha.

"Yes, sir," she said meekly.

Malaika would have continued, but Wolf chose that
moment to peer into the room.

"Captain, I think you'd better come take a look at
this. There is an object or objects on the screens
which I would say is a ship, or ships. I'd like your
opinion."

"*Nini?*" Malaika roared, whirling. "What!" He let

go of the two women. Both stood quietly, trying to create order out of the chaos of their clothing. Occasionally one would glance up at the other, but for now, at least, both were thoroughly abashed.

"It appears to be closing on us, sir. I do wish you'd come take a look ... now."

Malaika turned to face the erstwhile fighters. "Atha, you get fixed up and up front ... *upesi!* Sissiph, you go back to our cabin and stay there." Both nodded soberly and departed in different directions.

"Sociologist, you go and get your friend out of that semi-sleep, or whatever he calls it. I want you at full consciousness in case anything untoward happens. I have a hunch both of you have had at least a modicum of experience with deep-space ship maneuvers?"

Tse-Mallory had started off toward Truzenzuzex's cabin. Now he paused to smile back at the big trader. "Something of the sort," he said quietly.

"Fine. Oh, *kijana?*" Flinx looked up. "You keep a close eye on that pet of yours. Things might get a little bouncy around here. I don't know how excitable that little devil is, but I wouldn't want him underfoot and nervous around busy people."

"Yes sir. Have you any idea what it is?"

"Yes and no. And I'm afraid it's liable to be the former. And that's bad." He paused, thoughtful. "You can come up front, if you like, so long as you watch that snake. Tell our learned passengers they can too, if they so desire. There's enough room. I just don't want Sissiph around. The darling *pakadogo* has a tendency to get hysterical when things aren't where she can put a finger ... and other delightful things ... on them. But I think perhaps the others would like to be around when we find out what is what.

And they might have hunches to contribute. I value hunches highly. By the way, I don't suppose you can answer that question for me?"

Flinx concentrated, hard. It was a long way off, but there was nothing else around for light-years, so it came in strong, strong. "It" was malignant/strange/ picture of dry air, sun, blood/taste of salt/relief/ all wrapped in cold, clear thoughts like snow-melt fitted in only one type. . . .

He looked up, blinked. The merchant was watching him intently, with not a little hint of concern. He became aware then of the beads of sweat on his brow. He said one word, because it was sufficient.

"AAnn."

The merchant nodded thoughfully and turned for the door.

Chapter Eleven

The dot that indicated the presence of an operating posigravity drive field was clear now and far off to their "right"—about ninety degrees or so to the present x-plane. It was moving on a definite convergence course. They still could not be sure what it was, other than that at least one mind occupied a similar area of space.

An ancient aphorism someone had once recited to Flinx came back to him. As he recalled it, there had been two men involved, one old and one young. The younger had said, "No news is good news," and the other, a Terran holy man, had wisely replied, "That's not necessarily true, my young friend. A fisherman doesn't think he's lucky if he doesn't get a bite." He wasn't positive that the story was an appropriate analogy for the moment, because he found himself disagreeing with the holy man.

"Two of them, Captain," said Wolf. "See. . . ."

It was true. Even Flinx could see that as the large dot came closer it was separating into two distinct points. At the same time he sensed a multiplicity of similar minds to the one he'd first noticed although much weaker.

"*Two* ships," said Malaika. "Then my one guess is in error after all. Before shadows. Now, everything in the dark. *Usiku.* Still, it might be. . . ."

"What *was* your guess, Maxim?" asked Truzen-zuzex.

"I thought perhaps a competitor of mine—a certain competitor—had gotten drift of your discovery to a greater extent than I originally thought. Or that certain information had leaked. If the latter case, then I should suspect that someone on this ship is a spy." There were some fast, uneasy glances around the cabin. "That is still a possibility, but I am now less inclined to suspect it. I don't know of any combine in the Arm, neither the one I had in mind nor even General Industries, that could afford or would be inclined to put out two ships on what has a very good chance of being a profitless venture on merely spurious, secondhand information. Not even an AAnn Nest-Corporation."

"In which case," said Tse-Mallory, "who are our two visitors?"

"I don't know, sociologist, *hata kidogo*. Not at all. But we will no doubt find out shortly. They should be in reception distance momentarily, if they aren't already. If there were a relay station in this area we might have found out sooner . . . assuming of course that they wished us to know of their presence, and knew closely enough where we were. I think that I doubt that. . . ."

Atha was efficiently manipulating dials and switches. "I've got everything wide open, sir, and if they're beaming us, we'll pick it up, all right!"

They did.

The face that appeared on the screen was not shocking, thanks to Flinx's advance warning, but the garb it wore was because it was so totally unexpected.

"Good-morning to you, *Gloryhole*," said the sallow-

141

faced AAnn officer-noble who looked out at them. "Or whatever day-period you are experiencing at the moment. The illustrious and renowned Maxim Malaika captaining, I assume?"

"The puzzled and curious Maxim Malaika is here, if that's what you mean." He moved into the center of the transceiver's pickup. "You're one up on me."

"Apologies," said the figure. "I am named Riidi WW, Baron Second of Tyrton Six, Officer in the Emperor Maahn the Fourth's Circumspatial Defense Forces. My ship is named *Arr*, and we are accompanied in travel by her sister-ship, the *Unn*."

Malaika spoke in the direction of the omnipickup mike. "All that. Your mother must have been long-winded. You boys are a bit off your usual tracks, aren't you?"

The Baron's face reflected mild surprise. As Flinx suspected, it was mock. "Why, captain! The Blight is unclaimed space and open to all. There are many fine, colonizable, unclaimed planets here, free to any spacegoing race. While it is true that in the past His Majesty's government has been more involved in outward expansion, an occasional search for planets of exceptional promise does sometimes penetrate this far."

"A very concise and seemingly plausible explanation," whispered Truzenzuzex to Malaika from out of range of the audiovisual pickups.

"Yes," the merchant whispered back. "I don't believe a word of it either. Wolf, change course forty-five degrees x-plus."

"Done, Captain."

"Well, Baron, it's always nice to hear from someone away out in the middle of nowhere, and I am sure that two of his Majesty's destroyers will be more than

a match for any planet of 'exceptional promise' you
may happen to find. I wish you luck in your prospect-
ing."

"Your offers of good fortune are accepted in the
spirit in which they are given, Captain Malaika. In
return I should like to extend the hospitality of my
ship and crew, most especially of our galley. I am
fortunate enough to have on board a chef who works
wonders with the cuisine of thirty-two different systems. The fellow is a wizard, and would be proud to
have the opportunity to display his talents before
such discerning gourmets as yourselves."

Wolf's low whisper cut across the cabin. "They've
changed course to match our new one, sir. And accel-
erated, too."

"Keep on course. And pick it up enough to match
their increase. But do it subtly, *mwanamume*, subtly!"
He turned back to the screen.

"Truly a gracious offer, Baron, and ordinarily I
would consider it an honor and a delight to accept.
However, I am afraid that circumstances warrant we
decline this particular invitation. You see, we had fish
for supper last evening, and I am certain it was not
prepared half so well as your chef could manage,
because we have all been suffering from severe pains
of the lower intestinal tract today. If we may, I'll put
off your kind offer till a later date."

Away from the mike he whispered, "The rest of
you get back to your cabins and strap down. I'll try to
keep you up on what happens through your intership
viewers. But if we have to bump around a bit, I don't
want you all bouncing off the woodwork and messing
up my carpets!"

Flinx, Tse-Mallory, and Truzenzuzex made a
scramble for the exitway, being careful to stay out of

range of the tri-dee video pickup. But apparently Truzenzuzex couldn't resist a dig at a persistent and long-time enemy. The thranx had had dealings with the AAnn long before mankind.

He stuck his head into range of the pickups and yelled, "Know, O sand-eater, that I have sampled AAnn cuisine before, and that my gizzard has found it to be gritty to the palate. Those who dine upon rocks rapidly assume the disposition and mental capacity of the same!"

The AAnn bristled, the scales along its neck-ridge rising. "Listen, dirt-dweller, I'll inform you that . . . !" He caught it in mid-curse and recomposed himself with an effort. Feigning a sigh where he no doubt would have preferred a threat, he said, "I retain the courtesies while it is evident they have departed your ship, Captain. Have it your way. You cannot outrun us, you know. Now that we are within easy range, my detector operators will be most careful not to lose you. It will be only a matter of time before we come within filial distance of you. At that moment I would hope that you would have reconsidered my really exceptionally polite and generous invitation, and will lower your field. Otherwise," he said grimly, "I am very much afraid we shall be forced to open you up like a can of *zith*-paste."

The screen abruptly went blank.

In his cabin, Flinx lay down on his bed and began to strap into the emergency harness that was affixed permanently to its sides. He had Pip next to his left hand, curled around a bar on that side of the bed. He admonished it to be quiet. The snake, sensing that important things were happening, did as it was told with a minimum of fuss and bother.

When he had finished and settled himself into the

closest thing to a comfortable position he could manage in the awkward harness, he turned on the little screen which hung suspended from the roof of the cabin. It cleared instantly to reveal Malaika, Atha, and Wolf busy in Control. Unwillingly, he began to recall more familiar sights and smells. It embarrassed him, but at that moment he wished fervently he were back home in Drallar, juggling before an appreciative crowd and making small boys laugh by telling them the names of their secret loves. What he could interpret of the mind/thoughts of the AAnn commander was not pleasant. The feeling passed abruptly as though a cool rag had been drawn across his mind, and he settled himself grimly to wait.

In the huge, exotically furnished cabin which formed her quarters, Sissiph lay alone on the big bed, curled in her harness. Her knees nearly touched her chest. She felt very alone. The order to don harness had been delivered in a tough, no-nonsense tone that Maxy had never used with her before, and she was frightened. The luxurious accoutrements, the intricately carved furniture and sensuous cantilevered lighting, the king's ransom in clothing scattered about the room, all suddenly seemed as frivolous and flighty as the toys of a child. She had known, she had simply *known*, when she had chosen to try to replace that other little witch—what had been her name?—as Malaika's steady Lynx, that something terrible like this was going to happen. She had *known* it!

Merchants were so *damned* unpredictable!

She did not throw the switch which would lower the screen and put her in communication with Control and the rest of the ship. Let him survive without her for a while! Instead she buried herself as deeply as she could in the purrsilk pillows and promised

145

herself that if she survived this awful, horrible journey into no place, she was going to find some nice hundred-and-fifty-year-old man . . . on the verge of death. A senile, wealthy one, with whom she could look forward to a nice, quiet, comfortable, short, married life . . . and a long, wealthy widowhood.

Bran Tse-Mallory was lying in his bed quietly reviewing the hundred and five maxims of the state of Indifferent Contentment. It was originally invented by a brilliant graduate student to help nervous students relax for examinations. It would do duty in other situations. The current one, for example. But no matter how hard he tried, he couldn't get past twentyone. It kept repeating itself over and over in his mind every time he tried to concentrate on twenty-two.

"Mankind must without a doubt be the most conceited race in the universe, for who else believes that God has nothing better to do than sit around all day and help him out of tight spots?"

It was an unworthy thought for one who supposedly had mellowed so over the years, but how, oh, how he wished for the comforting grip of a gun—*any* kind of gun—under his fingers. They tightened and relaxed reflexively, making deep furrows in the softness of the blankets.

The Eint Truzenzuzex was lying quietly on his modified lounge, legs fully extended, foothands and truehands crossed on his chest in the proper *Oo* position. He tried to keep one half of his mind focused on the ship viewer, while the other half droned through the ritual.

"I, Tru, of the family Zen, clan zu, the Hive Zex, do hereforth pray that I shall not bring disgrace on my-our ancestors. I, Tru, of the family Zen, clan zu, the Hive Zex, do hereforth pray that in the coming Time

146

of Trouble I may reflect credit on my first-mother, clan mother, and Hive mother. I, Tru, of the family Zen, clan. . . ."

Atha Moon and the man called Wolf thought otherwise. They were much too busy for anything else. And Maxim Malaika, the man who was responsible for them all, did likewise. Also, he was too scared to have time for trivialities like worry. Wolf broke into his nonthoughts.

"They've closed to within five mils, sir. At this rate they'll be within particle-beam range in five, ten minutes."

"*Choovy*! And other unmentionables! Damn!"

Atha looked back at him worriedly. "Couldn't we try to dodge them, Maxim? I mean, captain?"

"*La, hasha*, Atha. No way. Those are AAnn destroyers out there. They're built to chase down and slice up ships much faster than we are. The *Gloryhole* is a rich man's whim, not a navy ship. But it *is* something of a speedster, *sharti*. Of necessity. With any kind of distance between us at initial contact we might have slipped out of detector range and lost them, but they were on top of us before we even knew who they were. Anyway, there are two of them. One, *labda*, we might still slip, but never two. Not at this range."

Atha thought. "Couldn't we just, well, surrender and take our chances? I mean, everything considered, that Baron didn't seem all that awful. Just impatient. And we aren't at war or anything with his people."

"*Ndoto*. A dream. The AAnn don't operate that way, Atha." His lips were firmed, tight. "At best they are . . . intolerant . . . with folk who cooperate with them. With those who don't. . . . If you're curious about details, ask Wolf. He was in an AAnn prison camp for five years, during the last real humanx-

AAnn conflict. There may be others who survived that long in one of those hell-pits and lived to tell of it. If so, I haven't met him."

"The captain is right, Miss Moon. I would much rather throw myself into space to blow up like a deep-sea fish than be captured by those again." He nodded at the screen, where the white dots continued their inexorable approach. "Among their other affectations, they are very adept at the more refined forms of torture. Very. It is something of an art form with them, you see. Most of my scars don't show. They're up here, you see." He tapped the side of his head. "If you wish some detailed descriptions. . . ."

Atha shuddered. "Never mind."

"This Riidi fellow seems fairly decent . . . for an AAnn, but to take the chance. . . . If I could spare Wolf from plotting, or myself from the computer . . . *tandunono*! No, wait!" He leaned over the mike pickup. "*Ninyi nyote*! Tse-Mallory, sociologist. And you, bug! Have either of you ever handled a spatial weapon before? Even in simulation?"

In his cabin Tse-Mallory nearly broke a finger struggling with his harness. And Truzenzuzex broke off his ritual in a place and manner that would have earned him the condemnation of every member of his clan, had they known of it.

"You mean you've got a *gun* on this tub?" shouted Tse-Mallory. "What kind? Where? Speak up, mercantilist! Implosion weapons, particle guns, missile tubes, explosive projectiles, rocks . . . Tru and I will handle it!"

"*Je*? I hope so. Listen to me. Behind your cabins, *naam*, storage compartment. There's a walkway, it opens into the cargo balloon. Then a pullway. Go to the end of the main pullway, you can't get lost. You'll find branches there. Be careful, there's no gravity in that part of the ship. Take the one that goes ninety degrees north of your horizontal. At the top you'll find a medium charge interstice laser, mounted on a universal belt encircling the ship. I'm powering it now." He paused momentarily while his hands did things below the range of the camera's pickup.

"It is a single-person mounting. Sorry, philosoph. But you could help him with the computer. If he doesn't have to watch the imageouts and battlescreen at the same time. . . ."

The two men of peace were already on their way.

Malaika uttered a silent prayer in the hopes that the two scientists wouldn't cut up the ship and turned back to his tables.

"How are we doing, Wolf?"

"They're still closing, sir. Not as rapidly now that we've picked up our own speed, but still closing. You want to go on maximum?"

"No. No, not yet. That's strictly our last gasp, if we need it. Let them continue to think the *Glory*'s just another freighter for awhile. First I want to see what our braincases can do with the popgun."

The braincases in question were making their way along the pullway at breakneck speed. Fortunately, there was no drifting cargo to impede their progress. The great metal-fabric enclosure was almost completely empty. A few cases drifted lazily in their spiderweb enclosures, giving the pale green cavern and its ghostly atmosphere a tinge of perspective. The feeling was enhanced by the lighting, or lack of it. Since this area of the ship, although by far the largest, was rarely visited except upon arriving or departing a cargo stop, the lighting was kept to a minimum. Even so it would have been lost in the cargo compartment of one of the great "Soaring Sun" class freighters.

They had no trouble locating the correct branch-way at the end nexus of the main one. It was the only strand headed remotely in the required direction. Tse-Mallory launched himself upward and began to float up to the rope. He reached out and began to pull himself rapidly upward, hand over hand. Truzenzuzex, he knew, would be right behind him. With its four hands the insect could go faster than he, but there was no reason for him to pass Bran since he couldn't operate the human-contoured gun nearly as well.

They reached the gun housing, a sphere of thick metal like a blister in the skin of the ship. It had its own emergency power and air supply. Far off to both sides he could see where the mounting's powered belt encircled the skin of the vessel. Moving along that belt the gun could cover an approaching threat from any angle. He had only a second to wonder what it was doing on a private yacht before he was inside the shell and buckling himself into the gunseat. Truzenzuzex secured the hatch behind them, moving to the computer imageouts to Bran's left. A more modern weapon would have had both combined in a single helmet-set that would fit down over the gun-ner's head. The insect began to cannibalize braces, locks, and belts from the emergency compartments, until he had built himself a reasonably solid harness opposite the 'puter.

Bran wrapped his right hand around the pressure trigger with all the fondness of a proud father caress-ing his newborn. His left went into the battlescreen sensory pickup. He let go of the trigger for a moment, reluctantly, to tighten the nerve sensors around his spread left hand. He flexed it once to make sure the pickups didn't pinch and then returned the right to the trigger grip. Next began a careful examination of the screen and dial scopes. It was definitely an early model, but then laser weapons hadn't changed much in their basic design for several centuries, and probably wouldn't in several more. The base design was too cheap and efficient. He had no doubt that he could operate this one effectively on the first try. Come to that, he'd damn well have to! Their pursuers weren't likely to give them a practice shot.

Under impulses from his left hand the battlescreen lit. He was gratified to see that his combat reflexes, at least, were still operative. On the screens were two dots the size of his thumbnail. For a moment he almost panicked, thinking he was back on the old Twenty-Five. If an opposing ship had managed to approach this close in a war situation they'd have been vaporized by now. But then, this wasn't a war situation. At least not yet. He put that unpleasant line of thought out of his mind. Something for the diplomats to sharpen their tongues on. Obviously neither of the approaching ships had expectations of meeting even token resistance. It was simply a game of catch-up. They came on openly and without caution. Possibly, hopefully, they also had their screens down or at least underpowered.

From his left Truzenzuzex began rattling off a stream of figures and coordinates. One of the destroyers was slightly nearer than the other. The sloppy formation was the inevitable result of overconfidence on the enemy's part. Bran began lining up a center shot. His finger hesitated over the trigger, and he spoke into the intership mike.

"Look, Malaika. These people are here after something, and since we've only got one something worth risking an interstellar incident over, they're going to want us in one piece. I don't expect them to start any reckless shooting. They're coming in as if all they expect to have to do is net us like a clipped *Geech* bird. I've played with the AAnn before. They're not overimaginative, but they think damn fast. That means one good shot and one only, and then we'd better run like hell. How close can you let them get while still giving us an outside chance to break their detection? Assuming they'll be sufficiently confused to let us."

Malaika calculated rapidly in his head. "Um . . . um . . . *mara kwa mara* . . . that Riidi fellow will have to decide whether to blow us to atoms or make another try . . . the latter, I don't doubt . . . *has* to take us alive, or not at all . . . I can give you another two mils distance. La, one and a half, now."

"Good enough," said Tse-Mallory, concentrating on the screen. It would have to be, he thought. "We'll know it back here when the 'puter hits it." Malaika didn't reply.

"That will bring us down almost to . . . to three," said Truzenzuzex.

"I supposed. Let me know when we reach three point one."

"Time enough?"

Tse-Mallory grinned. "Ole bug-wug, me friend, my reflexes have slowed down through the years, but dead yet they ain't! It'll be enough. Up the universe!"

"Up the universe!" came the even reply.

In Control, Malaika turned to Wolf, his face thoughtful.

"You heard?"

The shadow-man nodded.

152

"All right then. Start slowing down. Yes, slowing down! If he says he's going to get only one shot, he's probably going to get only one shot, and I want him to have as good a line as possible. So let's make it look nearly as we can as though we're giving up the chase."

Obediently, Wolf began cutting their speed. Slowly, but the AAnn computers would notice it.

"Three point seven . . . three point six . . ." Truzenzuzex's voice recited the figures with machine-like precision and clarity.

Bran's body was steady, but he was trembling ever so slightly inside. He *was* older.

"Tru, uh, did you spot any HIP drugs in that emergency locker?"

"Heightened IP? Three point five . . . you know that stuff's almost as carefully watched as the SCCAM circuitry. Oh, there's some of the bastard stuff back there, the kind that's available on any black market. All that will do, my friend, to borrow a saying, is 'screw up your bod' . . . three point four . . . not to mention your reflexes . . . screw it down, more likely. Relax."

"I know, I know!" His eyes never left the screen. "But, vertebrae, I wish I had some now!"

"Obscenity is better . . . three point three . . . pretend you're back at the University working over old man Novy's thesis. That ought to generate enough anger for you to take those ships apart with your bare hands. . . ."

Bran smiled, and the tenseness left him. Back at the University old professor Novy had been one of their pet animosities.

". . . three point two. . . ."

He could see the bastard's ugly face now. He won-

dered what had finally happened to the old boy after.
... His finger tightened on the trigger.

"... three poi. ..."

Already the pressure-stud was being depressed.

In the nothingness of nowhere a lancet of emerald
green brighter than a sun leaped from the *Gloryhole*
across a second of infinity. A milli-instant later it
impinged on the drive fan of the nearest AAnn warship, which happened to be the *Unn*. There was a
soundless flash of impossible scintillating gold flame,
like the waves of tortured hydrogen that march across
the skin of stars. It was followed by an explosion of
vaporized solids and an expanding, rapidly diffusing
cloud of ionized gas.

The battlescreen showed one white dot and one
tiny nebula.

In the gun housing, Bran was frantically trying to
reline the laser for a shot at the second ship, but he
never got a real chance.

At the instant of silent destruction, Malaika had
permitted himself one violent cry of *"Oseee-yeee!"*

Then, "Wolf, Atha, get us *moving, watu!*" Atha
slammed over a connection and the *Gloryhole* leaped
forward at her maximum acceleration.

On the still existing AAnn ship, the *Arr*, panic
reigned only in those areas of the vessel where Baron
Riidi WW's control was peripheral. Around him the
crew only reflected fatal resignation. The one pleasant thought in all their minds was what they would
do to the people on their quarry once the commander
and the techs had extracted whatever it was they
wanted from them. None glanced at the Baron's face
for fear of meeting his eyes.

The Baron's polished claws scraped idly at the

scales on his left arm. There was a voipickup set by
the right one.

"Enginemaster," he said calmly into the grid, "full
power, please. Everything you can spare from the
screens." He did not bother to inquire if they were
now up.

He turned back to the huge battlescreen which
dominated the bridge. On it a white dot had shrunk
rapidly but had not succeeded in disappearing completely. Now, it could not. Without taking his eyes
from the screen he addressed the crew over the
comm-system.

"No one is to blame for the loss of the *Unn*. Not
expecting interspace weaponry on a private craft of
that type, only debris screens were up. That error has
since been rectified. The enemy is faster than originally estimated. It apparently hoped to pass out of
detector range in the confusion engendered by the loss
of our sister-ship. This has not occured. It *will* not
occur. We are through playing polite. Bend your tails
to it, gentlemen, we have a ship to catch! And when
we have done I can promise you at least some interesting entertainment!"

Inspired, the crew of the *Arr* dipped to their tasks
with a will.

Bran cursed once, briefly, as the surviving AAnn
ship shrank out of range.

Truzenzuzex was busily disengaging himself from
his makeshift harness. "Relax, brother. You did as
well as we'd hoped. Better. They had their screens
down, all right, or they wouldn't have gone up like
that. We must have hit their generator dead on.
Metamorphosis, what a show!"

Tse-Mallory took the advice and relaxed as well as
he could. "Yes. Yes, you're perfectly correct, Tru. A

second time we wouldn't have been so lucky. If we'd had a second time."

"Quite so. I suggest now a return to our cabins. This toy will be of no further use. If we had a *real* gun, now . . . oh, well. After you, Bran."

Truzenzuzex had reopened the hatch and they dived down the pullway. Heading back through the murky green hollows they missed Malaika's congratulations as they poured over the now untended mike in the gunshell.

"Ships and novas, ships and novas! By the tail of the Black Horse nebula! They *did* it! Those effete, simple, peace-loving *nduguzuri did* it! Taking out a warship with one shot from that antique!" He shook his head. "We may not get out of this but, by *mitume*, the prophets, those lizards'll know they've been in a fight!"

Wolf brought the merchant back to reality. Not that his mind had ever really left it, but his spirit had—momentarily. It had been refreshing, anyway.

"They're beginning to pick up on us again, sir. Slower than before. Much slower. But we're running on everything we have and they're still making up distance on us."

Atha nodded concurrence. "The screen may not show it yet, but it's here in the readouts. At this rate we've got maybe three—no, four hours before they're within paralysisbeam range."

"*Je!* That's it, then. *Pepongapi?* How many evil spirits?"

He sat down in his seat. Once they got that close they'd make mummies out of everyone on board and then unwrap their minds at their leisure. The methods might vary, but they would undoubtedly be unique in their unpleasantness. That could not be permitted to happen. As soon as the AAnn got that close he'd see to it that everyone had a sufficiently lethal dose of something from med supply to insure that questioning would remain an impossibility. Or possibly a laser would be better. Burned down to ashes, the AAnn technicians, good as they might be, couldn't reconstruct. Yes, that was a better choice. After he finished with everyone else he'd have to make certain not to miss the brain. He'd have only the one shot. Better start looking for a mirror, Maxim!

If there were only some way they could pick up enough speed to swing out of detector range! Even if only for a few microseconds, it might be enough. Space was vast. Given that one precious interval the *Gloryhole* should easily shake her pursuers. Unconsciously, he put his hand over Atha's.

"There's *got* to be a way to pick up another half multiple!"

He didn't notice the way her hand trembled when his covered it, nor the way she looked down at it. He removed it abruptly without being aware of the effect he'd had on his copilot. It joined the other in digging at their owner's hair.

Flinx was also considering the problem, in his own way. He knew little about stellar navigation, and less about doublekay units . . . but Malaika had forgotten more than he might ever know. He couldn't match the merchant's knowledge, but he could remember for him. The links in the trader's mind branched a million ways. Patiently, he tracked down now this, now that one, bringing long-forgotten studies and applications to the surface where Malaika's own system would pick them up, look them over, and discard them. In a way it was like using the retrieval system at the

Royal Library. He kept at it with a steadiness he
hadn't known he possessed, until. . . .

"But *akili*! Commonsense . . . !" He paused, and his
eyes opened so wide that for a moment Atha was
actually alarmed. "*Atha*!" She couldn't prevent herself
from jumping a little at the shout.

He had it. Somehow the idea had risen from its
hiding place deep in his mind, where it had lain
untouched for years.

"Look, when the Blight was first reached, survey
ships went through it—some of it—with an eye
toward mapping the place, right? The idea was eventually dropped as impractical—meaning expensive—
but all the information that had originally been col-
lected was retained. That'd be only proper. Check
with memory and find out if there are any neutron
stars in our vicinity."

"What?"

"An excellent idea, captain," said Wolf. "I think . . .
yes, there is a possibility—outside and difficult, mind—
that we may be able to draw them in after us. Far
more enjoyable than a simple suicide."

"It would be that, Wolf, except for one thing. I
am not thinking of even a complicated suicide. *Mwal-
izuri*, talk to that machine of yours and find out what
it says!"

She punched the required information uncertainly
but competently. It took the all-inclusive machine
only a moment to image-out a long list of answers.

"Why yes, there is one, Captain. At our present rate
of travel, some seventy-two ship-minutes from our
current attitude. Coordinates are listed, and in this
case are recorded as accurate, nine point . . . nine
point seven places."

"Start punching them in." He swiveled and bent to

158

the audio mike. "Attention, everybody. Now that you two minions of peace and tranquility have effectively pacified half our pursuit, I've been stimulated enough to come up with an equally insane idea. What I'm . . . what *we're* going to try is theoretically possible. I don't know if it's been done before or not. There wouldn't be any records of an *un*successful attempt. I feel we must take the risk. Any alternative to certain death is a preferable one. Capture is otherwise a certainty."

Truzenzuzex leaned over in harness and spoke into his mike. "May I inquire into what you . . . *we* will attempt to do?"

"Yes," said Wolf. "I admit to curiosity myself, captain."

"*Je!* We are heading for a neutron star in this sector for which we have definite coordinates. At our present rate of speed we should be impinging on its gravity well at the necessary tangent some seventy . . . sixty-nine minutes from now. Atha, Wolf, the computer, and myself are going to work like hell the next few minutes to line up that course. If we can hit that field at a certain point at our speed . . . I am hoping the tremendous pull of the star will throw us out at a speed sufficient to escape the range of the AAnn detector fields. They can hardly be expecting it, and even if they do figure it out, I don't think our friend the Baron would consider doing likewise a worthwhile effort. I almost hope he does. He'd have everything to lose. At the moment, we have very little. Only we humans are crazy enough to try such a stunt anyway, *kweli?*"

"Yes. Second the motion. Agreed," said Truzenzuzex. "If I were in a position to veto this idiotic—which I assure you I would do. However, as I am not . . . let's get on with it, captain."

"Damned with faint praise, eh, philosoph? There are other possibilities, *watu*. Either we shall miss our impact point and go wide, in which case the entire attempt might as well not have been made and we will be captured and poked into, or we will dive too deeply and be trapped by the star's well, pulled in, and broken up into very small pieces. As Captain I am empowered to make this decision by right . . . but this is not quite a normal cruise, so I put it to a vote. Objections?"

The only thing that came over the comm was a slight sniffle, undoubtedly attributable to Sissiph (she had given in to curiosity and flipped on her unit). It could not be construed as an objection.

"*Je*! We will try it, then. I suggest strongly you spend some time checking out your harnesses and spreading yourselves as comfortably as possible. Provided that we strike the star's field at the precise tangent I am almost positive that the *Gloryhole* can stand the forces involved. If it cannot it will not matter, because our bodies will go long before the ship does. *Haidhuru*. It doesn't matter. Physiologically I have no idea what to expect. So prepare your bodies and your spirits as well as possible, because in sixty . . ." he paused to glance at the chronometer, "six minutes, it will be all one way or all the other."

He cut the mike and began furiously feeding instructions and requests into a computer auxiliary.

If they had one consolation, thought Flinx, it was that there would be no horrifyingly slow buildup of gravity within the ship. They would either fail or succeed at such a supremely high speed that it would be over in an instant . . . as Malaika had said, all one way or all the other. He did not care to imagine what would happen if they missed their contact point and dived too close to the star. Dwell in the well. Not funny. He saw himself and Pip mashed flat, like paper, and that proved unamusing also.

The chronometer, oblivious of mere human concerns, continued to wind down. Sixty minutes left . . . forty . . . twenty to . . . ten tofivetothreetotwo. . . .

And then, unbelievably, there were only sixty seconds left till judgment. Before he had time to muse on this amazing fact, there was a slight jar. A silent screaming from the farthest abyss of time flowed like jelly over the ship. He hung on the lip of a canyon of nothingness, while it tried desperately to ingest him. He refused to be ingested. REFUSED! A pin among other pins in a bowl of milk, while somewhere a million fingernails dug exquisitely scratching on a thousand hysterically howling blackboardsssscRRRR-EEEEEEEE. . . .

Chapter Twelve

On board the destroyer *Arr* the chief navigational officer blinked at his detector screen, then turned to stare up at where the Baron sat in his command chair.

"Sir, the humanx vessel has disappeared from my screens. Also, we are rapidly approaching a neutron star of considerable gravitonic potential. Orders?"

Baron Rüdi WW was noted for his persistence. The idea of a trapped quarry escaping him was most unappealing. Neither, however, was he a fool. His eyes closed tiredly.

"Change course thirty degrees, right to our present plane. Cut to cruising speed, normal." He looked up then, eyes open, at the battlescreen. Somewhere out there was a white dot. Out there also, an invisible bottomless pit of unimaginable energy masked an impossible retreat. Or a quick suicide. An inkling of the human's intentions percolated through his cells. He did not feel the least inclined to try to duplicate the event. Whether the idiot was alive or dead, he would not know for many months . . . and that was the most infuriating thing of all.

He flexed his long fingers, staring at the brightly polished claws whose length was suitably trimmed to that for a high member of the aristocracy. Colloid-gems shone lavalike on two of them. He locked them over his chest and pushed outward. Those among the crew who were more familiar with the actions of the nobility recognized the gesture. It indicated Conception of Impractical Power. Under the circumstances it constituted a salute to their departed foe.

"Set a return course for Pregglin Base and signal our industrialist friend the following missive. No, I don't wish an interstar hookup. Just send it. 'Intercepted anticipated vessel and made positive audiovisual identification. Repeat, *positive*. Chased to points . . . give our current coordinates, shipmaster . . . 'where contact with same was irretrievably lost due to,' " he smiled slightly, " 'an unexpected turn of speed on the part of the pursued vessel. In hostile action with same, the destroyer *Unn* was lost with all hands.' Add this note, communicator, and scramble it to my personal code. 'Sir. Your request has proven expensive in the extreme. Contrary to your indications we did not encounter, as you led me to believe, a terrified shipload of frightened moneylenders. As a result of your bungling, I now find myself in the uncomfortable position of having to account for my off-base time to my good friend Lord Kaath, C. How good a friend he is will now be put to a considerable test. As will your ability to place judicious bribes. I hope, for both our sakes, that the latter will be sufficient. Explaining the loss of the *Unn* will be rather more difficult. Should the true circumstances surrounding this idiocy leak out it would be more than enough to condemn us both to death by nth degree torture at the hands of the Masters. Kindly do keep this in mind.'

"Sign it, 'yours affectionately, Riidi WW, Baron, etc., etc.' And get me a drink."

Chapter Thirteen

It was autumn. Mother Mastiff had closed up the shop, packed a lunch, and taken them both off to the Royal Parks. It was a cloudless day, which was why. Literally cloudless. On Moth this wasn't merely a pleasant exception, it was an event. He could remember staring endlessly at the funny-colored sky. It was blue, so different from the normal light gray. It hurt his eyes. The thoughts of the animals, the birds, were odd and confused. And the hawkers sat listlessly in their respective booths, cursing softly at the sun. It had stolen all their customers. It was a softer sky, and softness of any kind was rare in Drallar. So everyone had taken the day off, including the king.

The Royal Parks were a great, sprawling place. They had originally been created by the builders of the first botanical gardens to use up the space left over from those great constructs. By some monstrous bureaucratic error it had been opened to the general public and had remained so ever since. The great flashing boles of the famous ironwood trees shot straight and proud to impossible heights over his boyish head. They seemed much more permanent than the city itself.

The ironwoods were molting. Every other week the royal gardeners would come and gather up all the fallen leaves and branches. Ironwood was rare, even

164

on Moth, and the scraps where far too valuable to be swept away. The guards in their lemon-green uniforms sauntered easily about the park grounds, there more to protect the trees than the people.

Children were playing on the marvelous gyms and tangles that an earlier king had set up. As long as the people had abrogated the park, he felt that they might as well enjoy it to the fullest. The kings of Drallar had been greedy, yes, but not exceptionally so.

He had been too shy to join the giggling, darting shapes on the funchines. And they had all been frightened of Pip, silly things! There had been one little girl though . . . all curls and blue eyes and flushes. She had shuffled over hesitantly, trying hard to appear disinterested but not succeeding. Her thoughts were nice. For a change, she was fascinated by the minidrag rather than repelled by it.

They had been on the verge of making introductions in the simple but very correct manner that adults lose so quickly, when a great leaf had drifted down unseen and struck him fair between the eyes. Ironwood leaves are heavy, but not enough to produce injury, even to a small boy. Only embarrassment. She had started giggling uncontrolably. Furious, he had stalked off, ears burning with the heat of her laughter, his mind frozen with her picture of him. He had thought momentarily of siccing Pip on her. That was one of the impulses he had learned to control very early, when the snake's abilities had been glass-gruesomely demonstrated on a persistent tormentor, a stray mongrel dog.

Even as he strode farther and farther away, the sounds of her laughter followed, ghostlike. As he walked he took vicious and ineffectual swings at the rust-colored leaves floating down uncaringly about him. And sometimes he didn't even touch them when they dropped brokenly to the ground.

Chapter Fourteen

Then the sky wasn't blue anymore. Nor light gray. It was pastel green.

He stopped flailing his arms and looked around, moving only his eyes. Pip stopped beating his pleated wings against his master's face and flew off to curl comfortably against the nearest bed-bar, satisfied with the reaction it had produced. The minidrag's tough constitution had apparently suffered few ill effects. Flinx didn't know yet whether to curse it or kiss it.

He tried to sit up but fell back, exhausted by the brief effort. Oddly enough, his bones didn't bother him at all. But his muscles! The tendons and ligaments too, all of the connective web that held the framework together. Felt like they'd been tied end to end, stretched out, rolled together into a ball, and pounded into one of Mother Mastiff's less palatable meatloafs.

It was a trial, but he finally managed to sit up. The events of . . . how long had he been out? . . . came back to him as he rubbed circulation back into benumbed legs. As soon as he felt reasonably humanoid again, he leaned over and spoke into his shipmike. In case the others were in less positive shape than he, he enunciated slowly and clearly so as to be sure to be understood.

"Captain? Captain? Control? Is anyone up there?"

167

He could sense all the other minds but not their condition, as his own was too addled to focus yet.

"*Rahisi, kijana!* Take it easy. Glad to hear you're back too." The trader's voice was a familiar healthy boom but Flinx could read the strain on his mind. In another minute his picture flashed onto the small viewscreen. The blocky face had added another line or two, the beard a few white hairs, but otherwise the craggy visage was unchanged. And although his body and mind looked wearied by the stresses they had undergone, the face reflected old enthusiasms.

"Wolf and I have been up, although not about, by *moyo. Uzito,* what an experience! It seems that our friend the hard-headed philosoph, who wears his bones inside out, stood it better than the rest of us. He's been up here rubbing us poor softies back into consciousness."

The voice of the insect came over the speaker from somewhere off-camera, but Flinx could place the thranx from the strength of its thoughts, which were indeed better organized than those of its companions.

"If the rest of your body was as hard as your head, captain, you, at least, would not need my aid."

"*Je!* Well, *kijana,* Tse-Mallory's been up the longest of us poor humans, and I believe Der Bugg is just now bringing Atha 'round ... yes, bless her flinty *moyo.* We were going to send him in to see you next, Flinx, but I see that's not necessary."

"Did we ... ?" but Malaika seemed not to hear and Flinx was too tired to probe.

"*Mwanamume* and *mtoto,* what a buggy ride! Sorry, bwana Truzenzuzex. No offense intended. It's an old Terran saying, meaning 'to go like blazes,' roughly. I know only that it's appropriate to our present situation. Perhaps it's designed to invoke a friendly

Mungu, *je?* Metamorphosis! Flinx me lad, me *kijana*, me *mtoto*, we went past that star so fast after hitting that field that our transversion 'puter couldn't handle it! The mechanism wasn't built to program that kind of speed, and I'd hate to tell you where the cut-off max is! If there were only some way this sort of thing could be done on a commercial basis . . . owk!"

He winced and gingerly touched a hand to the back of his neck.

"However, I must admit that at the present time there appear to be certain drawbacks to the system. *Uchawi!* I would have given much to have seen the face of our friend the Baron when we shot off his screens, *je!* Unannounced, as it were. I wonder if he . . . but unwrap yourself from that webbing, *kijana,* and get thee forward. I've a bit of a surprise for you, and it looks even better from up front."

Flinx could feel the tone beginning to return to his muscles. He undid the rest of the harness and slid slowly off the bed. There was an awkward moment as he had to grab the wall for support, balancing himself on shaky legs. But things began to normalize themselves quickly now. He walked around the room a few times, experimentally, and then turned and headed for Control, Pip curled comfortably about his left shoulder.

Malaika swiveled slightly in his seat as Flinx appeared on the bridge.

"Well? What's the surprise?" He noted that Truzenzuzex had disappeared, but could feel the insect's presence in another part of the ship.

Apparently Malaika noted his searching gaze. Or possibly he was becoming sensitive. He'd have to be careful around the big trader.

"He's gone to try to help Sissiph. She figured to be the last to return, *rudisha*."

That was undoubtedly true. Atha and Wolf he could clearly see busy at their instruments.

"*Kijana*, that big kick in the . . . boost we got shoved us far ahead of my anticipated schedule . . . on our prearranged path! I planned it that way when we were setting up the interception coordinates. No use wasting a brush with death if it can be utilized to profit also . . . but I honestly didn't think the *Glory's* field could hold us that steady. However, it did, and here we are."

"Which is where?" asked Flinx.

Malaika was smug. "Not more than ninety minutes ship-*nafasi* from our intended destination!" He turned back to his desk, muttering. "Now if there's only some way to make it commercially feas. . . ."

Flinx put together what he knew of how far they'd come when they were intercepted by the AAnn warship and how far they'd still had to go at that time. The result he came up with was an acceleration he had no wish to dwell on.

"That's great, of course, sir. Still, it would also be nice if. . . ."

"Um? If what?"

"If when we get where we're going we find something worth getting there for."

"Your semantics are scrambled, *kijana*, but I approve the sentiment. *Mbali kodogo*, a little way off, perhaps, but I do indeed approve."

Chapter Fifteen

The planet itself was a beauty. It would have been ideal for colonization if it hadn't been for the unfortunate dearth of land area. But even the fact that ninety percent of the land was concentrated in one large continent might not make such exploitations prohibitive. Oceans could be farmed and mined, too, as on colony worlds like Dis and Repler. And those of Booster, as they had named it, were green enough to suggest that they fairly seethed with the necessary base-matrix to support humanx-style sea-culture. Fortunately the chlorophyll reaction had proved the norm on most humanx-type planets found to date.

By contrast the single continent appeared to be oddly dry. Especially discouraging to Truzenzuzex, as the thranx would have preferred a wet, tropical climate. He confirmed this opinion by voicing it every chance he got.

As far as they were able to determine from orbit, everything was exactly as it had been described on the star-map. Atmospheric composition, with its unusual proportion of free helium and other rare gases, UV radicount (est. surf./sq.mi./ki.), mean and extreme temperatures, and so forth. There was only one fact their observer had failed to note.

As near as their probes could estimate, at no place on the surface of Booster did the wind ever blow less than 70 kilometers an hour. At certain points over the oceans, especially near the equator, it was remarkably consistent. But it did not appear to drop below that approximated minimum. There was currently one gigantic storm system visible in the southeastern portion of the planet. The meteorology 'puter guessed the winds near its center to be moving in excess of 780 kilometers per hour.

"Impossible!" said Malaika, when he saw the initial imageout. *"Mchawi mchanganyiko!"*

"Quite," said Truzenzuzex. "Definitely. Go fly a kite." The scientist indulged in the whistling laughter of the thranx.

Malaika was confused, by the laughter as well as the referent. "Translation, please?"

"It means," put in Tse-Mallory over the insect's laughter, "that it is more than possible." He was gazing in complete absorption at the sphere turning below. The unusual silver-gold tinge to the atmosphere had aroused interest in his mind. "And there might be places, on the single continent, for example, where canyons and such would channel even higher velocities."

The merchant took a deep breath, whooshed it out, and fingered the small wooden image that hung omnipresent about his neck. *"Namna gani mahaili?"* What kind of place? No wonder there's nothing more than one little continent and a few *visiwabovu.* Such winds would cut down high places like chaff!" He shook his head. "Why the Tar-Aiym would pick a place like this to develop their whatever-it-is I'll not guess."

"There is much we don't know of the Tar-Aiym and their motives," said Tse-Mallory. "Far more than we do know. From their point of view it might have been perfect. Maybe they felt that its very unattractiveness would discourage inspection by their enemies. And we have no final evidence as to what they considered a hospitable climate. We don't even know for certain what they looked like, remember. Oh, we've got a vague idea of the basics. The head goes here, the major manipulative limbs there, and so on. But for all we really know they might even have been semi-porous. A nice three-hundred-kilo-an-hour hurricane might have been as a refreshing bath to them. In which case I'd expect the Krang to be some sort of resort facility."

"Please!" said Malaika. "No obscenities. If that were true, why haven't we found such winds on any of the other planets we know the Tar-Aiym inhabited?"

Tse-Mallory shrugged, bored with the turn of the conversation. "Perhaps the weather has changed since then. Perhaps they changed it. Perhaps I am wrong. Perhaps I am crazy. In fact, there are times when my suspicions of the latter approach certitude."

"I've noticed," said Truzenzuzex, unable to resist.

"Agh! If I knew all the answers," said the sociologist, "I'd be God. In which circumstance I'd most certainly be outside this ship right now and not cooped up with the rest of you mental cases!" He returned his gaze to the screen, but Flinx could taste the humor in his mind.

"Captain?" broke in Wolf's quiet tone. "Preliminary readout from geosurv probes indicates that the continent has a basaltic base, but is composed on the surface primarily of sedimentary rocks, heavily calcinaceous, and with a high proportion of limestones."

"Um-hum. Figures. That would also tend to explain how the wind could knock down any mountains so quickly. In another million years, barring any rising of the ocean bed, there probably won't be a plot of land sticking above the waters of this planet. Fortunately I do not have to worry about that, too." He turned from the screen. "Atha, go and ready the shuttle. And get set to take us down. It doesn't appear that we're going to need airsuits, thank Mungu, but make damn sure the crawler is in good running condition. And see if you can't turn up something for us to use as eye protection against this infernal wind. So that we won't have to use the suit helmets. *Je?*"

She started to leave, but he halted her at the door, his face thoughtful. "And make sure we have plenty of rope. I've been on planets where the rain would eat right through a suit to your skin, if the fauna didn't get to you first, if the flora didn't beat the fauna out. But this makes the first one I've ever been on where my primary concern will be being blown away."

"Yes, captain." She left then, passing the arriving Sissiph on the way out. The two had recovered enough to glare at each other meaningfully for a moment but, aware that Malaika's eyes were on them, said nothing.

"I don't think we'll have much trouble locating this thing of yours, gentlesirs—providing it does indeed exist. There don't appear to be any canyons or other rugged areas where it could be hidden, and since your friend found it without seeming difficulty, I see no reason why we, with more sophisticated instrumentation, should not do likewise. Yes, we should get to it quickly, quickly. *Afyaenu*, gentlesirs. Your health!"

He clapped those huge hands together and the report they made in the enclosed space was deafening.

"He looks like a small child in expectation of receiv-

ing a new toy," Tse-Mallory whispered to Truzenzuzex.

"Yes. Let us hope that it is indeed of an aesthetic
rather than a lethal nature."

The shuttle had its own balloonlike hangar in the
bottom of the great cargo section. Sissiph, professing
ignorance of maneuvering the pullways, had to be
helped down. But the way she snuggled into an oblig-
ing Malaika suggested motives other than incompe-
tence. The powerful little ship was a complete space-
going vessel, albeit a far more streamlined and less
spacious one than the *Gloryhole*. It was powered by
rockets of advanced design and, for atmospheric, sub-
orbital flight, by ramjets. Being intended for simple
ground-to-space, space-to-ground flights, it had limited cruising range. Fortunately they had only a limited area of probability to search. Conducted from the
Gloryhole it would have been more leisurely, but
Malaika wasn't going to restrain himself any longer
than was necessary, despite the attendant inconve-
niences. He wanted *down*.

The fact that they wouldn't need the flexible but
still awkward airsuits would be a great help. Atha
had fitted them all with goggles whose original purpose was to protect the wearer from heavy UV. While
dark, they would serve equally well to keep dust and
airborne particles out of everyone's eyes. For
Truzenzuzex she had managed a pair from empty
polmer containers.

Off in a corner, Sissiph was arguing petulantly with
Malaika. Now that the fun of her escorted trip down
the pullway was over. . . .

"But I don't want to go, Maxy. Really I don't."

"But you will, my *mwanakondoowivu*, you will.
Njoo, come, we all stay together. I don't think our

175

playful AAnn friends will find us. I don't see how they could, but I still fear the possibility. In the event of that obscene happening, I want everyone in one and the same place. And I don't know what we're going to run into downstairs, either. We're going into the ruins of a civilization dead half a million years, more advanced than us, and utterly ruthless. Maybe they have left some uncouth hellos for late drop-ins? So every hand will be along in case it's needed. Even your delicious little ones." He smacked the collection of digits in question with a juicy kiss.

She pulled the hand away and stamped a foot (her favorite nonvocal method of protest, but ineffectual in the zero-gravity). "But Maxy . . . !"

"*Starehe*! Don't 'Maxy' me. A definite no, pet." He put a hand on her shoulder and spun her gently but firmly about, giving her a shove in the direction of the shuttle's personnel port.

"Besides, if I were to leave you on board all by yourself you'd likely as not erase the navigation tapes trying to order dinner from the autochef. No, you come with us, *ndegedogo*, little bird. Also, your hair will look so pretty streaming away in the gentle breezes."

Her caustic voice came faintly as they entered the lock. "Breeze! I heard you talking about the hurric . . . !"

Or, thought Flinx as he struggled with the gun and belt that Atha had given him, it is possible that our Captain hasn't forgotten how neatly the AAnn seemed to find us. Maybe he thinks dear, sweet, helpless Sissiph is not entirely to be trusted. He went quiet, sought within the mind in question for a hint, a relationship that might bear out the merchant's possible suspicion. If anything was there, it was too deeply buried or well-hidden for him to seek out. And there were other things that seeped in around the edges of his probe that embarrassed him, even a sixteen-year-old from Drallar. He withdrew awkwardly. Let Malaika keep the load on his mind.

He was far more interested in admiring the gun. The handle was all filigree and inlay, a good deal fancier than the practical destroyers he'd seen in the barred and shadowed gunshops of Drallar. Unquestionably, it was equally as deadly. He knew what this model could do and how to handle it. In those same shops he had fired this and similar weapons with empty charge chambers while the owners had looked on tolerantly and exchanged patronizing comments with the regular customers.

It was beautiful. Compact and efficient, the laser pistol could cook a man at five hundred meters or a steak at one. It could weld most metals, or burn its way through any form of conventional plastic barrier. All in all, it was a useful and versatile tool as much as a weapon. While he hoped he wouldn't need it down on the surface and still had Pip with him, the streamlined weight felt ever so comfortable hugging his hip.

At Malaika's insistence they had all also been issued a full survival belt. Even Sissiph, who had complained that the negligible weight distorted her figure. This prompted an unflattering comment from Atha which fortunately went unheard by the Lynx, or they might have had another minor cataclysm in the tiny vessel's lock.

The belt was equipped and designed for use on planets which varied no more than ten percent from the humanx norm. Besides hefting the mandatory gun, the belt contained concentrated rations and energy pills, sugarsalt solution, their portable communicator units, a tent for two which was waterproof, conserved body heat, and folded to a package smaller than one's fist, charges for both comm and gun, tools for finding direction, making nails, or planting corn, among other things. There was also a wonderfully compact minimicrofilm reader, with some fifty books on its spool. Among the selections were two staples: the *Universal Verbal Communications Dictionary* (in seven volumes, abridged), and the Bible of the United Church, *The Holy Book of Universal Truths, and other Humorous Anecdotes.*

If he had had his entire apartment and all its accouterments from Drallar, he would have been less well off than he was with that single fabulous device encircling his waist.

The tremendous winds and jetstreams that flowed unceasingly around the planet should have made their descent difficult. Under Atha's skillful handling, however, it was almost as gentle as it might have been in the *Gloryhole*. The only rough moments came as they passed through the silvery-gold impregnated sections of the atmosphere. The natural layers of air-borne metallic particles (there were two) seemed unusually dense to the two scientists, but as long as they remained on rockets, not dangerously so.

Unlike the luxury craft which had lifted them from Moth's surface, this shuttle was equipped more for carrying cargo than folk, and so wasn't provided with as many ports. Despite the smallness of the scattered plexalloy sections, however, Flinx still had some view of the land below. The one continent rambled from the north pole down to a point just below the equator. It was mostly red-yellow at this height, with here and there large splotches of dull green. Small rivers, faint and insignificant in comparison with the coppery blues of the planetary ocean, meandered lazily down among the low hills. Naturally there were no river canyons. Any such would have disappeared millenia ago under the punishing onslaught of the untiring winds.

He had been momentarily worried about Pip, who had adamantly refused to be fitted with a tiny pair of makeshift goggles. Close inspection revealed that the reptile was equipped with transparent nictitating membranes, which slid down to protect the eye. He'd never noticed them before, probably because he'd simply not looked. He berated himself mentally for not realizing that an arboreal animal would naturally come built with some such type of natural protection against wind-carried objects. But then, neither of the two scientists had, either. Actually, Pip was more of a glider than a flyer. If he could master the winds down there he'd no doubt be more at home on Booster's surface than any of them.

A small intercabin comm conveyed the voice of Malaika back to them from Control. The tiny piloting cabin barely had space enough for the two pilots, and the big trader crowded it unmercifully. But he had insisted on remaining "on top of things." It was literally put.

They had been cruising on jets for only a short while when his excited cry broke the cabin's silence.

"*Maisha*, there it is! Check out the ports to your right."

There was a concerted rush to that side of the ship. Even Sissiph, her natural curiosity piqued, joined the movement.

They were still high, but as they banked the ruins of what had been a good-sized city, even by Tar-Aiym standards, came into view. They had built well, as always, but on this planet very little could remain in its original state for long. Still, from here it seemed as well preserved as any of the Tar-Aiym cities Flinx had seen on tape. As they dropped lower the alien city pattern of concentric crescents, radiating out from a fixed point, became as clear as ripples from the shore of a pond.

But even at this height the thing that immediately caught everyone's attention and caused Truzenzuzex to utter a soft curse of undefinable origin was not the city itself, but the building which stood on the bluff above the metropolis's nexus. A single faceless edifice in the shape of a rectangular pyramid, cut off squarely at the top. Both it and the circular base it rose from were a uniform dull yellow-white in color. The very top of the structure appeared to be covered with some kind of glassy material. Unlike the rest of the city it looked to be in a state of perfect preservation. It was also by far the tallest single structure he had ever seen.

"*Baba Giza!*" came Malaika's hushed voice over the speaker. He apparently became aware that his speaker pickup was on. "Take your seats, everybody, and fasten your straps. We are going to land by the base of that bluff. *Rafiki* Tse-Mallory, *rafiki* Truzenzuzex, we will explore the entire city beam by beam if you wish, but I will bet my *majicho* that your Krang is in a certain building at the top of a certain hill!"

Nothing like understatement to heighten anticipation, thought Flinx.

They landed, finally, on the broad stretch of open sandy ground to the left of both city and bluff. Atha had wisely elected to use replaceable landing skids instead of the wheeled gear, being uncertain as to the composition of the land they were going to set down

on. There had been no clear, paved stretch of territory nearby. They had had a quick glimpse of the ruins
of a monstrous spaceport off to the rear of the city's
last crescent. Malaika had vetoed landing there, wishing to land as close as possible to the ziggurat itself.
He felt that the less distance they had to travel on the
ground and the closer they could remain to the ship
itself, the safer he would feel about roaming around
the ruined city. The great spaceport had also no
doubt served as a military base, and if any unpleasant
automatic devices still remained to greet unautho-
rized visitors, they also would probably be concentrated there. So their landing was a bit rougher than it
might have been. But they were down now, in one
piece, and had received another benefit none had
thought of. It would have been obvious had anyone
reflected on it.

The wind came in a constant wall from behind the
building and the bluff below which they had landed.
While by no means perpendicular, the bluff proved
steep enough to cut off a good portion of the perpetual gale. It would mean easier working conditions
around the shuttle itself, in addition to eliminating
the possible problem of having to tie the ship down.
The ship's branch meteorology 'puter registered the
outside windage at their resting point at a comfortable forty-five kilometers an hour. Positively
sylvan.

"Atha, Wolf, give me a hand getting the crawler
out. The rest of you check over your equipment and
make sure you've got an extra pair of goggles apiece."
He turned to Tse-Mallory. "*Je!* They built their city
behind the biggest windbreak they could find. Sort of
gives the lie to your 'caressing wind-bath' theory,
kweli?"

181

"Do not abuse my guesses, captain, or I'll make no more." His eyes and mind were obviously focused elsewhere.

"Wolf?"

"Here, captain." The skeleton came out of the fore cabin, looking even more outré than usual in his silver belt and goggles. The expression on his face was odd, because *any* expression on his face was an oddity.

"Captain, there's an active thermal power source somewhere under this city."

"Not nuclear?" asked Malaika. A gravitonic power plant was of course impossible on any body with a reasonable field of its own. Still, there were known aspects to Tar-Aiym science that humanx researchers couldn't even begin to explain.

"No, sir. It's definitely thermal. Big, too, according to the sensors, although it was a very fast check-through."

Malaika's eyebrows did flip-flops. "Interesting. Does that suggest any 'guesses' to you, gentlesirs?"

Tse-Mallory and Truzenzuzex pulled themselves away from their rapt contemplation of the monolith above and considered the question.

"Yes, several," began the philosoph. "Among which is the confirmation of a fact we were fairly certain of anyway, that this is a young planet in a fairly young GO system. Tapping the core-power of a planet is difficult enough on the youngest, which this is not. But anyone can *tap*. The problem is to keep it under sufficient control to be able to channel it without causing planetwide earthquakes or volcanoes under major Hive-centers. We're still not so very adept at that ourselves. And only in the most limited sense."

"And," continued Tse-Mallory, "it suggests they

needed a hell of a lot of power for something, doesn't it? Now this is a fairly good-sized Tar-Aiym town, but it also seems to be the only one on the planet." He looked at Malaika for confirmation and the trader nodded, slowly. "So for the mind of me I can't see what they had to go to all that trouble for, when their quasinuclear plants would have provided more than enough power for this one city. Especially with all the water that's available."

"Captain," said Truzenzuzex impatiently, "We will be happy to hypothesize for you at length—later. But now I wish you would see about removing our surface transportation from the hold." His head swiveled to a port and the great golden eyes stared outward. "I have little doubt that your unasked questions and, hopefully, most of ours will be answered when we get inside that *Tuarweh* on top of this bluff."

"*If* we get into it," added Tse-Mallory. "It is just possible that the owners locked up when they moved, and left no key behind."

Chapter Sixteen

The crawler was a low, squat vehicle, running on twin duralloy treads. It also had a universal spherical "wheel" at its center of gravity to facilitate turning. Atha had made a few preliminary safety calculations and had come up with the fact that it would remain relatively stable in winds up to two hundred and fifty kilometers per, at which point things would start to get sticky. Flinx, for one, had no desire to put her calculations to a practical test. Nor did Malaika, apparently. He insisted on filling every empty space on the machine with objects of weight. If the winds got *that* bad, all the paraphernalia they could stuff into it wouldn't help. But it at least provided them with something of a psychological lift.

Not the least of these "objects of weight" was a heavy laser rifle, tripod-mounted.

"Just in case," the merchant had said, "opening the door proves more difficult than it might."

"For a peaceful trader traveling on his private racer you appear to have stocked quite an arsenal," Truzenzuzex murmured.

"Philosoph, I could give you a long, involved argument replete with attractive semantic convolutions, but I will put it, so, and leave it. I am in a very competitive business."

He cocked a challenging eye at the thranx.

"As you say." Truzenzuzex bowed slightly.

They boarded the crawler, which had been maneuvered close to the cargo port to minimize the initial force of the wind. The big land cruiser held all of them comfortably. It had been designed to transport heavy cargo, and even with Malaika's "objects of weight" scattered about there was plenty of room in which to move around. If bored, one might take the ladder up to the driver's compartment, with its two beds and polyplexalloy dome. There was room up there for four, but Malaika, Wolf, and the two scientists occupied it immediately and were disinclined to give it up. So Flinx had to be content with the tiny ports in the main compartment for his view of the outside. He was alone in the quiet spaces with the two women, who sat at extreme opposite ends of the cabin from each other and exchanged deathly thoughts back and forth. A less congenial atmosphere would have been difficult to imagine. Try as he would, they were beginning to give him a headache. He would far rather have been upstairs.

They were making their way up the slope of the bluff now, zigzagging whenever the incline grew too steep for even the crawler's powerful spiked treads to negotiate. Their progress was slow but steady, the machine after all having been designed to get from point A to point B in one piece, and not to race the clock. It did its job effectively.

As might have been predicted, the ground was crumbly and soft. Still, it was more rock than sand. The treads dug in deeply and the engine groaned. It slowed their advance somewhat, but assured them of excellent traction in the teeth of the wind. Still, Flinx would not like to have faced a real blow in the slow device.

They finally topped the last rise. Looking back into the distance Tse-Mallory could make out the crumbled spires and towers of the city, obscured by eternal dust and wind. It was more difficult to see up here. Gravel, dirt, and bits of wood from the hearty ground-hugging plants began to splatter against the front of the dome. For the first time the howl of the wind became audible through the thick shielding, sounding like fabric tearing in an empty room.

Wolf glanced at their anemometer. "A hundred fifteen point five-two kilos an hour . . . sir."

"*Je*! I'd hoped for better, but it could be worse. Much worse. No one is going to be taking long walks. *Upepokuu!* In a gale we can manage. A hurricane would be awkward."

As they moved farther in from the edge of the bluff the air began to clear sufficiently for them to catch sight of their objective. Not that they could have missed it. There wasn't anything else to see, except an occasional clump of what looked like dried seaweed. They rolled on, the wind dying as they moved farther into the lee of the building. Three pairs of eyes leaned back . . . and back, and back, until it seemed certain it would be simpler to lie down and stare upward. Only Wolf, eyes focused on the instrument board of the massive crawler, failed to succumb to the lure of the monolith.

It towered above them, disappearing skyward in swirls of dust and low clouds, unbroken by ledge or window.

"How *huyukubwa*?" Malaika finally managed to whisper.

"How big do I make it? I couldn't say too well," answered Tse-Mallory. "Tru? You've got the best depth vision among us."

The philosoph was quiet for a long moment. "In human terms?" He lowered his eyes to look at them. If he could have blinked he would, but thranx eye-shields reacted only in the presence of water or strong sunlight, so he could not. His improvised goggles gave his face an unbalanced look.

"Well over a kilo at the base . . . each way. It looked a perfect square from the air, you know. Perhaps . . ." he took another brief glance upward, "three kilometers high."

The slight jolting and bumping they had been ex-periencing abruptly disappeared. They were now traveling on the smooth yellow-white circle on which the structure was centered.

Malaika peered down at the substance they were traversing, then back at the building. The heavy crawler left no tracks on the solid surface.

"What do you suppose this stuff is, anyway?"

Tse-Mallory had joined him in looking down at the even ground. "I don't know. When I saw it from the air my natural inclination was to think, stone. Just before we grounded I thought it looked rather 'wet,' like certain heavy plastics. Now that we're down on it I'm not sure of anything. Ceramics, maybe?"

"Metal-reinforced, surely," added Truzenzuzex. "But as for the surface, at least, a polymer ceramic would be a good guess, certainly. It's completely dif-ferent from anything I've ever seen before, even on other Tar-Aiym planets. Or for that matter, from any-thing I could see of the city as we came in."

"Um. Well, since they built their city in the lee of this bluff, as a windbreak, I don't doubt, I'd expect any *mlango* to be on this side of the structure. *Je?*"

As it turned out shortly enough, there was, and it was.

Alan Dean Foster

Unlike the rest of the mysterious building the material used in the construction of the door was readily identifiable. It was metal. It towered a good thirty meters above the cab of the crawler and stretched at least half that distance in either direction. The metal itself was unfamiliar, dull-gray in color, and possessed of an odd glassy luster. Much like the familiar fogs of home, for Flinx. The whole thing was recessed several meters into the body of the building.

"Well, there's your door, captain," said Tse-Mallory. "How do we get in? I confess to a singular lack of inspiration, myself."

Malaika was shaking his head in awe and frustration as he examined the entrance. Nowhere could be seen the sign of a single joint, weld, or seam.

"Drive right up to it, Wolf. The wind is practically dead here. We'll have to get out and look for a doorbuzz or something. If we don't find anything that's recognizably a handle or a keyhole, we'll have to unlimber the rifle and try a less polite entrance." He eyed the massive square dubiously. "Although I hope that alternative doesn't become necessary. I know the stubbornness of Tar-Aiym metals."

As it turned out, the problem was solved for them.

Somewhere in the bowels of the colossal structure, long dormant but undead machinery sensed the approach of an artificial mechanism containing biological entities. It stirred sleepily, prodding resting memory circuits to wakefulness. The design and composition of the approaching vehicle was unfamiliar, but neither was it recognizably hostile. The entities within were likewise unfamiliar, albeit more obviously primitive. And there was an A-class mind among them. Likewise unfamiliar, not hostile. And it had been *such* a long time! The building debated with itself for the eternity of a second.

"Hold it, Wolf!" The merchant had noticed a movement in front of the crawler.

With a smoothness and silence born of eternal lubrication, the great door separated. Slowly, with the ponderousness of tremendous weight, the two halves slid apart just far enough for the crawler to enter comfortably. Then they stopped.

"*Utamu.* We are expected, perhaps?"

"Automatic machinery," mumbled Truzenzuzex, entranced.

"My thoughts also, philosoph. Take us in, Wolf."

The quiet man obediently gunned the engine and the powerful landcraft began to rumble forward. Malaika eyed the sides of the narrow opening warily. The metal was not a reasonably thin sheet. It was not even a moderate one.

"A good nineteen, twenty, meters through," said Tse-Mallory matter-of-factly. "I wonder what it was designed to keep out."

"Not us, apparently," added Truzenzuzex. "You could have played your toy on that for days, Captain, and burned it out before you scratched the entrance. I'd like to try a SCCAM on it, just to see which would come out the winner. I've never heard of any artificial structure resisting a SCCAM projectile, but then I've never seen a twenty-meter-thick Hive-block of solid Aiymetal before, either. The question will undoubtedly remain forever academic."

They had rolled perhaps a few meters beyond the door when it began to slide heavily shut behind them. The silence of it was eerie. Wolf glanced questioningly at Malaika, hand on throttle. The merchant, however, was at least outwardly unconcerned.

"It opened to let us in, Wolf. I think it will do so to let us out." The doors closed. "In any case, *kwa nini* worry? It doesn't matter now."

They got another surprise. Unless they were hollow, which hardly seemed likely with that door, the walls of the pseudoceramic material were a good hundred and fifty meters thick. Far more than was needed merely to support the weight of the building, great as it was. It bespoke much more an attempt at impregnability. Such had been found before in the ruins of Tar-Aiym fortresses, but never approaching this in scale.

Flinx did not know what he expected of the interior. He'd been scanning consistently ever since the great doors had opened, but had not been able to detect anything thinking inside. And he'd lamented his purely sideways view from the crawler. He didn't see how the inside could possibly surprise him any more than that unmatched exterior.

He was wrong.

Whatever it was he had anticipated in his wildest thoughts, it was nothing like the reality. Malaika's voice drifted down to him from above. It was oddly muted.

"*Katika* here, everyone. Atha, open the lock. There's air in here and it's breathable, and light, and no wind, and I don't know whether to believe it myself or not, even though my *majicho* tells me . . . but the sooner you see it. . . ."

They didn't need further urging. Even Sissiph was excited. Atha scrambled to the small personnel lock and they watched while she cracked the triple seal, cutting the flow of liquid at the three prescribed points. The heavy door swung itself outward. The automatic ramp extended itself to touch ground, buzzed once when it had made firm contact, and turned itself off.

Flinx was first out, followed closely by Atha and the two scientists, Malaika and Sissiph, and lastly, Wolf. All stood quite silent under the panorama spread before them.

The interior of the building, at least, was hollow. That was the only way to describe it. Somewhere above Flinx knew those massive walls joined a ceiling, but strain his eyes as he might he couldn't make it out. The building was so huge that despite excellent circulation, clouds had formed inside. The four gigantic slabs pressed heavy on his mind, if not his body. But claustrophobia was impossible in an open space this large. Compared to the perpetual swirl of air and dust outside the utter calm within was cathedrallike. Perhaps, indeed, that was what it was, although he knew the idea to be more the feeling imparted by this first view than the likely truth.

The light, being intended for nonhumanx eyes, was wholly artificial and tinged slightly with blue-green. It was also dimmer than they would have preferred. The philosoph's naturally blue chiton looked good in it, but it made the rest of them appear vaguely fishlike. The dimness did not obstruct their vision as much as it made things seem as though they were being viewed through not-quite-clear glass. The temperature was mild and a bit on the warm side.

The crawler had been halted because it could proceed no farther. Row upon row of what were indisputably seats or lounges of some sort stretched out from where they stood. The place was a colossal amphitheater. The ranks extended onward, unbroken, to the far side of the structure. There they ended at the base of . . . something.

He took a glance and risked a brief probe of the others. Malaika was glancing appraisingly about the limits of the auditorium. Wolf, his permanent nonexpression back on his face, was sampling the air with an instrument on his belt. Sissiph clung tightly to Malaika, staring apprehensively about the disquieting silence. Atha wore much the same look of cautious observation as the big trader.

The two scientists were in a state as close to Nirvana as it was possible for scientists to be. Their thoughts were moving so fast Flinx was hard-pressed even to sample them. They had eyes only for the far end of the great room. For them a search had been vindicated, even if they didn't know what it was they had found. Tse-Mallory chose that moment to step forward, with Truzenzuzex close behind. The rest of them began to file down the central aisle after the scientists, toward the thing at the far side.

It was not an exhausting walk, but Flinx was grateful for the opportunity to rest at the end of it. He sat on the edge of the raised platform. He could have taken one of the seat-lounges below, but they were nowhere near contoured for the human physiology and doubtless were as uncomfortable as they looked.

Large steps led up to the dais he sat on. At its far end a flawless dome of glass or plastic enclosed a single, unadorned couch. A large oval doorway opened in the dome facing the auditorium. It was a good meter higher than their tallest member and far wider than even Malaika's copious frame would require. The bench itself was tilted slightly to face the amphitheater. A smaller dome, shaped like a brandy glass, fitted partway over its raised end. Thick cables and conduits led from it and the bottom of the couch to the machine.

The "machine" itself towered a hundred meters above them and ran the length of the auditorium, melting into the curved corners. While the exterior of the structure was remorselessly acute, the interior was considerably rounded off. Much of the machine was closed off, but Flinx could see dials and switches catching the light from behind half-open plates. Those he could make out had obviously not been designed with humanx manipulative members in mind.

From above the dull metal plating of the machine an uncountable profusion of chromatically colored tubes ran toward the distant roof. Azure, peach, shocking pink, ivory, Tyrolean purple, chartreuse, orange, mutebony, smoke, white-gold, verdanure . . . every imaginable shading and tone, and not a few unimaginable ones. Some were the size of a child's toy, small enough to fit over his little finger. Others looked big enough to swallow the shuttle with ease. In the corners they merged into the fabric of the structure. He turned a slow circle and saw where bulges in the walls, extending even above the entrance way, indicated the presence of more of the colossal pipes. He reminded himself that he had no way of being certain they were even hollow, but somehow the impression of pipes persisted. Sometimes his talents operated independent of his thoughts.

"Well," said Malaika. He said it again. "Well, well!"

He seemed uncertain of himself, a rare state. Flinx smiled at the merchant's thoughts. The big man wasn't sure whether to be pleased or not. He definitely had *something*, all right. But he didn't know what it was, let alone how to market it. He stood while everyone else sat.

"I suggest we obtain whatever supplies we'll need for our investigations." Truzenzuzex and Tse-Mallory were examining everything in minute detail and hardly heard him. "This has passed over my head, and so from my hands. I trust you gentlebeings can find out what this thing does?" He waved a broad hand to encompass what they could see of the machine.

"I do not know," said Truzenzuzex. "Offclaw, I would say that our acquaintances the Branner had the right idea when they spoke of this thing as a musical instrument. It certainly looks like one, and the arrangements in here," he indicated the amphitheater, "would tend to support that assumption. For my wings, though, I can't see as yet how it operates."

"Looks like the ultimate product of a mad organbuilder's worst nightmares," added Tse-Mallory. "I wouldn't say for sure unless we figure out how to operate the thing."

"*Will* you?" asked Malaika.

"Well, it seems to be still partially powered, at least. Wolf recorded the power source, and something operated the doors, turned on the lights . . . and keeps the air fresh, I hope. It wasn't designed according to conceptions we'd find familiar, but that thing," and he gestured at the dome with its enclosed bench, "looks an awful lot like an operator's station. True, it might also be a resting place for their honored dead. We won't know till we dig a lot deeper. I suggest that we move everything we'll need from the shuttle in here. It'll be a lot simpler than running out in this gale every time we need a spanner or a sandwich."

"*Mapatano*! I agree. Wolf, you and I will start

transferring things from the shuttle. It will go quickly enough, once we unload some of that junk I piled into the crawler. It appears we are going to be here for a bit, *hata kidogobaya!*"

Chapter Seventeen

It was an odd feeling to be constantly within the building. Not confining, for the door worked perfectly even for one person—provided he carried with him at least one item of recognizably metallic artificial construction. It was a peculiarly satisfying sensation to approach the great bulks, comm unit or gun extended in front of one, and have a million tons of impregnable metal slide gently aside to reveal a personalized passageway a meter wide and thirty meters high.

It was better outside at night, but not much. In spite of the goggles the dust eventually worked its insistent way into eyes. And it was chilly.

Tse-Mallory and Truzenzuzex had been pouring over the immense apparatus, prying behind those panels in the slate-gray wall which would open, ignoring those which would not. There was no point in forcing entry and risking breakage to the intricate device. Not when they could spend years on the unresisting portions. And they didn't have years. So they continued to dig into the exposed guts on the Krang without disturbing a single wire from its proper place, treading with the utmost care lest they nudge some vital circuit from its proper alignment. While the scientists and Malaika labored over the enigma of the machine, Atha and Flinx would sometimes take the crawler into the vast city. Wolf remained behind to help Malaika, and Sissiph to be near him. So Flinx had the crawler's observation dome practically to himself.

He found it hard to believe that structures which even in ruin and under a centuries-old coat of dust could remain beautiful had been raised to house the most warlike race the galaxy had known. The thought cast an unshakable pall over the quiet ruins. Little in the way of decoration was visible on the sandblasted exteriors of the structures, but that didn't necessarily mean much. Anything not integral to the actual support of the edifice would long since have been worn away. And they were cruising far above what had once been a main boulevard. The street itself was somewhere far below, buried under a millenia of shifting sand and soil. They recognized it as such only because of the absence of buildings. Probably this city had been covered and uncovered at least a hundred times, each new cycle grinding away some portion of its original aspect. They had soon discovered that a mild electrostatic field came up regularly every evening and cleared the days' accumulation of dust and debris from the base of the Krang for the width of the yellow-white circle. But no such care was visible in the city. In the evenings, as the sun set, the sands turned blood-red and the hulks of hollowed buildings sparkled like topaz and ruby in a setting of carnelian. The constant, unceasing wind spoiled the illusion of beauty, and its rise-and-fall moan seemed an echoing curse of all the vanished races ever subjugated by the Tar-Aiym.

And they didn't even know what they had looked like.

Chapter Eighteen

A week later they were all gathered in informal conference on the dais. A small, portable cookstove, powered by an aeternacell, had been set up nearby, giving the place an incongruously domesticated look. Next, thought Flinx, they would be hanging out laundry. It had been found more convenient for the scientists to sleep and eat by their work, instead of making the daily hike to the crawler. They could have brought the cruiser right up to the base of the dais, but for all they knew the seats themselves might play some crucial part in the operation of the Krang. Besides, reducing parts of the place to rubble hardly seemed the proper way to go about resurrecting its secrets. It was just as well that they hadn't, because the sleepy machine would have noted the gesture as hostile and taken immediate and appropriate action.

The odors of frying bacon and eggs, and juquil for Truzenzuzex, added to the homey atmosphere. At the moment, Atha and Sissiph were managing the cooking for the scientists. This was proved a necessity after all the men had demonstrated a monumental ineptitude with the device, which did 90 percent of the work itself. Knowing full well he could operate it better than any of them, Flinx had pleaded ignorance when offered the chance to try it. He had no desire to be tied down with the job of cook, not when he could spend his time watching the two scientists dissect the amazing innards of the machine.

"This thing grows more incredible by the day." Tse-Mallory was talking now. "You know, we found walkways at each corner of the building, where the machine disappears into the walls."

"I'd wondered where you two had disappeared to," said Malaika.

"They extend I don't know how far beneath us. To the center of the planet for all I can tell, although I'd think that the heat would make that a prohibitive development even for the Tar-Aiym. Nor do we have any idea how far it extends on the horizontal level, either. To the ocean? Under it? We didn't have an easy time of it down there, you know. There are steps and ladders and ramps, and none designed for human or thranx hands. But between the two of us, we managed. There must be mechanical lifts somewhere, but we couldn't find them."

"We first went down three days ago . . . apologies for worrying you. I suppose we should have mentioned where we were going, but we didn't really know ourselves, and certainly didn't expect to be gone as long as we were. The excitement of the moment overcame our time-sense.

"We went more or less straight down, pausing only twice, for three hours and sleep-time. These pipes, or whatever," he indicated the rainbow giants ranked above them, "are continuous below this flooring, and descend to levels we didn't reach. Not even at the farthest point of our journey. Most of the machinery was completely unfamiliar to us, and I daresay we two are as familiar with Tar-Aiym design as anyone in the Arm. But the majority of this stuff was way past us."

"Near the surface the machinery is practically solid. Farther down it thins out to a sufficient degree to become recognizable as to its individual components. All of it looked brand-new. In many places the metal was warm, confirming what we've suspected all along. Power is being fed into it continually. And there must be a billion kilometers of wire down there.

"Still, we have no idea what it does, captain. I am sorrier than you could ever be, but you can console yourself in the knowledge that whatever it is, it is far and away the biggest and best of its kind."

This last from a tired-looking Truzenzuzex. The philosoph had been working at an incredible pace the past week, and his age was beginning to show. On the ship he had kept it well masked with his energy and youthful spirits.

"Couldn't you discover *anything* about its function?" pleaded Malaika.

Tse-Mallory sighed. He had been doing a lot of that, lately. "Not really. We both incline to the musical instrument theory, still. There are many arguments against it that bother us, though." He looked at Truzenzuzex, who nodded confirmation.

"*Je?*" Malaika prompted.

"For one thing, we can't quite bring ourselves to believe that in a time of such stress a race as war-oriented as the Tar-Aiym would devote so much effort and material to anything of a nonlethal nature. The metal for that door, for example, must have been required for the construction of warships. Yet it was brought and used here. On the other hand, we know they were artistically inclined in a gruesome sort of way. Their tastes did run strongly to the martial. Possibly they felt the need of a project to stimulate patriotic fervor, and this was their way of doing it. It

200

would also have possible psychological benefits we can't begin to imagine. If that seems unlikely, consider the lack of evidence we have to go on. I'm not ready to believe any of my explanations myself."

"And another thing. Did you happen to notice the unusual silvery-gold tinge to the atmosphere as we were coming down?"

"No . . . yes!" said Malaika. "I've seen it before on other planets, so I didn't think it too out of the ordinary. These . . . there were *mbili* layers, if I remember aright . . . seemed thicker than most. And better defined. But I don't view that as a cause for surprise. I've seen quadruple layers, too. And the unusual thickness of these could easily be accounted for by the scouring effects of these *wachawi upepo*, sorceror's winds."

"True," Tse-Mallory continued. "Windglitter, I believe they call it. As you say, there could be natural explanations for the odd thickness of the layers. The reason I bring them up at all is because on one of the levels we reached we found what appeared to be at least a portion of a great meterological monitoring station. Among other things, several of the instruments appeared to be occupied solely with keeping information on those two levels in the atmosphere. We only had time for a fast look at it, as our prime concern was making speed downward. But the only reason we noticed it at all was because the metal was quite warm there, gave off a lot of heat, and seemed to be running at full power. That's something we observed in only a very few other places. We now think that those layers have something to do with the actual function of the Krang. What, I can't imagine."

"To be more specific," said Truzenzuzex, "this thing," and he pointed at the transparent dome and the lounge within, "takes on more and more the aspect of a center control for the operation of the entire apparatus. I know it seems difficult to imagine this monstrosity being operated by a single being lying on that slab, but evidence seems to support it. I am skeptical, myself. There is not a switch, dial, or similar device anywhere near the thing. And yet its location alone, and isolation, seem to support its importance.

"Close examination of that helmet, or headdress, or whatever it is, shows that it's lined with what might be some form of sensory pickups. If the machine is indeed still capable of more than partial activation, then theoretically mere proximity to those pickups ought to do it. Actual physical contact with the operator wouldn't seem to be necessary. So the fact that the size and shape of our heads in no way corresponds to that of the Tar-Aiym . . . in all probability . . . shouldn't hinder us."

"You're thinking of trying it, then," said Malaika.

"We must."

"But suppose it's geared to respond only to the electromagnetic patterns generated by a Tar-Aiym mind?"

"We have no indication that 'electromagnetic patterns' are even the type of whatever is necessary to activate the machine," retorted Tse-Mallory. "But if that does prove to be the case, then unless you can produce a live and cooperative Tar-Aiym, I am very much afraid that we might as well pack and go home." He shrugged. "Tru and I feel we've more or less reached a dead end as far as mere circuit-tracing goes. We could continue to poke around in this pile of complexity for a thousand years—fascinating as that might be—and not come any closer to making it work."

"Trying it ... couldn't that be awfully dangerous?" asked Atha.

"It could very well be lethal, my dear. We decided that long ago. For instance, there might be a feedback which could . . . for that very reason, and for several others, I shall try it first. If we have still failed to activate it and no obviously harmful results are forthcoming, I see no reason why everyone here should not have an opportunity to try the same."

"Not *me*!" said Sissiph loudly.

"Now wait a minute!" began Malaika, ignoring her.

"Sorry, captain." Truzenzuzex, now. "*Starhe*! Don't bother, as you would say. Bran is correct. Our training may not exactly qualify us as operators of this thing, but our familiarity with the works of the Tar-Aiym and what little we know of their psychologies might help us cope with any unforeseen problems that could develop. Such designs might arise which would overwhelm a complete novice. Sorry, but there is too much involved to permit you to make the initial attempt, at least. We are not on board ship. You are momentarily overruled, captain."

"*Je*!" rumbled Malaika.

Tse-Mallory stepped to the entrance of the dome. "Let's be on with it, then."

"You mean, *sasaa kuume*?" asked Malaika.

Tse-Mallory paused. "I don't see why not." He hesitated again at the entrance, looked back. "I don't expect much to happen, let alone anything dangerous. And if it does I wouldn't expect this to be much protection, but for my own psychological comfort, everyone off the dais, please. It certainly ought to be safe enough in the seats, or lounges, or whatever they are. Obviously the Tar-Aiym used them when this thing was in operation, so they *should* be safe for us as well. Theoretically speaking."

"Sociologist, theoretical injury I don't mind." Malaika smiled in what was intended to be a reassuring manner and joined the others in moving off the raised area into the rows of "seats" below.

Truzenzuzex was the only other one to remain on the platform. Ostensibly he was there to observe, but both he and Tse-Mallory knew that if anything went wrong the insect's aid would not likely be of much use. He took the proverbial and ritual deep breath and entered the dome.

The ceramic-plastic slab was now familiar from days of prolonged and minute inspections. He climbed up onto the smooth, cold surface and turned, facing out and slightly up. From inside the dome the roof of the monolith seemed almost visible. Possibly the transparent material had an actual slight magnifying effect. It did not seem significant.

The slab was much longer than was necessary to hold his lanky frame. It wasn't heated, though. He found himself squirming uncomfortably on the hard, chilly surface and wishing it were a bed. This was too much like the molds in a cryogenic suspension lab. Do it quick, his mind told his body! Digging into the unyielding surface with his heels, he shoved himself upward. In one motion his head was fully within the helmet.

Flinx didn't know what to expect. Explosions, earthquake, a collapsing building, perhaps. In any case the results were disappointing, if safe.

The helmet took on a pale red tinge, shifting to yellow, and thence to a light green. Also, a slight humming sound became audible. Apparently it came from within the slab itself. That was all. No fireworks, not even a few simple flashes of lightning.

Tse-Mallory's face within the dome was twisted, but it was obviously in concentration and not pain. Oddly, his mind was unreachable to Flinx. If nothing else the dome blanketed the thoughts of whoever lay within.

Twenty minutes later he was out of the dome, shaking his head while the others crowded around.

"*Je?*" asked Malaika.

The sociologist looked irritable. "*Je?* Well, we proved one thing. If this machine is still capable of functioning as it was intended, that helmet is certainly the initiating point."

"I can't believe that this entire insanity was built just to make pretty colored lights in a plastic head-dress!"

"No, of course not." Tse-Mallory looked wistfully back at the slab and the once-again transparent helmet. "It seems as though I was able to activate it, but only a very little. Apparently there's a necessary something missing from my mind. Or maybe it merely takes a kind of training we know nothing about. I don't know. I tried everything I could with my mind. Self-hypnosis. Yoga. The Banda exercises. Total objective concentration. An open subconscious. You saw the results. Or rather, the lack of them."

"Could you feel anything, anything at all?" asked Flinx.

"Umm. Yes, it was peculiar. Not painful or threatening. Just peculiar. Like something was trying to get inside my head. A tickling of the outside of the brain, barely noticeable. And when I tried to concentrate on it, it went away and hid. I must say I'm disappointed."

"*Je*? You think perhaps you've got a monopoly on it?" The merchant looked upset, as well he had a right to be. "What now?"

"Now I suggest the rest of the humans give it a try. I believe that I've amply demonstrated its harmlessness, if nothing else. Keeping it attuned to one type of mind might have a beneficial cumulative effect."

One at a time the rest of them took a turn under the innocuous helmet. Excepting of course Sissiph, who refused even to go near it. Malaika managed to generate a strong yellow glow in the transparent material. Flinx did as well (or as poorly, no one could say) as Tse-Mallory, only his coloring also possessed an uneven pulsing. As if to counter Tse-Mallory's claim, he emerged from the domed chamber with a definite headache. Atha and Wolf could each manage a light red, almost rose color. They had better luck when Truzenzuzex at last made his attempt.

The second that aging, iridescent head entered the zone of effectiveness, the soft colors immediately ran from pink up to a deep blue. Tse-Mallory had to remark on it to get everyone's attention. Repeated failure had led to discouraging boredom. But no one was bored now. Even outside the dome the humming from the base of the slab was clearly audible. On one of the open panels of the great gray bulk of the machine, lights were beginning to glow faintly. The helmet had by now turned a deep lavender.

"Look at the dome!" Flinx pointed.

For several inches of its height the dome was glowing a solid and unwavering crimson. Every now and then the cottony light would creep upward a few millimeters, only to sink back and disappear into the floor.

An hour later Truzenzuzex staggered out of the

dome. Tse-Mallory had to support the philosoph around the b-thorax, as the old insect's legs proved too shaky to manage on their own. The philosoph was visibly tired. Together they lurched down to the first row of alien benches. Truzenzuzex's visage did not wrinkle as did a primate's, but the usual healthy glow of his eyes was more subdued than before.

"You certainly labeled it correctly, brother," he finally gasped, "when you said there was something trying to get inside your head! I felt like a youth again, trying to break out of my crysalis. Whew! I could tell it did no good, though."

"Not true," said Flinx. Malaika nodded confirmation. "You had the dome itself glowing red—around the base, anyway."

"I did?" The whistling thranx laughter followed. "I suppose that is an accomplishment of sorts. I could not detect it from the inside. I was concentrating rather deeply, and my optics weren't the nerves I was working with. Does that mean perhaps we are on a proper track?" He turned to face Malaika. The tone was gradually returning to his muscles. "Captain, I retract my earlier statement. Give me another three or four weeks at this and I believe I'll be able to tell you, one way or another, whether this thing can ever be operated by man or thranx. Or whether your investment has proved itself a loss."

Malaika looked resigned rather than frustrated. His own unsuccessful strivings with the Krang had produced a little patience, if no other results.

"*Bado Juzi*. 'Yet the day before yesterday.' An old saying in my family, gentlemen. You've done already much more than I had a right to hope. Take your time, gentlesirs, take your time."

Far below in the secret places of the planet the

consciousness of the Krang stirred sluggishly. It considered more fully the impulses which had awakened the Prime Nexus with feeble, childish probings and pressures. Even in its semisomnolent state it was reasonably certain (+prob., 90.97, —prob., 8.03, random factoring, 1.00) that there was an A-class mind present above. One fully capable of arousing the Krang to the state of *Naisma*, or total effectiveness. Apparently it had chosen not to reveal itself yet. The machine considered and allowed the sections of itself which controlled intelligence to lapse back to dormancy, ready.

When the mind was ready, the Krang would be.

After all, it had been built that way.

Chapter Nineteen

As it developed, Truzenzuzex did not get his month. Nor his three weeks. They had been pouring over the accessible portions of the machine's innards for only three days when Malaika's comm signaled an extra-atmosphere incoming call. As a matter of safety his portable comm was hooked to the big transmitter in the crawler. Flinx was present when the signal came in, helping the two scientists with the more physical aspects of their work. Sissiph, Atha, and Wolf were back in the crawler, rearranging their supplies in its cavernous hold.

In order to facilitate their work, two cots (one modified) had been placed next to the scientists' portastove. The others still found it more comfortable to sleep within the familiar confines of the crawler, despite the attendant daily walk it engendered.

Both scientists paused in their work the moment they spotted the strange expression which had come over Malaika's face. Flinx picked it up from the sudden confusion of the merchant's thoughts. He had been watching them labor over strange markings and unfamiliar alien switching devices all morning. Nine tenths of what they were trying to do mechanically eluded him. He had been able to help them with the more delicate portions of their operations, having, as they put it, a certain "feel" for where things were located. And as always, their conversation on both the vocal and mental level had been fascinating.

"Captain . . ." began Tse-Mallory.

"We're being called," the merchant replied. "Extra-atmospheric."

His thoughts reflected suspicion as much as disbelief. He flipped over the broadcast switch of the tiny communit.

"Wolf, are you monitoring this?"

"Yes, captain," came the unmodulated reply from the distant crawler.

"All right. Send an acknowledgment and put it over. Someone *knows* where we are. Not much use denying it." He turned to the others. "We might be being monitored now, although I doubt it's possible through these walls. But then, I also doubt we're receiving a call from another starship, and that is the case. *Haidhuru*. Nothing matters. Leave your comms off and listen on mine, if you wish. No point in broadcasting how many units we have in operation. If they don't know already."

It was the first time Flinx had seen the merchant so downcast. Obviously the strain was taking a bigger toll of his resources than he cared to show. At any rate, all he said into the comm was, "Yes?"

The voice that responded was naturally high. But if the tone was slightly effeminate, the words were not.

"Captain Maxim Malaika, House-Head and Pluto-crat? I bring you greetings, sir, from Madame Rashal-leila Nuaman and Nuaman Enterprises." Malaika's lips twisted in a subvocal oath which made Flinx blush. "Congratulations!"

That superciliousness was sufficient to stimulate the merchant's tongue.

"Damned decent of you. And who are *ninyi ny-ote*?"

"Pardon? Oh, *I*. I am of little consequence. But for purposes of facilitating further conversation . . . which, I assure you, *will* be forthcoming . . . you may know me as Able Nikosos."

"*Je*, Mister Nikosos. I agree wholeheartedly that your personage is doubtless of little consequence. I am curious as to how you got here. This planet seems to be acquiring a universal notoriety."

"How so? Umm. As to your question, Captain, why," and the voice reflected mock astonishment, "we followed you. Most of the way from Moth. At a discreet distance, of course. Speaking of which, you certainly changed your course a good deal at the beginning of your journey. Yes you did. But after the first week we had no trouble plotting your approximate course. You know, this is the fourth system in this sector with planets that we've visited. We knew more or less where the one we wanted was, but not its exact coordinates. It made it hard on us, yes hard, when we lost you completely. Those coordinates were on a bit of material which. . . . but never mind that. That's long in the past now, isn't it?"

"You didn't by any chance get some help from a certain AAnn baron?"

"An AAnn baron?" The squeaky voice reflected surprise. Malaika glanced at Flinx.

"He's telling the truth, sir. And they're definitely in a set orbit."

The two scientists looked in surprise at Flinx. Neither said anything, but he could sense a mild resentment of his secrecy in their thoughts. He wanted desperately to tell them of how necessary it was to maintain that secrecy. Even today, psi-sensitives were not universally popular, a fact he had found out early and painfully as a child. Now was not the time, though. The voice on the comm continued.

"What would we have to do with the AAnn? Nasty people, those, nasty! No indeed, sir. We found you all by ourselves, in spite of the difficulties your disappearance occasioned us. But we did find you, didn't we? So no harm done. Besides, no use trying to share the blame, and I refuse to share the credit. Not that it should matter to you in the long run. Or even the short one." A brief giggle broke the commentary. "My ship is parked a couple of field-lengths from your *Gloryhole*. We beamed it first. When we did not receive a reply and when the lock refused us entrance—how clever of you, captain!—we assumed you had already made your drop to the surface. A glance at your shuttlebay confirmed it."

"*Thelathini nguruwe!* Thirty pigs. Which is the ultimate number which can be fitted into a standard captain's cabin, in case you didn't know."

The voice seemed immune to insult as well as to modesty. "Tut, tut, Captain. You'll offend my modest nature."

"Small chance of that."

"Anyway, the emanations from your components would have revealed your location to us even if you had declined to acknowledge our call. As I am sure you were well aware."

"Captain," said Flinx, "I thought you said. . . ."

"Forgot about the relay to the shuttle's comm. That's what they'd pick up. They could hardly miss us anyway." He was already setting up a last-ditch defense in his mind.

"Where are you now, friend Nikosos, other than in orbit?"

"A good guess, Captain. Why, we're drifting over this moisture-poor continent. Rather close to you, I've no doubt. We should be down in a short while, at which time I hope to greet you personally." The voice paused, then resumed again. "Whatever you are hiding in must really be something. We're having no end of trouble picking up your signal."

"You've traveled a long way for a lot of nothing, Nikosos. We've been working on this 'whatever,' as you so accurately say, for weeks now. We haven't been able to figure out what it does, much less how it does it."

"Certainly, captain, certainly!" The voice carried a humoring tone now. "Personally, whenever the cold of space affects me too deeply, I like to fly through the nearest M supergiant to warm my chilly bones. As I said, we'll be seeing you shortly."

"He doesn't believe you," said Flinx.

Malaika nodded. "And then?"

"Well, that does pose a problem, eh? I certainly can't wave you on your happy way home, because then all my hard work would have been for naught, wouldn't it? But then, assassination really isn't my line, either. Perhaps something can be worked. . . ." Malaika cut the comm. He turned to the others.

"*Je,* you heard. Where new planets are concerned, possession is nine tenths of the ancient law. I doubt Rasha will leave me be to call in a Church Evaluation Force." He switched the comm to interpersonnel frequency.

"Wolf, you heard everything?"

"Yes Captain." The shadow-man's reply was even. Flinx wondered if the pilot were capable of an excitement he never showed. "I fear that your pet took it rather hard, though. She's fainted. Miss Moon is caring for her now."

"*Je*! She will be quiet for a while then, anyway. We're going to join you shortly. We'd best all remain *pamoja*." He flipped off the comm again.

"What do you propose?" asked Tse-Mallory.

"Not much I can, sociologist. Even if this Nikosos person should be *mjinga* enough to come down without a portable defensive screen, it would be awkward to attempt to fight our way out. Although we are not," and here he looked directly at Flinx, "without surprises of our own. However, I am certain the men he leaves on his ship—only one this time, for a change —will be monitoring everything that happens. We'd be at their mercy in the shuttle. If this Nikosos doesn't bring a screen, and if we could surprise him and get off a crippling few shots before they had time to warn their starship, and if we could slip up to the *Gloryhole* under their detectors, and if we could get inside and get the generator powered before they noticed—why, we might have a good chance of sneaking off or fighting them."

"Too many 'ifs'," said Truzenzuzex unnecessarily.

"*Kabisa*, quite. Still, we have other weapons. Rest assured I'll try them. Bribery, for one, has often proven more effective in war than nucleonics. But I fear that Rasha wouldn't send a creature that vulnerable on such an important mission. Not one who'd be tempted by total bribery, anyway. Partial, now. . . . There is only one other thing I can think of to do. There's only one *mlango* to this building. Set up the rifle and blast the first being to enter it. As long as he has no certain idea of how we are equipped for supplies and guns he might be impatient enough to dicker with us. Unfortunately we don't have much, even with what we could move in here from the shuttle. *Mibu*, all he has to do is burn the shuttle and take a leisurely safari back to Nineveh with coordinates for the Registry!"

"Why doesn't he do that anyway?" asked Flinx.

"Not his assignment, *kijana*, or he wouldn't even have bothered to call us. Simply disabled the *Glory* and been on his way. Obviously he needs to find out everything he can about the Krang." He gestured at the two scientists. "Rasha knows about you two. I told her myself, *chura* that I am. She could hire experts of her own, but she knows your reputation. Rasha never neglects her homework. So I'm not worried for your lives. Only your reputations. I believe I can also manage something for myself. Too many people would ask awkward questions if I were to disappear suddenly. . . . even on a trip of exploration in an unspaced area. And he *can't* make that much *fedha!* Oh, he still couldn't afford to let any of us go free. Most likely he's been ordered to keep us comfy someplace until Rasha's investment here is tied up six ways in four dimensions. That veiled hint at 'assassination' was probably his way of opening bids."

"A suggestion, captain," said Truzenzuzex.

"*Ndiyo?*"

"Assuming all you've said to be true, why not simply accede quietly and give him what he wants?"

"What!" Even Flinx was startled.

"I assure you that the Krang will remain useless to both him and his employer. I was pessimistic when I said I would require three weeks to evaluate the machine's potential usefulness. We could learn much about the Tar-Aiym from it, of that I've no doubt. I think that I can also say with a great deal of certitude right now that it will otherwise never be more than an outstanding curiosity for archeologists and *touristas*."

"*Lakini*, but . . . you got it working! Part of it, anyhow."

"What I did was no more than polishing the drive coils of a Caplis generator. I succeeded in warming it up, perhaps, and appearing functional, but I doubt that I could ever, ever bring it to even partial operation. And we still have no more idea of what it's supposed to do than we did before. No being could go further, I think . . . no matter who your Madame Nuaman engages."

"If you're positive—" began Malaika.

Truzenzuzex looked questioningly at Tse-Mallory and both turned back to the merchant. "Nothing is positive, Captain, but I will not bandy Church maxims with you. Without hesitation, I concur with my brother's evaluation."

"*Mbwa ulimwengu!* Very well, then. We will forgo destruction in favor of more subtle maneuvers." He activated the comm for a wide broadcast channel. Now that he was on familiar ground once more, his voice had the old ring back. "Nikosos!"

There was a hiss, sput, pause, and then the mousey voice had returned. "No need to shout, captain. You have thoughts?"

"Look, agent. I will give you the opportunity to gain what you wish and perhaps save a few lives in the process. I have a fully operational six millimeter laser rifle here, and plenty of charges, but I don't see anything worth fighting over. I wish you luck in making it perform if you can, which I doubt. The whole city is yours. I wish only to leave this *nukia* as rapidly as possible. You may have our notes, if you wish. Everything we've found out about the Krang itself . . .

which amounts to very little. But I've a boy and two women here, and I want them out of this."

"How touching! I did not expect such admirable altruism from you, captain. Yes, despite my orders I think a financial agreement satisfactory to all concerned can be arranged. Blood tends to upset my liver, anyway. Although I'm sure you'll understand when I say that you and your companions must remain as my guests for a short while. A minimal amount of time, really, but very necessary."

"Naturally, I understand the necessity and will be glad to sign. . . ."

"Oh no, captain, that won't be required. I trust your word. Your reputation precedes you. Personally I find honesty in our profession somewhat nauseating, but in this case it is to my advantage. No, much as you'd like to have such an agreement in words, I'd rather not have such a missive in existence. Such things have a habit of disappearing and turning up later in the most *distressing* places. Shortly, now.

"Our flight has been interesting so far, captain, but I fear I should find this planet boring. If you would be so kind as to leave your transmitter on standby, we will follow its pulse in. This entire distasteful business can be speeded to completion. I am certain you have even less desire than I to prolong it." He clicked off.

"Captain," came Wolf's voice over the comm, "this makes me ill. Is there no other way . . . ?"

"No other way, Wolf. I would rather fight too, but. . . . Leave open the transcomm for them to follow down, as he requested. At least our work here appears to have been fruitless, or I wouldn't consider such an alternative. We can wish them much of the same. Whatever they find in the city they are welcome to. It's been something of a wild *mbizu* chase after all."

"But he as much as threatened murder . . . !"

"Wolf, please, I know. *Jua* is hard. Still, we've little choice. I don't trust him, either. But he *could* simply leave now and return for our emaciated corpses later. No, I'm betting he'd rather pick up the extra credit my offer holds. Why shouldn't he?" He shrugged, despite the fact that Wolf couldn't see it.

"Wolf, if the odds weren't so *nyani*-sided . . . !" He sighed. "House rules."

"I understand, captain."

Malaika switched off and sat down heavily on one of the alien benches, looking suddenly very old and tired.

"Of course, if you gentlesirs had discovered how to make this *mashineuzi* work, I wouldn't even consider. . . ."

"We understand, too, captain," said Tse-Mallory. "A bad choice is no choice. We never worried for ourselves. He must at least display us to Nuaman to convince her of our uselessness. And our abrupt disappearance, too, would cause discussion in certain quarters."

"Nuaman. *Damn* that bitch!" He looked upward. "This day I forget forever that creature is human and *mwanamke*!" He noted Flinx's glance. "She ceased to be a *bibi*, a lady, *kijana*, long before you were born."

Chapter Twenty

Kilometers above, a very satisfied Able Nikosos leaned back in his lounge in the plush shuttle cabin and relayed orders to his pilots. He rubbed his hands together. Things had gone nicely, nicely. Almost as nicely as if he had received that map as scheduled, back on Moth. The presence of Malaika already down on the planet made things a mite more complicated, but not overmuch. It appeared that it would make things more profitable. Besides collecting a fat bonus from the old witch for successfully carrying out a mission more difficult than originally assigned, there would be the matter of the wealthy Malaika's ransom . . . payable in advance. As preplanned, the two braincases would be shipped off to Nuaman. As soon as a decent amount of the ransom had been paid—wasn't Malaika's word good now?—the boy could be shunted out the nearest lock. As for the two women, well, the ancestral homestead was in need of a few new toys. The price of healthy young women had gone up insufferably in the past few years. Insufferably! All the fault of those damned priggish Churchmen. "Violence is unsanitary," indeed! At the rate he used them up his hobby was becoming prohibitively expensive. Shameful! The addition of two new, free faces (and bodies, oh yes!) would therefore be a financial as well as an aesthetic bonus. He did not doubt but that they would both prove young and attractive. Otherwise what business would they have with the roguish Malaika?

If they weren't his type, quite, he could still use them. Less artistically, perhaps, but they might still remain servicable. And he was not known as a connoisseur for nothing.

The shuttle's delta wings began to unfold as it dipped toward atmosphere.

Chapter Twenty-one

Malaika, Tse-Mallory, Truzenzuzex, and Flinx were making their way slowly back to the crawler. No one spoke. Flinx had already determined not to let his gun be taken from him without argument. He could prove equally adept at treachery! He'd read the confusion and little piggish thoughts Nikosos had been having, difficult as it had been with their owner moving so rapidly above the planet's surface. He trusted him now about as far as he could throw the *Gloryhole*. That the two scientists and Malaika would get off safely was a possibility, but from the agent's thoughts the chance that he and the women would do likewise seemed small in the light of what he had read. In the final analysis he would not count—no, not *expect* the merchant to put his life on the line for him, or for the women, or even for the scientists. Survival is an argument that morals do not even belong in the same class with. So he'd best plan on taking some action on his own. It was an unflattering but logical evaluation of their present situation. That scared him almost as much as the reality of it did. He shivered slightly, despite the warmth.

Something had been bothering him for the last few minutes, in addition to the expected quota of fearful anticipation. He shrugged his shoulders despite the lack of an itch there. That was it! Not an itch, but the lack of a persistent and familiar one. The minidrag was elsewhere. In the absorption of the past moments and his concentration on the agent's mind, he'd not noticed that the reptile was missing. He turned abruptly.

"Pip? Where's Pip?"

"Just to be certain," murmured Malaika, not hearing Flinx's low inquiry. He flipped his comm. "Wolf, I don't like to play without at least a few cards. Break out the rifle and set it up facing the entranceway."

"Yes, *captain*!" came the enthusiastic reply.

"If this fellow has us so neatly tied up and packaged," said Tse-Mallory, "why bother with the gun? I thought you'd given up once and for all the idea of our fighting our way out of this?"

Flinx searched the air around them. The snake was still not visible. He felt naked without the familiar reptilian presence.

"So I have, more or less. We know that he has us packaged, and he knows that he has us packaged, but he doesn't know that we know he has us packaged."

"Simplify that, please."

"*Ndiyo*. Sure. Put it this way. A man negotiates with considerably less arrogance than he might when he knows he's sitting under the gun of a man who fears for his life. We've little enough in the way of levers so that we've got to use the slightest we can find."

Despite Flinx's varieties of calls, whistles, and entreaties the minidrag had not shown itself. It was unusual, but not unprecedented. Sometimes the snake had a mind of its own. Truzenzuzex couldn't duplicate the stuttering calls Flinx was using, but the insect was helping with the visual portion of the search. It served to take his mind at least temporarily off their unfortunate circumstances.

"Where would he be likely to hide, lad?" asked the scientist.

"Oh, I'm not sure, sir. Different places." He was becoming honestly concerned now and listened with only one ear to the philosoph's questions. He could not sense the minidrag's presence and that alone worried him. "He doesn't do this sort of thing often. I suppose the depression in the atmosphere got to him. He's sensitive to that, you know. He does prefer cool, closed-in places. Like. . . ."

He broke off in shock. In the distance he could see the minidrag. Even as he watched, it fluttered about the transparent dome. Its natural curiosity got the better of it then, because despite a warning thought from Flinx it poked its head under the attractive shape of the helmet. What happened next surprised both watchers. The minidrag did an awkward turn in the air and seemed to fall in on itself, collapsing into a tight curl at the very highest point of the helmet. It lay still, unmoving, within the structure, which now pulsed an uncertain yellow.

All thoughts of their immediate difficulties were instantly discarded in a paroxysm of fear for his life-long companion. Heedless of Truzenzuzex's cautions he plunged forward at a run for the place they'd just left. Malaika turned and uttered an oath, charging after the boy. His bandy legs were no match for those of the youth but moved at a respectable speed none-theless.

As he neared the dome Flinx noted a slight but definite tremor underfoot. He paid it no heed.

Truzenzuzex did. He glanced at Tse-Mallory.

"Yes, brother. I felt it too." His voice was reflective. Another tremor, stronger this time.

"What occurs?" said a puzzled Truzenzuzex. "I thought we'd established that this part of the planet, at least, was plutonically secure." He stared uneasily at the vaulting walls, gauging their strength and stability.

The gentle shaking started again, only this time it was somewhat less than gentle. And it didn't stop. It grew progressively louder and more forceful, and although no one noticed it, it did so as Flinx drew closer to the dome.

The steady vibration was felt, no, *sensed*, more than heard. It bespoke power somewhere deep below.

"What *is* going on?" whispered Tse-Mallory.

"*Elitat*! I'm not sure, replied the philosoph in equally subdued tones, "but I think perhaps our puzzle is setting about answering itself."

Flinx had mounted the dais and was moving toward the dome. Pip had still not moved. He barely noticed the tremors which were shaking the structure. As he neared his motionless pet the odd buzzing which had begun in his head began to get worse. He shook his head impatiently to clear it but with no effect. There was an odd feeling of euphoria alternating with the pain.

Don't fight it, something seemed to whisper. He heard waves on a beach, breaking softly. The mini-drag's eyes were shut tightly. It appeared to be jerking to the strains of some silent song. His first thought was of convulsions, but the reptile's movements, although irregular, seemed too even for that. He started to reach under the great helmet for his troubled pet.

The buzzing increased and he reeled backward under a startling attack of dizziness.

DON'T . . . FIGHT . . . YOU!

Pip's in . . . trouble. Trouble.

He shook his head again and this time it seemed to give him a little relief. Blurred, his thoughts were blurred. He focused watery eyes on the snake and plunged drunkenly under the helmet.

E*P*I*P*H*A*N*Y.

Inside his skull an ancient dam, weakened by chance and evolution, collapsed. The surge of stuff behind it was awesome.

The normally transparent structure of the dome exploded in a mass of scintillating, brilliantine auroras. From crown to base, all the colors of the visible spectrum . . . and probably those of the invisible also. Purples, greens, golds dominated the reds, blues, and other primes. A corruscating maelstrom of angry, almost metallic iridescence wove intricate and indecipherable patterns within the material of the dome itself. Faerie grids of phosphorescence, foxfire, and ball-lightning etched spiderwebs of light in the air within the building.

On the bench within the dome within the building that was the Krang, Flinx lay stilled in seeming unconsciousness next to his now quiescent pet. The helmet above them pulsed a deep and fiery violet.

"Captain. . . ." Wolf's voice fluttered distorted by waterfalls of static over the crackling communit, but Malaika didn't notice. He had pulled up short in astonishment as soon as the dome had begun its eye-blinding display.

The gigantic pipes of the machine pulsed with anvillike ringings, circlets of lambent electricity crawling up their sides like parasitic haloes. They crackled viciously, much as ripping plastic foil.

". . . interspace call . . . !" Wolf didn't have a chance to pick up Malaika's acknowledgement, for the voice of Nikosos overrode the pilot's on the channel.

"What are you trying down there, merchant? No tricks, I warn you! I will have my men destroy your ship! I wish only a transmitter signal. A whole section of the continent to your east is . . . glowing, yes, glowing, under the surface, it seems. The place looks like it's on fire. I don't know what you're up to, man, but if you so much as. . . ."

The voice disappeared in a Niagara of interference. At that moment the world became filled with H's, U's, N's, and for some reason, especially G's.

Malaika took one step forward and dropped to the floor as if he'd been axed. At least, later, he thought he'd fallen. For all he could actually remember, he might have floated. The air in the ampitheater suddenly seemed to exert its presence, forcing him back and down. He was drowning in it. *Msaada!* Funny, they'd never noticed how dense it was. Dense. His head was imprisoned in a giant vise . . . no, not a vise. A thousand million jackboots drummed alien marches on the sides of his head while a conspiracy of laughing electrons tried to pull his scalp off. He smelled burnt-orange.

As he rolled on the floor trying to keep his head together while it insisted on flying apart, he caught a glimpse of Tse-Mallory. The sociologist was in similar shape. His face was a terrifying sight as he battled the force that was pushing them all toward gentle madness. Deprived of full rational control, the tall body twisted and flopped on the pale white floor like a suffocating *samaki*. Truzenzuzex, on the other hand, was sprawled motionless on his back. His eye membranes were closed for the first time the merchant could recall. Nowhere could he see what might have stimulated the reflex. The philosoph's legs were extended straight out and stiff, but the hands and foothands waved feebly in the electrostatically charged air.

Down below, the trillion kilometers of circuitry (and other things) that was the dormant mind of the Krang stirred, awoke. A-class mind, yes. But *blocked*! *Naturally* blocked! And what's more, unaware of itself! It was unheard of! An A-class mind could be reduced, yes, but only artificially. Blocked? Never! And *naturally*! The situation was . . . unnatural. It conflicted with the Law.

The Krang found itself confronted with a Unique Circumstance. It would be forced to the ultimate mechanical decision. Taking the initiative. But it could not operate itself itself. The mind above was essential/needed/required. It probed gently. Once the blocks were removed . . . cooperation. . . .

ADJUST YOUR CELLS, ORGANISM . . . SO!

Gently, gently.

Above, the body of Flinx jerked once.

I can't do that!

YOU MUST. IT IS . . . NECESSARY.

It hurts!

IGNORANCE HURTS. TRY.

Flinx's inert body squirmed again. His head throbbed unmercifully, seeming to grow to impossible proportions.

I . . . can't!

The Krang considered. Stronger pulsation could remove the blockage forcefully . . . and possibly destroy the mind forever. Consider alternatives. If blocked,

227

how was the mind able to stimulate initial activation in the first place?

It required the fraction of a nanosecond to locate the answer. There was a catalyst mind nearby. That Explained. In referents the Krang was familiar with. Working swiftly through the moderating channels of the C-mind, the great machine made the necessary adjustments/tunings in the A-class brain. Gratefully, it sensed the barriers go down/dissolve. It was easy, this time. They had been weak and perforated to begin with. ETTA energies started to flow in the waiting floways. Further intervention was no longer required.

E*N*T*R*O*P*Y*R*E*A*L*I*Z*A*T*I*O*N.

In an instant of falling glass shards Flinx perceived the entire universe. It appeared as a very small, opaque ball of crystal. The instant passed, but he saw things clearly for the first time. Yes, much more clearly. He sensed things only half-noticed, suspected, before. And things not noticed at all. He saw the marvelous structure that was the Krang. He perceived the marvelous structure that was himself. Certain energies were required fully to awaken the instrument. Only a tiny part of it pulsed with awareness now. Here, and here, yes.

The Krang awoke. To full awakefulness for the first time in half a million years. Hymn-march. Glorianus! The threnody that flowed from the now attuned activator-mind was an unfamiliar one and crude in technique. But the Krang realized that in five hundred millenia tastes might have changed. The important thing was that the Screen had gone up automatically the instant the tune had supplied the necessary keying impulses.

The Krang's sensors instantly scanned the sky for

light-years in all directions. Since the activator had done nothing on an instructional level except to broadcast sensations of danger, the machine instituted a general optimum scan pattern and hoped it would prove sufficient. It recognized the activator now as a novice. He would have to be guided. Somewhere a minor circuit dutifully noted that a single ship of alien construct had been pulverized at the moment of Screen activation, caught as it went up. A close call! Again the Krang regretted it could operate at only partial consciousness until the moment of full stimulation. Fortunately, the vessel had not penetrated. No harm done. The activator was informed and concurred. Another ship—no, two—lurked just outside the Screen. Although it remained stationary and made no hostile gestures, the activating mind directed the Krang to focus on the area of space occupied by the larger of the two vessels. Obediently, the machine complied.

Its field of effective close-range focus was a minimum thousand-kilometer sphere. It would have no trouble impacting the single indicated craft while missing the other. Those incredible sensors could line up the necessary cone of projection within a meter of any desired point. That was far more than necessary. It drew the necessary information as to specifics from a now cooperating A-mind. If the Krang had had feet, it would have been tapping them.

Above, the rhythmic pulsations that were making a pulp of Tse-Mallory's thoughts let up momentarily. They were instantly transformed into an utterly indescribable cross between a modulated screech and a bellow. The supersonic shriek of a bat amplified a million times and made audible, backed with electric trumpets and kettledrums. Even so, it did not press as intolerably onto his skull as had the other. The sociologist was able to roll onto his back and lie still, panting and gasping irregularly for the hostile air which seemed intent on evading his lungs.

Painfully, he turned his head. He fought to keep the skreeling moan from penetrating too deep, knowing that if he eased up and allowed it to gain deep purchase, the knife-edge of the sonics would begin slicing up the nerves and neurons therein. He was able to stave it off.

Apparently Malaika was stronger in his resistance than any of them. Somehow he staggered to his feet and began to lurch and sway in the direction of the platform. He had made half the distance when the building moved.

At the moment of the first thrum, Wolf had gunned the crawler's engines and made a dash for the door. Fortunately the big cruiser had been pointing in that direction. When the first full note struck him he had tumbled from the control seat, clasping his ears. But the crawler, set on its course, continued on dumbly. As they had before, the great doors parted. The moment they closed behind the crawler, the torture stopped.

Wolf pulled himself slowly into the chair and managed to halt the machine's headlong plunge before it sent them hurling over the bluff. He didn't know what had happened—too quick! But he did know that the captain and the others were still inside. He made a quick check of the cargo area. Both women were sprawled among the supplies, mercifully unconscious— whether from the effects of the "thing" or their precipitous exit he couldn't tell.

What to *do*. Sprawled helplessly on the floor of the crawler, beating at the metal in agony, he would be little help to the captain or anyone. For the moment, returning inside was out of the question. A try at the communits produced only an ocean of static. Maybe he could find something in the shuttle that would screen his mind enough to permit him to re-enter that hell. He wasn't given time to ponder the problem.

The building, every million-ton of it, was shifting its position. It leaned backward and for a horrible moment he feared it was going to topple onto the miniscule crawler. It did not. It hung poised in the swirling sky for a second and then turned slightly to the south. It began to hum, deeply. The vibrations could be felt through the floor of the cab—or in one's teeth. Miles up in the dust-laden air he could see the upper hundred meters or so of the structure begin to glow a rich ebony. He'd never seen anything glow black before and was fascinated by the phenomenon. It continued for some thirty seconds. The circular base on which the building rested also seemed to brighten slightly. The air for some distance around took on a momentary rose color. Then it stopped.

The Krang recorded the dispatch of the second vessel as matter-of-factly as it had the first.

The entire process, from initial activation to now, had taken a little under two minutes.

Impatiently the Krang waited for further orders from the activation Nexus. The directive to destroy the other alien spacecraft did not come. In fact, the mind then and there removed itself from control of the Nexus.

The machine debated with itself. It had been a long, long time since it had existed at full consciousness. It had discovered again that it rather enjoyed the sensation.

But its imprinted instructions were clear and left no

room for logical evasions. In the absence of an activating mind it was to return to a state of powered-down dormancy. This meant deactivation of all but the most elementary maintenance functions. The Krang sighed. The purposes of its builders had often seemed at variance with their desires and it had not now been shown reason to change that opinion. But it knew what a Frankenstein was, if it utilized a different reference. The great vanes in the depths of the limestone caverns which channeled the planet's unceasing gales began to shift down. The generators which drew power in countless ergs from the molten core of the planet throttled back, and the bubbling iron-nickel center calmed.

Slowly but efficiently, the Krang went about the necessary task of turning itself off.

Chapter Twenty-two

Flinx rolled over and picked himself up. His head still throbbed but the actual pain had almost disappeared. He'd been drunk only once in his life. The memories of the monstrous hangover he'd suffered as a consequence came back to him now, incongruously. He stared around. After their close swing around the neutron star it had been his muscles which had been beaten and mauled. Controlled by the piano-string tautness of his outraged nervous system, it was now the marrow of his bones which vibrated in remembered sympathy with the ton-tones of the abruptly silent Krang. He looked inward, unconsciously rearranging certain cellular structures, fluids. The pain drifted away, leaving only a lot of light.

Aided by his friend, Truzenzuzex was slowly getting to his feet. Flinx didn't care to imagine what the insect, with its unprotected exoskeleton, had gone through. Malaika had been thwarted in his attempt to reach the dais by the unexpected angling of the building. He was sitting on the edge of a bench now, rubbing a knee and carefully checking the ligaments and tendons to make certain that nothing critical had been damaged. Otherwise he seemed unharmed, for a multiplicity of oaths in a remarkable number of languages flowed in unceasing profusion from his thick lips.

Assured that his humanx companions were all right, Flinx turned his attention to his pet. The small, leathery body was curled tightly under the activation hood. It gave sign of neither motion nor life. Careful not to get his head under that quiet object, he lifted the solid little form from its resting place. Still it did not stir. With his newly stimulated mind he probed gently within the small body. He had been pushed, indeed shoved into a new and unfamiliar universe and was still a little uncertain (honest now, frightened) of his abilities. He probed deeper. The minidrag had served as a conduit for forces beyond its own capacity to handle. Like an overloaded capacitor, certain rearrangements and adjustments were in order.

Flinx set about making them.

The others had gathered together and were standing off to one side, watching silently and having the courtesy not to offer sympathy. With an unoccupied portion of his mind he searched theirs, briefly. All three were still stunned by the events of the past few minutes. Almost as much as he, he reflected wryly. He could feel the empathy radiating outward from them and it made him feel better.

A last readjustment, a stubborn artery . . . no, there! One thin eyelid flickered, raised. An oil-black eye peered out and around. It swiveled up to where it encountered Flinx's own, was joined by its twin. In slow, jerky motions the minidrag began to uncurl. Flinx stuck out his tongue. Pip's darted out to make contact with it in an old gesture of familiarity and affection. He could feel the tension begin to slip from the muscular coils, the life-pulse to strengthen.

He had dropped the habit of crying at about the time he had discovered it did nothing more than clean his pupils. Still, there was a suspicious moisture at the corners of his eyes. He turned away so that the others might not be offended by it. If he had remained facing the other way or had bothered to probe he might have noticed that Truzenzuzex's expression was something more than merely sympathetic.

Chapter Twenty-three

The shuttle had not been harmed and they made the ascent into the upper atmosphere with more ease and certainty than they had managed the trip down. Atha and Wolf were at the controls. The others were in the rear cabin, their minds intent on the present instead of the future for the first time in some while.

"Well, sir," said Truzenzuzex to Malaika, "we apologize. It seems as though your investment has proven singularly unprofitable. I confess that it was not really a concern of ours from the beginning. But after the expense and danger you have been through I do wish you could have realized something in the way of a more substantial increment from it."

"Oh now, you are unnecessarily pessimistic, my hard-shelled *rafiki*." The merchant puffed vigorously on an incredibly foul-smelling pipe. "I have a city that is no doubt filled to overflowing with priceless Tar-Aiym artifiacts and inventions . . . if I can ever dig them out of that infernal sand! A fine, inhabitable planet. With a thriving native aqueous ecological system, probably compatible to the humanx norm. I think that this planet might even bring back the sailing ship, *ndiyo*!"

"The reference eludes me," said the philosoph.

"I'll show you trioids when we get back. One of the more poetic bits of man's technological past. No, no, from the *fedha* standpoint I am not ready to count this journey a bust! And there is always the Krang to play with, *je*? Even if our young friend insists it was a freak accident that he had nothing to do with." He looked questioningly at Flinx, who studiously ignored them all. "But for you two, I am afraid, it was a real disappointment. You must be even more frustrated now than when we landed, *je*?"

"It all depends on how you choose to view it," said Tse-Mallory. "When we started on the trail of this thing we really had no idea what we expected to find, other than something big. When we found that, we didn't know what we'd found. And now that we've left it . . . well, when you get ready to come back and dig out those artifacts," he glanced at his ship-brother, "Tru and I will be more than happy to help you with the sorting, if not the excavating. And we still, as you say, have the Krang itself to 'play' with. It will at least form the basis for many a lengthy and infuriating scientific paper." He smiled and shook his head. "The psychological and sociological implications alone . . . eh, Tru?"

"Unquestionably, brother." The thranx tried hard to convey a human attitude of profound reflection, failed, and substituted one of nostalgic unconcern instead. The result did not quite come off.

"It seems as though the legends of both the Branner and our primitive hominids had some validity to them. Who would have suspected it? The Krang is both a weapon *and* a musical instrument."

They had left the atmosphere now and Atha was setting an orbit that would bring them up on the *Gloryhole* from below and behind. The blackness poured in on one side while the sun, filtered down automatically by the photosensitive ports, lit them from the other. Despite the equalizing effects of the cabin lights, it tended to throw facial features into unnaturally sharp relief.

"It tells us a lot about the Tar-Aiym . . . not to mention going a long way toward explaining their interest in two such seemingly divergent fields as war and art. I can't say that I care for their tastes in music, though. Myself, I prefer Debussy and Koretski. No doubt to their ears . . . or whatever they used . . . such sounds were pleasing and exciting, nay, patriotic."

"Subtle sounds of death resound, and lyres smote as children drowned," Tse-Mallory recited.

"Porzakalit, twenty-third sonnet," said Truzenzuzex. "It *would* take a poet."

"I may be overly dense," said Malaika, "but I still don't understand how the *kelelekuu worked*!"

"You are not alone in that respect, captain, but rather the member of a large minority. If you wish, though, I could hypothesize."

"Go ahead and hypothesize, then!"

"Apparently," continued the thranx, discreetly waving away the noxious effluvia produced by the carbonized weed in the merchant's pipe, "the machine generates some form of vibration . . . I confess myself hesitant to label it 'sound waves.' Probably something partaking of those characteristics as well as those of wave forms we could not identify—although their effects were noted! You recall that on our initial passage through the atmosphere I remarked on the unusual density of the double layer of windglitter?" Malaika nodded. "Probably those layers are kept artificially reinforced. The wave forms—let's call them 'k-waves' for want of a better, or more accurate, term—

were generated by the Krang. These waves passed through the lower layer of the metallic windglitter but not the higher, denser one. Accordingly, they were then 'bounced' along between the two layers, as they were by now sufficiently weakened to be incapable of breaking back through the lower one. All around the planet, I'd wager. Perhaps more than once, constantly being rejuvenated by the generators of the Krang."

"Oh, now I know they're probably not sound waves," said Malaika, "but planet-wide circulation in the atmosphere? From a single generating source—maintenance of a certain minimal strength—the power requirements. . . . You really think it possible?"

"My dear Malaika, I regard anything as possible unless clearly demonstrated otherwise . . . the more so when *this* machine is involved."

"Even simple sound waves," put in Tse-Mallory. "Back on Terra itself, old calendar eighteen eighty-eight, there was a volcanic explosion in the major ocean. An island called Krakatoa blew up rather violently. The shock waves traveled several times around the globe. The sound of the explosions—simple sound waves, remember—was heard halfway around the globe. Given the Tar-Aiym's abilities and the fact that these were much more than mere sound waves, I should consider the production of such forms an elegant possibility. Besides, I should think you'd need little convincing after that highly spectacular demonstration we had."

"A conclusion after the fact," said Truzenzuzex drily. "Very astute of you, brother. However, as I am only slightly more knowledgable in this regard than you. . . ."

"Disputed!"

". . . I let the matter drop. The Tar-Aiym were fully capable, as you say, of amplifying on nature—pardon the pun."

"I would suppose that explains what became of our *rafiki* Nikosos, then," murmured Malaika. "Once his shuttle entered the region of effective vibrations. . . ."

"Destructive oscillation?" added Tse-Mallory.

"Shaken to pieces? Possibly," said Truzenzuzex. "Or maybe they cause a breakdown or weakening of the atomic structure. Even in what was probably the safest place on the planet the vibrations—'music' if you must—near to shook my skeleton off. Not an impossible device. Fantastic, yes, but not impossible. Myself, I am much more interested in the method used to eliminate their starship."

"*Ndiyo*," said Malaika. "How about that? It was nowhere near the atmosphere and so could not have been trapped in the windglitter layers."

"In addition to maintaining an impenetrable defensive screen around the planet, the Krang would be no more than a stalemate device if it did not have offensive capabilities as well," continued the thranx. "A device wholly defensive in nature would be contrary to everything we know of Tar-Aiym psychology. And you are all aware of how the quality of vibrations changed ever so significantly toward the end of our ordeal. Now then, Flinx, you say you sensed the destruction of the other starship, yet there was no sign of an explosion? No flare, nothing?"

A safe question, and one he could hardly deny. "That's right, sir. It just . . . vanished."

"Um. A possibility suspected that will probably never be confirmed, but . . . remember that our ship was a very short distance away, yet apparently has not been affected. I suspect gentlesirs, that the Krang is a gravitonic generator—but of power undreamed of even by the ancient Gods." He faced Malaika squarely. "Captain, what would happen if a gravity field approximately one centimeter in diameter with a field equal in strength to the surface of a neutron star impinged on a real mass?"

Malaika's swarthy face reflected puzzlement, revelation, and astonishment in amazingly brief succession. His voice reflected all three.

"*Manisa!* That would trigger a Schwarzchild Discontinuity! But that's . . . !"

"Impossible?" Truzenzuzex smiled. "Pardon, captain, but how else might you explain it? The power necessary to generate such a field would need a planet-sized ship . . . much simpler to use a planet, eh? And remember there was no evidence of an explosion. Of course not. Not even light could escape a field of such strength! And gravity follows an inverse square law, so naturally our ship was not effectively endangered. A more perfectly selective weapon would be hard to imagine. A mere kilometer away and you would not even notice such a field. But touch it and poof! Instant nonexistence! I hope that one might have the sense not to tamper with such a device overmuch, captain." The thranx's voice was steel-solemn. "We do not know anywhere near enough about the operation of such a field. Suppose we did not discover the way to 'uncreate' such a field? The Krang obviously can do that—how, I cannot begin to imagine. But if such a field were to be released, uncontrolled, it would simply wander around the universe gobbling up . . . everything."

Alan Dean Foster

It was too quiet in the cabin, now. "But I think there's little chance of that," he continued more spiritedly, "unless our young friend can activate the mechanism once again. Not to mention," he added, "directing it as successfully."

Flinx had read the veiled accusation coming for some time now. He knew it would have to be countered. They must not think him capable of operating such a threatening weapon. Especially, he reminded himself, when he wasn't sure if he could!

"I told you sir, I don't know what happened. The machine controlled *me*, not vice versa!"

"Still," the thranx said significantly.

It would have been easy to rearrange the insect's mind so that he would simply take Flinx's explanation of the ocurence at face value. Too easy. The Krang had not affected his sense of ethics. Besides, the idea of deliberately tampering with another's deepest centers of thought was mildly repulsive, as well as a bit frightening. Especially when the mind in question was recognizably wiser than his own. Power, he reminded himself, is not knowledge. He would need a lot of the latter in the future.

"Look. . . ." He was thinking rapidly. It was easy, now. "As far as 'directing' the device goes, you said yourself that the machine was composed of infinitely sophisticated circuitry. Once started up, it would be fully capable of handling the situation to its own satisfaction. I was merely like the hydrogen 'plug' that starts the KK drive."

"Um. And how do you account for its taking the actions it did?"

"Maybe Nikosos' ship made a movement that the machine interpreted as hostile, and it responded ac-

242

cordingly. Perhaps it was just keyed and ready when I entered it. I'm certainly not that much different from anyone else here." (Lie!) "Probably my gift or talent or whatever you want to call it had something to do with it. Remember, it didn't do anything the first time I entered it."

"I have a hunch your own fears at the moment had a lot to do with it too. Yes, that's plausible."

"Right," Flinx continued, grateful for the opening. "I was scared when I entered it this time . . . really scared." (Truth.) "My emotional strain *had* to be picked up by the machine. It's an artistic device, too! Probably any of us could have stimulated it under those conditions." (Possible, not probable.) "In any case, it's finished now and I've no desire, not the tiniest, to try it again!" (Mixed truth.)

"Enough lad! You are too aggressive for my poor, senile mind." (Baloney!) "I am satisfied, for the nonce." (Flinx read otherwise, but it did not matter.) "You have convinced me in fair and equal oral combat. Try me at personality chess and I'll beat the freckles off you! Yet. . . ." He glanced at the minidrag, then back to Flinx. "You say you feel unchanged? No aftereffects?"

Flinx shook his head with a confidence that would have made Mother Mastiff proud. "No. I really don't know what happened. My mind was. . . ." He broke off as the outside light was abruptly extinguished. The shuttle had slipped into her mooring dock in the cargo hold of the *Gloryhole*.

"And that is that," said Malaika, unnecessarily. To everyone's great satisfaction, his pipe had gone out. "I'd love to discuss this all further with you gentlebe-ings, but at some future *nafasi, ndiyo*? If I do not get something of a recognizably liquid consistency down my throat very soon, you'll be able to scatter me in orbit with the windglitter, for I shall dry up to dust!"

He moved down the narrow aisle between them and opened the small personnel lock. The pale green light of the cargo balloon sifted inward. A pullway drifted conveniently nearby. Sissiph in hand he began hauling the two of them up its swaying length. Atha went next, followed by the two scientists. Flinx plucked Pip from where the minidrag lay coiled comfortably about a chair arm and placed him on his shoulder. He hurried out of the ship. Even now the figure of Wolf was still one he wished to avoid. He followed the others up the pullway.

On reaching the gravitized section of the ship, everyone went his separate way. Atha and Wolf to Control, Malaika and Sissiph to their cabin. The merchant had not yet had a drop of intoxicant, but he had escaped a ransom and gained a planet. Even if he never realized a cent off his investment, that alone was enough to make him slightly drunk. The two scientists prepared to resume their endless game of personality chess as though they had never been interrupted.

"That was not a legal psychosis," said Tse-Mallory, his voice drifting back to Flinx. "And you are well aware of it!"

"Why, Bran, how can you say that? Surely when I instigated a jump of four places in that secondary childhood fear piece. . . ." Their voices faded as he turned the corner leading to his cabin.

Flinx glanced down at this shoulder. The minidrag, the effects of its ordeal now apparently catching up with it, was fast asleep. He paused after a moment's hesitation for twice that in thought. Then he shrugged, grinned. Whistling a famous and delightfully ribald tune, he sauntered off in expectation of the biggest pseudosteak the ship's autochef could produce. He had much to think about.

And much to do it with.

Chapter Twenty-four

Rashalleila Nuaman lay back in her huge bed and idly examined the bedraggled, seminude figure of her niece. The girl had obviously used more force than good sense in protesting madame's request for her presence.

"Teleen," she said, sighing, "I am awfully disappointed in you, you know. Stupidity I can sometimes understand, but sloppiness is inexcusable. I knew about your amusing plan for doing away with me, of course."

The girl started at this and her eyes darted around the room in search of an escape route. Even assuming she could evade the grasp of the two giants who stood impassively to either side of her, there was nowhere on the airless moon to escape to.

"Oh, don't let it bother you, child. It didn't me. Actually I thought it rather an admirable attempt. Showed some spunk, for a change. But that you should undertake to interfere with *business* . . . that, my dear," and her voice dropped dangerously, "was ill-chosen on your part. I would perhaps have more sympathy for you had you succeeded. And with the AAnn, too. Dear, dear! I suppose you are aware they are the closest thing to a hereditary enemy mankind has?"

Teleen's tone was bitterly sarcastic. "Don't foist pa-

triotic mush on me, you sanctimonious crank! You'd
sell babies to the Devil if you thought he was more
than a superstition . . . and enough profit."

"You are being absurd, girl. Also impertinent. I
certainly would not. At least, certainly not for spite,
as you did. Being branded an enemy of the Commonwealth and excommunicated by the Church would
require promise of a considerably greater potential
return than such pettiness as you aspired to. And on
top of everything else, your adolescent ineptitude will
force me to tolerate an unbearable amount of ridicule
from a very old and dear friend. Who incidentally, I
am informed, has long since sewn up the registry of a
certain planet by interspace relay, beyond argument
of any kind. I will now be forced to fall back on legal
means to obtain what was rightfully mine in the first
place. As you may know, such procedures are notoriously unfair.

"However, we are not here to discuss that. What we
are here to determine, dear niece, is what I am to do
with you. I fear that your attitude has taken rather a
dangerous turn. I do not fear it, but my men are
capable of error too. Accordingly, I am forced to
send you on vacation, until such time as you have
been persuaded to channel your considerable energies
into more productive pursuits. You shall be given
ample time to repent and readjust your rebellious
attitudes. There is a very excellent and renowned
mental institution in the Qatar system. It is operated
by a group of exceptional therapists who have aided
me often in the past. While their methods have often
been questioned, most notably by the Church, their
successes cannot be denied. The director is a personal friend of long standing."

"Rory," said Teleen imploringly.

"I am sure they will be more than happy to accommodate you as a guest for awhile. Unfortunately, they specialize in childhood neuroses and sexual maniacs of the most extreme kind. Now, which section do you suppose you would find more comfortable for your stay?"

"Rory!" The girl's voice was frightened and shrill, now.

Rory Mallap van Cleef stood quietly by the foot of the bed in silk loincloth and beads.

"Oh, you needn't badger your accomplice and confidant, my dear. Darling Rory knows what side of the bed his butter is on." She smiled sweetly.

His voice was even and mild. Almost neutral, in fact. "I *am* sorry, love." He flexed a bicep. "I still love you, of course, but I don't see why we should both be made to suffer for this unfortunate setback. I'll wait for you." Then, after a thoughtful pause. "I do hope this doesn't complicate our relationship."

Teleen's answer was unprintable.

"Tch! Such language. And after all those expensive schools, too. Yes, I am certain you will be placed in the section most suitable to your attitude, child. I see no reason why you shouldn't take the opportunity to add to your education at the same time as we are about improving your disposition."

She waved a hand negligently and the girl was dragged spitting and squalling from the room.

"Remember now, dear, I am depending on you to show your hosts the true Nuaman spirit! Come back to us in one piece, won't you?" She shook her head mournfully after the closing doors had cut off the sound of the girl's fading shrieks. "Tch. I'm not sure that girl will ever be ready to take over the company reins. Everything devolves upon me, and I am old.

But not that old." She extended a hand. "Rory . . . come here. . . ."

They were halfway home and proceeding smoothly for Moth. Flinx looked up from his game of crystal solitaire, now grown childishly simplistic. The sense of thoughts in violent conflict had grown too strong to be ignored. As it was a normal sleep shift he was the only one in the lounge, and the commotion surprised him.

A rather disheveled-looking Atha stepped into the room. She obviously hadn't expected to encounter anyone and was noticeably upset by Flinx's presence.

"Well," she began awkwardly, simultaneously trying to adjust her clothing, "we've, uh, almost finished our journey, Flinx. I imagine you're looking forward to getting home . . . and to that credit slip Malaika's prepared for you!"

"Yes, to both. You're on your way to relieve Wolf at Control, I assume?"

"Hmmm? Oh yes, naturally!" He had to hide his amusement at the way she had pounced on the excuse. "Yes, I've just come from making some alterations, uh, in the arrangement of the ship's supplies. They were becoming unwieldy. I had to ... work on the problem at some length to get things right."

"And did you?"

Her smile was broad. "Oh, yes. Everything should now be in its proper place." She disappeared forward.

A short while later a much more disheveled Sissiph, clothes and self in nearly equal disarray, staggered into the lounge. The expression on her face was murderous, interrupted only when she grimaced at a particularly painful bruise. She spared him one unfocused glance before weaving off in the direction of the big cabin she shared with Malaika.

Apparently then, everyone had profited from the expedition, with the exception of an attractive and furious minority of one. He sighed and returned to his game, its attraction dimmed. There were many things to do, and he wasn't sure how to go about doing them. If he couldn't have any fun. . . . Malaika, he knew, was preparing great things for him. He could not see himself in the role the merchant had envisioned for him. Dressing up for gala conferences, withering competitors with his astonishing insight. Perhaps a compromise might be arranged. But that might mean leaving the markets, and his friends there. Mother Mastiff would probably have no trouble adapting to such a life. He grinned. Could High Society survive her? More seriously, how would he adapt? With everyone these days convinced of his own righteousness and secure in the knowledge that "his was the proper way of doing things."

He'd also seen what un-nice people could do to the nice, enough to want to modify the situation. Out there were minds which would resist such efforts. And who was he, to arbitrate the lives of others? Did he *want* to play God? He didn't think so. Besides he was only . . . well, he *was* almost seventeen, wasn't he? He had talent, and one innocent man and two probably guilty ones had died because he hadn't used it properly. Now he had Power, and who knew how many had died in space because of it? Power. Fagh! He wasn't one tenth the Man Tse-Mallory was! He'd need men like that to help him or he'd likely make some horrendous mistakes. Now they might prove deadly. Could he handle what he was now? Did he *want* to?

Still, the whole universe was out there and it seemed a shame not to take a look at it.

Now that he could see.